FAN ART

Also by Sarah Tregay
Love and Leftovers

FAN ART

sarah tregay

KATHERINE TEGEN BOOKS
An Imprint of HarperCollins Publishers

Katherine Tegen Books is an imprint of HarperCollins Publishers.

Fan Art
Text copyright © 2014 by Sarah Tregay
Illustrations copyright © 2014 by Melissa DeJesus
All rights reserved. Printed in the United States of America.
No part of this book may be used or reproduced in any manner whatsoever
without written permission except in the case of brief quotations embodied in
critical articles and reviews. For information address HarperCollins Children's
Books, a division of HarperCollins Publishers, 10 East 53rd Street, New York,
NY 10022.

www.epicreads.com

Library of Congress Cataloging-in-Publication Data
Tregay, Sarah.
  Fan art / Sarah Tregay ; illustrations by Melissa DeJesus. — First edition.
    pages cm
  Summary: "High school senior Jamie has a crush on his best friend and
finds ways to share that news with the help of several friends"— Provided by
publisher.
  ISBN 978-0-06-224315-7 (hardback)
  [1. Love—Fiction. 2. Best friends—Fiction. 3. Friendship—Fiction.
4. Homosexuality—Fiction. 5. Coming out (Sexual orientation)—Fiction.
6. High schools—Fiction. 7. Schools--Fiction.] I. Title.
PZ7.T713Fan 2014   2013037292
[Fic]—dc23   CIP
                                                                    AC

The artist used PaintTool SAI (for inking) and Photoshop to create
the digital illustrations for this book.
Typography by Michelle Gengaro-Kokmen
14 15 16 17 18   LP/RRDH   10 9 8 7 6 5 4 3 2 1
❖
First Edition

For art geeks everywhere

FAN ART

ONE

"Nah," I say about the brunette at the next table. "Isn't she more your type?" But the truth is, even though Mason's my best friend, I don't know his type. He doesn't date—he says it's just asking for drama.

His lip twitches upward as if he's suppressing the urge to laugh. "What about Juliet Polmanski?" he asks, trudging through the not-very-long list of girls who don't have dates for prom.

I groan. Juliet is extremely shy—so shy I've never heard her say anything but "sorry" and "excuse me." Prom with Juliet would be one long awkward silence.

Mason pops a ketchup-covered fry in his mouth and scans the cafeteria for another subject while he chews. "I know!" he says. "Lia Marcus. You both do *Gumshoe* so you could talk about literary magazine stuff."

"I heard she was going to ask Michael Schoenberger," I say, stealing two fries from Mason's plate.

"Jamie, every girl without a date is asking the Schnozbooger."

"Huh?" I ask. Michael Schoenberger isn't exactly cute—he's got this, well, huge schnoz. And, for as big as his nose is, he's always breathing through his mouth like he has a cold.

"He's safe," Mason explains. "Safer than asking some guy you have a crush on, right?" He grins, showing me a row of almost-but-not-quite-straight teeth.

"Wait." I hold up a finger. "What?"

"Come on, Jamie," Mason says. "Everyone thinks Michael's gay."

"Gay?" I echo. *Whoa.* We are not talking about this. Mason and I don't talk about gay.

Mason shrugs as if it's no big deal. He picks up the last fry and points it at me. "Michael has a date. I have a date. You, my friend, still need a date."

"You have a date?" I ask. "Since when?"

"Since I asked Bahti Rajagopolan in physics."

"Huh?"

"*You're* the one who wants to go to prom," he says, as if breaking his streak of all studying and no girlfriends was my fault. "So I'm going."

"Thanks, but I still need find someone to go *with*." I drop my head into my hands.

"We don't have to go," Mason whispers. "We could do something else."

I look up.

"Like what?"

"I dunno," he says. "Go to McCall. Stay in Frank's condo."

"We never have any fun there," I say. Frank is my stepfather. He's taken us to McCall a few times—male bonding and all that—complete with hikes in the woods, canoeing on the lake, and once, fishing. It's boring. We'd have a much better time at prom.

"Without Frank," Mason says, and glances down the length of our table to where our friends Brodie and Kellen are sitting.

Now I get it—my stepdad's condo without my stepdad. *That's an improvement.*

"Maybe invite some of the guys?" he adds, looking hopeful.

"You kidding me?" I ask, knowing our friends. "It'd turn into a total kegger. My parents would flip—" I stop because the spark in Mason's eyes dims as I speak. "We should go to prom. I mean, Bahti's counting on you."

"Yeah, probably," he says. "She's cute. Right?"

"Mmhmm," I say in a noncommittal way. Because none of my memorized hot-girl comments really apply to the third runner-up for valedictorian, Bahti Rajagopolan. She's Malaysian, with high cheekbones, big brown eyes, and a light-up-the-room smile.

The bell rings, and Mason gives me a questioning

look as if to say, *And?*

"Yeah, cute," I say. "Great smile."

Mason stands, looking relieved. "You think?"

I nod enthusiastically.

"I love you, man." Mason whacks me a good one on the shoulder.

I laugh, picking up my tray. He's not serious. We say it all the time—and not just us. All the guys say it.

It began during my sophomore year, when the goalie of the varsity soccer team died. His name was Jordan Polmanski. He was a senior. I didn't know him and I hardly knew his sister, Juliet, even though she was in my grade.

He died in a car wreck on Freezeout Hill, a long, boring section of highway that's icy from Halloween to Easter. That's when it happened. Easter. Driving home from his aunt and uncle's house, Jordan rolled his pickup off into the sagebrush. And didn't survive.

I didn't go to his funeral. I didn't have to. It was on the five o'clock news, and even though I wanted to change the channel, I couldn't. Someone from my school died. *Died.* So I watched as teary face after teary face— male and female—told the camera, "I loved him, man."

That's when Jordan's friends started saying, "I love you, man," to one another. They were seniors, varsity athletes, popular with steady girlfriends—so no one dared make fun of them. But then other guys started saying it too—juniors and sophomores like me, mostly because we wanted to be like the cool seniors, but also because it felt right. Sure, we weren't serious—but we were taking back our right to say we care about our friends. After years of tormenting one another about being wusses, pussies, or fags, collectively we said, "Screw it!" We told ourselves it was okay to love our friends—in a teasing, mocking way, of course.

And we owe it all to Jordan Polmanski.

"Hey," Eden says as I slide into my seat next to hers at a table in the art room. She and I are pretty much friends—we've been sitting together all year—but we don't do stuff outside of school. "You decide on your self-portrait medium yet?"

"Pencil."

"Pencil? Ms. Maude said no to Photoshop?"

I nod. "It has to be done in a tactile medium."

"I'm doing pen and ink," Eden says. "And Chuck Close."

The assignment was to choose a medium and an artist for inspiration, then draw or paint a self-portrait. And it's supposed to reveal something about you. At first I thought I wanted to choose a graphic designer for inspiration, but Paul Rand's poster for the film *No Way Out* was a little too obvious. And I just couldn't picture myself on a Toulouse-Lautrec poster. So I was going to do a Norman Rockwell triple self-portrait, until I found this Belgian designer, Maxime Quoilin, who merges two photographs into one, so you see the person's profile and the front of their face at the same time. I'm pretty sure I'll be able to BS my way through what this reveals about me—that there are two sides of me or something.

Eden gets out her pad of tracing paper. She pulls a sketch from between the pages and puts it on the table between us. It's a picture of her, without her glasses, taped over a piece of graph paper, the little squares showing through. Her eyes look huge.

"No glasses?" I ask.

"I hate my glasses," she says, and tucks a strand of strawberry-blond hair behind her ear.

"So your self-portrait is revealing this fact?"

"No." She sighs as if I'm stupid. "The grid reveals all the little pieces of me—that I am complex and multi-faceted."

I suppress the urge to laugh. That's exactly the type of thing Ms. Maude would fall for. I take out my sketches and the photos of myself that I was working from. They're awful.

Eden turns one sketch right side up. "Very Picasso."

"I'm not doing Picasso," I say, even though sometimes I feel a little like his paintings—arms, legs, and thoughts all at weird angles to one another and not quite fitting into the picture frame.

"Maybe you should," she says, and giggles.

"Very funny," I say, because I'm not about to reveal all my feelings for some art class assignment.

After school I plop my stuff on a desk in Dr. Taylor's classroom for the *Gumshoe* meeting. I say hi to Lia, Holland, and DeMarco while I get out my laptop.

Michael nods at me, smiles.

I think of what Mason said about him at lunch and smile back. Michael may not be model material, but he's not Frankenstein.

Michael inhales a noisy breath and begins the meeting. "As you all know, the deadline for submissions is Friday—so Jamie will have time to do the layout—but between now and then, we need to encourage people to send stuff in."

"Our video is running on the announcements for the rest of the week," DeMarco says, his tall frame slouched low in his chair. He's one of those black kids everyone thinks should play basketball just because he has to duck through doorframes, only he chose the literary mag and band over sports. Maybe it's because he and Holland were flirting with each other back in September when he signed up. Now they're an item. The only junior on staff, he will inherit the literary magazine next year.

"And I've got new posters," I say, passing them

around. They're green and have an illustration of a detective tiptoeing around a column of type that reads, *Don't let the* Gumshoe *deadline sneak up on you. Submit your art and writing by Friday.*

When I'm finished, Lia pats a ragged stack of papers on her desk. "We've got stuff," she says. "But it's not gonna win any prizes."

Gumshoe won an excellence award last year, the only student literary magazine from Idaho to place. But last year people were excited about it because it had just been resurrected—a victim of budget cuts from a decade ago. This year *Gumshoe* is old news.

Lia starts sorting the pile into art, poetry, and short prose. Since I'm the graphic designer, I get the art. I peer at what's going into my pile: a manga-style drawing, two landscapes, and a still life of an apple, peacock feathers, and a skateboard—the crap piled up in the art room. *Ugh.*

Lia adds another one, a realistic nude. It's good, drawn on bark-colored paper in Conté crayon with highlights sketched in white over the model's cheekbones, but I pretend not to see the obvious—that the model is male. And naked. I wonder if it was someone's self-portrait for Ms. Maude's assignment and decide the lack of clothing reveals a lot about a person. Literally.

By the end of the meeting the others have decided on five new poems, two flash fiction stories, and two drawings for me to add to the Adobe InDesign layout on my laptop. Lia says she'll email me the pieces that were submitted online and type up the one handwritten poem. I tell her I can do it and slide the poem between the keyboard and the screen of my computer. I put the nude and a landscape into my folder as the others start to pack up their things.

I'm halfway to the door when Michael says, "Hey, Jamie."

I turn around. "Yeah?"

"You going to prom?"

I open my mouth. No words come out. *Is he asking me to prom?*

"I take that as a no?" Michael guesses.

"No— Yes." *What am I saying?* "I was thinking about going. It'll be fun. You know, dancing . . . ," I babble.

When I manage to stop the tumble of words, Michael says, "Awesome."

I wait for more. For a question. For some idea of what this conversation is about. "Yeah."

"You want to share a limo with me and Lia? Holland and DeMarco are in."

I parse the equation and figure out that he isn't asking me on a date. Lia is his date. "Sure. Yeah. A limo."

"Cool. Let Mason know." Michael cuffs my shoulder.

There's no zap of romantic connection, no gentleness, no lingering touch. It's simply friendly. And not at all gay. "Yeah, I will. Thanks."

"And you got that hard-copy submission, right?"

I tap my laptop. "Yeah."

"Thanks for typing it up," he says, and turns in the direction of his locker. I head to the music wing to pick up my trumpet, letting out a breath I didn't know I was holding.

Crossing Jordan
by Juliet Polmanski

This stretch of nothing highway
just past the roar and cheer of the racetrack
is as quiet as a cemetery
and dotted with white crosses.

I drive as slow as a funeral procession
looking for mine,
my brother's,
my hero's.

I pull onto the shoulder,
step out into the silence
to untangle the tumbleweed
from my faded silk flowers.

With a Sharpie,
I darken the letters of his name—
Jordan, like the river of tears
flowing into the dead sea.

I'm done with asking why,
and pray only that he knows
I love him. Loved him.
More than silk flowers

can ever say.

TWO

"Hey, Mom," I call as I shut the front door behind me. I let my backpack fall to the floor and kick off my sneakers.

"Hi, honey," my mom says from the kitchen, her voice as chirpy as the beep of the microwave. "How was school?"

I don't have time to answer before my two-year-old twin sisters assault my knees.

"Jamie, Jamie," Elisabeth greets me, hugging one knee.

Ann Marie doesn't bother with words; she just shrieks and tugs on my jeans.

I try to move, but Elisabeth is doing a good job as an anchor. I peel her from my leg and carry her into the kitchen, following an excited Ann Marie. Ann Marie shows me her doll—who is taking a bath in the spaghetti pot.

"School was school," I tell my mom. "And we finally got some decent art for *Gumshoe*."

"About time," she says, and holds up a box of frozen chicken nuggets. "How many?"

"Six," I answer, although I don't particularly care for processed chicken bits.

"'Icken," Elisabeth says.

"Yeah," I tell her. I couldn't agree more. This is my mom's idea of cooking: chicken nuggets, tater tots, pork 'n' beans, mac 'n' cheese—anything with an 'n' instead of a real word. It's been this way since she went back to work and Frank started working out of state.

He's home for the moment, which makes my mom happy—she has her husband back—and nervous—because if he's here, he isn't working. And if he isn't working, he isn't getting paid.

I pick up the spaghetti pot and my laptop, and take the girls into their room, leaving Mom with a few minutes of peace while she heats up dinner. I play dolls with Ann Marie while Elisabeth packs a toy purse with plastic pork chops and alphabet blocks. I don't know if she's ever seen a real pork chop, so maybe it all makes sense to her.

Settling in to watch them, I sit on the floor and lean back against their toy chest. I open InDesign and scroll through the pages until I find a blank one. Reading Juliet's poem, I type it in. Then I proofread my version against

13

hers to check that I've copied it exactly. Unfortunately, I have. It's about Jordan, and it leaves a little ache in my heart.

I look up at my sisters and put my computer down. I crawl over to where Ann Marie has abandoned her dolls and is unpacking Elisabeth's purse.

"Pork chop," I say, and pretend to take a bite. I hold it out to her.

She leans forward and pretends to eat too.

Elisabeth joins in, and the three of us make sloppy chewing sounds until we burst into a fit of giggles. I start a tickle war but soon regret it. They pin me and wiggle their small hands under my arms. Mom pokes her head in, wondering if I need to be rescued.

Later I help the twins into their booster seats and slide their chairs up to the kitchen table. They've got bibs, plastic plates, sippy cups, and little kid silverware, as if dinner is a sport that needs safety gear.

"Jamie," my stepdad says while stabbing a chicken nugget with his fork, "I was talking with my friend Sal, and he said he needs some guys to fill out his crew this summer."

Sal started a landscaping business back when construction took a nosedive. His crew fixes sprinklers and mows lawns—not my idea of a fun summer job, but I don't say so.

"Frank," Mom says. "Jamie has a summer job all lined up—"

"I know, I know. But this is outside. Fresh air and sunshine," Frank explains to Mom. Then he fakes a punch to my shoulder. "Build up those muscles, get some color, huh, bud?"

I fake a smile. And wince inside. That's so Frank— built, tan, construction contractor Frank with sawdust on his clothes and dirt in the laces of his steel-toed boots. And so not me—beanpole tall and prone to sunburn. Sure, I used to love tagging along to construction sites where he'd show me my mom's designs being built. The last day was always my favorite—and not because of the new Day-Glo green grass—but because the signs would be up: shiny letters stating the name of the business inside, rows of numbers on the doors indicating the address, bright neon curls announcing that it was open.

I have no interest in mowing lawns this summer. I *want* to work at my mom's architectural firm, running errands, redoing the website, updating the brochure, and photographing projects. And I want to remind Frank that I flipped burgers and asked people if they wanted "fries with that" all last summer to buy my Mac—tell him that I've earned this job.

But Frank is, as usual, trying too hard at the stepdad thing, as if he wants to be my receding-hairline superhero. "I thought you'd like to earn a few bucks. Sal pays more than your mother does."

"Hey," my mom says.

"It's not about the money," I say instead of *hell no*. "I want to work for Mom."

A look of dejection crosses Frank's face. "I put in a good word for you with Sal, that's all."

"Thanks, but I get all the lawn-mowing fun I need around here." I do. He's always away at a job site or just getting home or about to leave again. And I mow the lawn.

"Exactly!" His face bounces up into a smile. "That's what I told Sal. That you have experience."

I close my eyes and let my head fall into my hands. He doesn't get it. He never gets it.

"Now, honey," my mom says to me. "It would be nice to have a little extra to put toward tuition in the fall."

That's what happens when you get a new stepdad at fifteen, followed by two baby sisters and a Honda for your sixteenth birthday. Don't get me wrong: I love my sisters. And my car might be a POS, but it's mine. The college tuition money my mom had carefully saved for me, though, is no longer all mine. It's divided three ways. And the new guy that lives down the hall? He's not my dad no matter how hard he tries. And Mom? I have to share her, too.

My dad? He never married her. They were college sweethearts, but after graduation they found jobs in different cities and promised each other they'd work something out. They never did. Sure, he visited a few times when I was a kid, sent child support when he could. But that stopped the day I turned eighteen. He and I were always on tectonic plates, slowly drifting apart, from father and son to nothing over the course of eighteen years.

THREE

In gym class the next morning, a rough-and-tumble game of two-hand touch is tied at 21–21. Coach Callahan has given up on the soccer unit and let the guys play football instead. It's shirts vs. skins and Brodie Hamilton vs. Kellen Zalaba. They look like they're having fun—not that I want to join them. The skins part of shirts vs. skins can be a little distracting when you're trying to catch a ball and run at the same time—oh, and not run into Lincoln High's defensive MVP, Nick O'Shea, a six-foot-three wall of muscle. His friends call him Red and everyone else refers to him as the Redneck—and not just because he drives a vintage two-tone Chevy Silverado. He's the kind of guy you don't want to run into on the field or off. In fact, guys like DeMarco, Michael, and I walk wide circles around him. So I've opted out of the game in favor of running a mile.

Today I walk an extra lap to cool down and, on my

way back inside, I find Mason staring up at the sky. His back is to me, the game ball tucked under one arm. He looks like a modern day Greek god in a faded John Deere T-shirt—his dark curls his personal brand of halo.

I stand beside him and follow his gaze. A plane passes overhead, its contrail neatly dividing the brilliant blue sky in two. The line is as crisp and as white as the snow lingering on Shafer Butte.

"I can't wait to get outta here," he says. "Live my own life."

"So with you, man," I agree. "Frank wants me to mow lawns all summer."

"Lawns, as in plural?"

"Yeah. For his friend Sal."

"And you don't want to, I take it."

"Bingo." I bump his shoulder and start toward the doors.

"Jamie," he calls out, and when I turn, he tosses me the ball.

I catch it, backpedal, and launch it to him in a graceful arc.

He snatches it from the air and runs toward me, zigzagging as if to dare me to tackle him.

I bend at the waist and spread my arms out to my sides.

Mason fakes left and zigzags right.

I catch him by the waist and his momentum spins us

around. In a dizzying flash, he grabs my arm and holds it tight against his ribs. I feel them shake as he laughs. One more revolution and we stumble to the ground.

"Dork," I tell him, and flop onto my back. "I was tackling you."

Spread out like he's making a snow angel in the grass, he lifts the ball from under his arm. "Nah, total touchdown."

"Touchdown? Not even close," I protest, and reach for the ball.

But Mason points up at the split-in-two sky. I lie back to look.

We watch the contrail as it fades away. I wonder about college next year and the million things that will change in our lives, like living away from home, on our own without parents and siblings. I wonder if college will feel like home, if I'll make new friends, if coming out will finally let me feel like I fit in.

I know Mason's itching to leave, probably because he shares a room with his older brother, Gabe. And his sister, Londa, can be a royal pain. He'll be the first one to go away to college. (Gabe works at the family garage, and Londa goes to Boise State; they both still live at home.) One thing's for sure: he'll be glad not to be working for his father.

"Just a few more weeks," I say.

"I hope I survive," Mason says. "Five APs and Purdy's

exam. It all just might kill me."

"You'll ace 'em," I say.

Mason chuckles. "Thanks, man."

I stand up. I reach for Mason's hand and pull him to his feet. "So, about prom. You want to share a limo with me, Holland, DeMarco, Lia, and Michael?"

"Don't you need a date first?"

"Ouch," I say, and clutch my chest.

This makes him smile. "See?" he says. "McCall."

"No McCall," I tell him. "Bahti will kill you if you back out, and I told Michael we'd share a limo."

Grinning as if he's pulling my leg, he shakes his head and walks toward the building.

I follow him through the door. I'm so confused. He says he's going to prom because I'm going to prom, but then he goes and mentions McCall again—like he doesn't want to go to prom. I don't get it. I don't know about him, but I want to get dressed up, ride in a limo, dance, and party until sunrise. It'll be one of those things you never forget. Besides, I've never gone to a school dance because of the lack-of-date problem. But I like to dance. Well, I think I'd like to dance. I want to go to prom, and I know it'll be one hundred times better with Mason there. "It'll be fun," I say, trying to convince him. "Promise."

"*McCall* would be fun," he says, and walks down the hall toward the locker room, leaving me standing there, looking at the back of his green T-shirt and at how the worn fabric is pulled taut across his shoulder blades. He runs one hand through his hair, his bicep rising in a smooth hill of honey-colored skin. I watch, mesmerized, as his hair tangles between his fingers and springs free again, one curl, then another.

What is up with him?

What's up with me?

I didn't just check out my best friend. *Did I?*

FOUR

No. No, no. No.

I did not just do that. *I can't believe I just did that!* Mason and I have been friends since third grade, and I have never looked at him like that. Other guys, yeah, but not him. It should be in the Bible. *Thou shalt not check out thy best friend.*

I wait a minute to catch my breath and the last shred of my sanity before I follow Mason into the locker room. I head for the sinks and splash water onto my face in an attempt to straighten out my thoughts. I'm okay with bent thoughts—I have them all the time—but checking out Mason? That's going too far. He's my best friend. And everyone knows friend crushes are the worst—even guy-girl friend crushes—drama, angst, broken hearts, you name it. It's bad—real bad. And straight-guy-gay-guy friend crushes? I don't even want to think about that apocalypse.

I take a deep breath and watch as the water collects along my upper lip. I mouth the words, *Mason. Is. Not. Cute.*

But I'm *so* lying to myself. Under his glasses, mop of curls, and total lack of fashion sense is a square jaw, a straight nose, and an amazing smile. And, well, totally kissable lips. *Mason. Is. Not. Cute. Not cute. Not cute.* I chant in my mind as I splash more cold water on my face and then rub it dry with the hem of my shirt.

I check out my hair in the mirror. It's in need of a major overhaul. Sweat is so not a hair product. I pick a piece of dandelion fuzz from over my left ear and stick my head under the tap. I pull off my T-shirt and dry my hair with it. I grab my emergency hair gel from my locker and run a dollop through my shortish sandy-blond hair, arranging it into a perfect, just-rolled-out-of-bed sexy mess. Satisfied, I get dressed and apply half a stick of deodorant.

By the time I'm done, Mason is gone.

In art class, I sit in my usual seat next to Eden.

"Challis was looking for you," she says.

"In a good way?" I ask with a flicker of hope. Maybe Challis will ask me to prom. That would save me a whole lot of trouble in the date-finding department—she's the president of the Gay-Straight Alliance and clearly batting for the home team. We'd go as friends.

"Not exactly," Eden admits.

I see Challis, tall and thin, stomping into the room like a moody runway model.

She whips out a sheet of paper then slaps her hand down on it, cementing it to the table in front of me. "You rejected my drawing!"

I peer around her fingers and recognize the image on the paper: the manga-style drawing from yesterday's *Gumshoe* meeting. "We vote by committee?" I say, but it sounds more like a question.

She barks half a laugh. "No, you don't. You do art. Lia, poetry. Holland, flash fiction. Michael, shorts."

I ease the drawing out from under her hand. It's a guy dressed like Magellan, only wearing a beret and holding a paintbrush. He looks familiar, like he's from a game or a book.

Eden leans over to get a better look. "Nice," she says, admiring the picture.

"You have something against Leo?" Challis accuses.

Now I recognize him—a young Leonardo da Vinci from *Assassin's Creed*. "No, but I am looking for original characters, not fan art." *Phew*. A legitimate reason actually popped into my brain and came out of my mouth!

Challis's arched eyebrows form a straight line.

"And"—I fish for another brilliant answer—"I'm really looking for art that I can pair with writing, like a story set in the Renaissance and a painting inspired by da Vinci—that'd be cool."

This explanation does nothing to lift the eyebrow frown from her face.

I try again because I like Challis. "And I'd kill for a graphic short—give me one of those, and I'll get it in."

"A graphic short story?" she echoes.

I nod. Truth is, I admire Challis, maybe even wish I was more like her—out, proud, and in the GSA. Plus, she's an amazing artist.

"Any topic?"

"Um—" Eden chimes in, as if warning me against agreeing to this.

"Anything I can get past Taylor. So, like, no f-bombs, okay?" I clarify, already imagining how a comic would look awesome in *Gumshoe*.

Challis bites her lip while the corners of her mouth curl up into a smile. "You'll accept it?"

"Uh-huh."

"'Cause it'll be a ton of work," she explains.

"Yeah," Eden says. "Original characters are more time consuming."

"Promise," I tell Challis. "Original characters, and it's in."

After school Mason sags into the locker next to mine. "Gabe got my shift," he says about his brother. "Wanna save the world from the zombie apocalypse?"

"Sounds great," I say, and glance over at him. He looks like he always does at the end of the day, tired but content, and as if he just put an X through the calendar square in his day planner. His curls have straightened a little, and they hang in a curtain around the frames of his glasses. *See,* I tell myself. *He's not that cute. No way I have a crush on him.*

I throw my books in my backpack, and we walk out to the student parking lot, grumbling about the pop quiz in government. Mason tells me the correct answers, and I calculate that I scraped by with a C. I drive the three blocks while Mason cranks the radio.

After a few hours of Mason killing zombies and my character getting killed by them, Mason's cell chirps with a text. He pauses the game to read it. He frowns.

"What?" I ask.

"My mom's working late," he says.

Mason's mom works at the twenty-four-hour supermarket, and late can mean really late. But this isn't why he's frowning. "And I'm hungry."

Personally, I'm famished. One of Mrs. V's home-cooked meals would have really hit the spot.

"She said there's hamburger in the fridge," he adds, standing up.

Soon we have a couple of burgers sizzling in a skillet on the stove, and rolls are toasting in the oven. Mason

27

has his head buried in the pantry, looking for a can of chiles, when his dad and Gabe come in.

"Smells good," Gabe says. "What's for dinner?"

"Ham—" Mason starts to answer, appearing again with a can in hand.

But Mr. V cuts him off, asking questions in his rapid-fire Spanish. Not angry but not kind, either.

"At work," Mason manages to answer one before another round of questions begins.

I pull two or three words from the volley: *little girls* and *cooking* or maybe *kitchen*.

Mason presses his lips together, his skin darkening with embarrassment or anger before he tries to hide it. He opens a drawer and rummages around for a can opener.

Mr. V continues, gesturing to the backyard and saying something about *huevos*.

I flip the two burgers over, getting the gist. We are, in his opinion, playing house like little girls by cooking in the kitchen instead of grilling like real men.

Gabe finds two beers in the fridge and gives his father one, ushering him out of the kitchen. "Put on another two, would you, Mace?" he asks on his way out.

"Effin' A," Mason mutters. "Make your own goddamn dinner."

We eat our chile-and-cheese-topped hamburgers on the steps that lead to the backyard, sharing a bag of chips and drinking orange soda from cans. We're quiet for a while, and I remember when Mason went from idolizing his father to antagonizing him.

The summer after seventh grade—the summer Mason spent in Mexico—was the worst summer of our lives. Mine because Mason was gone. His because he dug up a family secret. See, Mason's father has two families: one here and one in Mexico. Mason is the youngest of five children total, Londa and Gabe being his full brother and sister.

His half sister, Clara, had come to visit the summer before. The trip was a birthday present. She had just turned twenty. She made the best tortillas, and we ate our fill while teaching her dirty words in English. We said she'd need to know them now that she was living in the States. She laughed, ruffled Mason's hair, and said he was just like their brother Pedro. He'd shrugged off her comment, thinking he was nothing like Pedro. Pedro, he imagined, was more like Gabe, a tall, muscular teenager interested in cars and girls. Or maybe girls, then cars.

But when he met Pedro the awful summer that followed, he learned Clara was right. Pedro wasn't older than Gabe like he had thought he would be. He was fourteen—just a year older than Mason and me. And the math was off. Seriously off.

Gabe confirmed Mason's suspicions—that Pedro was their half brother and, yes, his father had cheated on their mom with Clara's mother. Pedro was the result. Mason asked Gabe why no one in the family ever told him about the affair. And Gabe said, "You've always known about Pedro. I just didn't know you thought he was eighteen."

In Mason's mind, Pedro's age changed everything.

He had heard the family story that his father wasn't there when he was born—a month premature. He knew that his mom had named him Mason and that his father didn't like it—he had planned on naming him Diego so all five of them would have Spanish names. Now Mason knew about Pedro, and—according to Londa—that their father had been in Mexico with Pedro instead of at the hospital with their mom.

Mason is his mother's maiden name, and it fits—because he is pretty brick-headed sometimes. That summer, Mason built a wall between himself and his father. He stopped speaking Spanish. Not a word. He signed up for French the following year, even though he could have tested out of all the foreign language credits, like Gabe and Londa did. And now? Exchanges between Mason and his father sound pretty much like what just happened in the kitchen.

"Do you think Sal would hire me?" Mason asks, breaking the silence.

"You want to mow lawns?"

"More like I don't want to work for my dad."

"Probably," I say. "I'll tell Frank you're interested."

"Thanks," he says, and takes a bite of his burger. When he's finished chewing, he changes the topic. "You should ask that art-geek girl to prom. I think she likes you."

"Challis? She's a lesbian. And pissed that she didn't get into *Gumshoe*," I say, even though Challis would be a perfect prom date. If she wasn't mad at me.

"No. The other one. The one you sit with?"

"Eden O'Shea?"

"Yeah."

"Eden likes me?" I never got that vibe from her. I mean, we're strictly platonic.

"In a googly-eyed-fan-girl way, yeah."

"It's not like that."

Mason presses his lips together, but the corner of his mouth curls up in a grin.

I elbow him.

"Sooo . . . ," he drawls. "You're just friends, huh?"

"Yeah. Just friends."

"Girls don't want to go as friends, though," Mason says. "They want romance, slow dancing, hotel rooms."

"Hotel rooms?" I hadn't thought of that.

"Yeah, duh. Why do you think prom is at the Riverside Hotel?"

The color has probably drained from my face. There is no way I'd be caught dead in a hotel room with a girl.

Okay, well, maybe if I *were* dead.

"Kidding," Mason says quietly, bumping my shoulder.

I bump his shoulder back and let the silence fall around us once again. We don't talk, just eat. Our elbows brush each other's on occasion, but neither of us moves away.

FIVE

Michael has a date. Mason has a date. The popular guys like Brodie and Kellen have had dates since elementary school. I still do not have a prom date.

But this doesn't stop me from marching up to the prom ticket table after school. "Two please," I say to Bahti.

"We're sharing a limo," she says in her British-tinged accent.

"Yeah." I hand her the money.

"Who's your date?" she asks, friendly because we know each other from band.

"Dunno."

"You don't know?" she asks. "Prom is a week and a half away, Jamie. All my friends are taken."

Thank God, I almost blurt. Because Bahti's friends are supersmart—like Mason—and I don't want to spend the evening comparing GPAs. (For the record, I am not a runner-up for anything.)

Then I remember my manners and say, "That so?"

"So sorry. Good luck." She hands me my tickets with a smile that's edged with pity.

At home I drop my backpack on the floor, shout "I'm home," and head to the kitchen for a snack. I make a triple-decker PB&J with raspberry jam, take the carton of milk into the living room, and collapse on the couch in front of the TV. A *Jerry Springer* rerun is on, and I watch it on mute—Mom doesn't want the twins to hear people argue like that. It's funnier this way, anyway. A heavy chick's arm flab jiggles as she jabs a finger at a rapping midget.

Ann Marie waddles in, holding out my English notebook as if it were some sort of present.

"Thank you," I coo to her sweetly, while my mind says, *Oh crap*.

The twins got into my backpack. Or, well, Elisabeth has it hiked up over one shoulder and is dragging it around behind her, upside down, its contents spilling out in a slow-motion avalanche.

I take another bite of my sandwich and tiptoe after her—so she won't break into a run.

"Oh, honey, thank you," Mom says in the other room. Ann Marie must have given her some of my homework to do.

I coax my backpack away from Elisabeth by convincing her it's time to play baby dolls, then I sweep my stuff back inside before Ann Marie returns for another load.

I'm sitting on the floor of the twins' room, rocking a doll in one arm while Elisabeth holds a bottle to its lips, when my mom appears in the doorway.

"Who's the lucky guy?" she asks, fanning herself with my prom tickets.

"Mom!" My cheeks grow warm.

"Oh, you don't have to tell me," she says. "I was just curious."

"It's just that— Well, I don't know yet."

She laughs gently, then asks, "Can I pay for your tickets anyway?"

I nod, not having the heart to tell her that I'll probably chicken out and ask a girl, not a guy, to prom. Which I could, technically. But it doesn't seem worth the fuss, even if I liked someone, which I don't. Lincoln High isn't exactly crawling with cute gay guys, except maybe a sophomore or two. I wonder if Mom will be disappointed. She's been this way—eager—ever since I came out to her, as if she can't wait for me to bring a boyfriend home to meet her.

"Burp," Elisabeth says.

I shift a doll over my shoulder and pat its back absentmindedly.

I never had baby dolls, never played dress up in my

mom's high heels, and never wanted to join the cheer-leading squad, so it wasn't like my mom knew I was gay. So I had to come out to her and Frank. Believe me, it was the worst thing ever. It's not like they kicked me out of the house or sent me to boarding school or any-thing, but it was awful. I wanted to tell them before they got married, just in case big guy's guy Frank had a problem with having a gay stepkid. But as the weeks and months passed by, they picked out flowers, hired a pho-tographer, and ordered cake—and I kept choking on the words. The longer it dragged on, the harder it got to say. I couldn't sleep at night, and my stomach was a constant knot of worry. I lost a few pounds, dragged myself out of bed in the morning, and watched way too many talk shows after school.

My mom was convinced that something was wrong with me and made a doctor's appointment for me. Then, when the doctor confirmed that I was physically fine, she made me an appointment with a counselor. And coun-selor is a nice word for shrink. So I said it. In the car, on the way to the shrink's. "Mom, I'm gay."

She pulled over—right there on Capitol Boulevard—and gave me a great big hug. She started crying, and I thought it was because she was upset. No one wants a gay kid, right? All parents want is weddings and daughters-in-law and grandchildren, right? Well, no. My mom was happy about it! She asked if I was seeing anyone. And her face fell a little when I said no. But I was in ninth grade, for Pete's sake.

"You have to tell Frank and Grandma," I informed her. Coming out once was all I had in me.

"You sure?" she asked, mopping up tears with a yellow Wendy's napkin she found in the console. "It's your special news."

And while I spent the next fifty minutes talking to that counselor about anything but being gay, my mom called Frank.

To this day I don't know how he pulled it off. But when we came home, the kitchen was decorated. *Decorated!* With two dozen balloons, rainbow streamers, and pink heart-shaped confetti. There was an ice-cream cake with rainbow sprinkles and *Way to go, Jamie!* written on it.

I was mortified.

I couldn't tell him that coming out was private—to me, anyway—and celebrating it made me cringe inside. So I tried to sneak upstairs to my bedroom and crawl back in the closet, but Frank cajoled me into staying with a stack of brightly wrapped presents.

I should have gone upstairs.

They were books. Embarrassing books with titles like *The LGBTQ High School Survival Guide*, *Your Sexuality and You*, and *Queue: Authors Line Up Tell Their Coming-Out Stories*. My mom got *Parenting Your Gay Teen*, and for Frank, *The Dummies' Guide to Stepparenting an*

LGBT Child. He must have bought the whole shelf at the bookstore.

I grabbed Frank's book and paged through it furiously. I was looking for the idiot box where it told him to throw me a party. I didn't find one. And my heart sank. I would have felt better if he had done this because some dummy told him to.

But he came up with it on his own.

imagined
—E. K. O.

there's this boy in my class
who's matt-damon adorable,
with idaho summer-sky blue eyes,
the same turned-up nose
smattered with freckles,
and lips quick to reveal
his famous, nervous smile.

all the girls are in love with him,
but he doesn't know it,
and perhaps this is what
we love about him.

or maybe we love
how he and his best friend
are perfect for each other,
only they don't realize it.

and maybe, just maybe,
this is what we love about him.
the idea of them together—
walking side by side, hand in hand
under an idaho-blue summer sky,
across an emerald hayfield
smattered with wildflowers,
his lips quick to say
a nervous "i love you."

six

I find a poem in my locker when I get to school. And even though I know it's someone's *Gumshoe* submission, I don't read it, but rather pretend for a minute that it's for me from a secret admirer and slip it into my pocket. I imagine it's full of intimate details, like how he likes my hair or my ridiculously childish freckles. It ends with a clue—there'd have to be a clue—of where to meet and when. We'd both show up, of course, and sit on a blanket under the stars, the warm April air having nothing to do with the shiver running down my spine.

Too bad imaginary secret admirers don't make viable prom dates.

In art, Ms. Maude has the lights off and the projector on, and we're flying through art history at breakneck speed. We started the semester with the cave paintings in Lascaux and, with three weeks of classes to go, we are up to Marcel Duchamp and his urinal. Ms. Maude is certain we'll get up to present-day art by the end of the term, but the class has a bet going—most of the girls say she will and the guys say she won't.

I write *$1* in my notebook and slide it across the table to Eden.

In my pocket, she writes back.

I'm about to write *No way* when Ms. Maude leaps ahead half a decade and sums up Dadaism in one sentence. *No fair.* She segues to the Bauhaus, and I know I should be listening. Those Bauhaus dudes are the founding fathers of graphic design.

But I'm not listening. *You going to prom?* I write. Again I slide my notebook to Eden.

She looks at me, an are-you-crazy? expression on her face.

I gesture at the note.

She writes something. Slides it back. *No.*

Why not? I scribble.

She doesn't wait for me to pass the notebook; she just reaches over and writes. *No date.*

Be mine.

She looks at me again, then writes: *I thought you were gay.*

I freeze. *How the hell does she know?*

Eden takes the paper back before I write anything. *And you want to go to prom with me?*

Yes.

Not possible, she scribbles.

Why not?

Ms. Maude glances our way, and Eden pretends she's taking notes on the lecture. When she slides my notebook back, it reads: *You're out of my league. Not to mention the wrong gender.*

The wrong gender? I try not to look surprised and I ignore that part. *What league?*

The popular one.

I'm not popular. I'm in band.

Eden sighs as if I'm clueless, and she pushes my notebook back at me without an answer.

Please, I write. I didn't know dating involved so much persuasion.

Why?

Because you're cool. I offer her the notebook.

She reads my note and shakes her head.

I try again. *Because I want to get to know you better.*

She fake gags on her finger.

Because I'll have a good time if you're there.

Eden smiles.

And I have a prom date.

"Here's the thing," Eden says as we pack up our stuff after class. "My parents are überstrict about stuff I do—they don't usually let me go to school dances."

All that work and she can't go? *Dang it.*

"But since it's prom and you're a guy, I think it'll be okay."

Phew.

"But before I can go anywhere with you, you'll have to prove you're an upstanding citizen."

"How am I supposed to do that?"

"We'll start with just my mom. You come over, and we'll go somewhere like we're dating."

"Yeah," I say. "That's how prom works. I pick you up. We go to prom."

"Before prom. Like, today. Or tomorrow."

"Okay," I agree, because if finding one prom date was this difficult, finding a second one is out of the question. And besides, Eden and I are sort of friends. We could do stuff outside of art class.

Eden takes my hand, turns it palm up, and writes down an address.

"Four thirty," she says.

When I find the address that Eden wrote on my hand, I'm relieved not to see her brother's truck parked in the driveway. Seeing him once a day is about my limit.

After I've answered no fewer than twenty questions for Eden's mom, including if I have taken the Lord Jesus Christ as my savior—which, well, I might have lied about—Eden and I are seated in a booth at a Shari's.

"When did you *know*?" Eden asks me, her emphasis implying everything.

"Huh?" I play dumb. If she thinks I'm going to come out to her just so she'll go to prom with me, she's going to wait until the second coming.

"Oh," she says, suddenly interested in the menu. "Sorry, I just thought we had something in common. I can totally relate, you know?"

This is why I don't date girls. They're weird. They talk about everything and assume you want to too. I don't get it. It's as if their bras are filled with words.

"In sixth grade I had a crush on a girl in Sunday school," she offers up as proof to my theory.

"How'd that work out for you?" I ask.

"Not good," Eden says. "This other girl squealed when she saw us kissing behind the boathouse at church camp."

"Bummer."

"Nothing brings down the wrath of God faster than two girls kissing," she says.

I wonder about two boys kissing, but I don't say anything.

"I haven't been allowed to go to church camp since."

The waitress comes to take our orders. I get a burger and fries. Eden just orders a soda.

"So you're out with your parents?" I ask when the waitress is out of earshot.

"Tried to be," Eden says. "But they don't believe in lesbians—for them, it's something I did, not something I am. And, well, their daughter can't possibly be one."

"That's pretty weird," I say.

"I've tried to educate them, but every time I bring it up, my mom gets really upset."

I nod sympathetically.

"So Nick can do whatever he wants—as long as he goes to church on Sunday. Has his own truck. And me? They won't let me out of their sight. They wouldn't want me to be tempted by the she-devil."

The waitress brings us our drinks.

"Yeah," I say. "You wouldn't want a girl like you to step out the house. She might drink a soda at Shari's."

Eden laughs. "I know. I am such a rebel."

My burger arrives, and we share the fries and gab about prom—the limo plans and who is going with whom.

An hour later I pull into Eden's driveway behind the Redneck's truck. She doesn't open her door right away, as if she's waiting for something.

"You okay?" I ask, following her gaze and feeling a flicker of worry in my gut.

She's watching her house.

Then I see what she sees. Her mom is watching us from a window.

Eden turns her head quickly—catching me off

guard—and plants a lip-gloss-sticky kiss right next to my mouth.

"Ew!" I reach up to wipe off the strawberry-scented slime.

"No, you don't," Eden says, catching my hand on its way to my face.

"Why'd you do that?" I ask.

She rolls her eyes and juts her chin toward the house.

I don't see her mother anymore, and I imagine she's telling Nick to unlock the gun safe and drop a bullet into the chamber of a shotgun. I imagine him storming out the door, ready to take aim at the boy who appears to be taking advantage of his little sister.

"Don't do that again," I say, touching my cheek. My fingers get slimed with lip gloss. "It's—" I stop myself before I say "gross," because I don't want to sound like a little kid.

"Come on, Jamie. I didn't even touch your lips."

I wipe the lip gloss from my cheek, and I can taste the strawberry. My face bunches up as if I'd bit into a lemon.

"Don't look at me like that!" Eden says. "I don't have cooties. Or mono."

"I know," I say. "I'm sorry. It's just that, well, I—"

"You don't like kissing girls?"

"Yeah, and . . . ," I trail off.

But from the look on my face, Eden deciphers my *other* secret. "Oh. My. Gaga. You've never kissed anyone!"

"Hey!" I say. But it's true. I've never kissed anyone in a romantic way.

"Jamie, you're a senior in high school! And you've never been kissed?"

I didn't need her to point that out. "I'd hardly call that ambush a kiss."

Eden puckers her lips and I duck behind my hands. I hear her making smoochy sounds.

She stops and I peek at her.

"You're adorable, Jamie Peterson," she says, and opens the car door. "I had a nice time. So thanks."

I back out of the driveway and drive home. I rest my forehead on the steering wheel and close my eyes. I feel drained of energy.

And then it hits me.

I told her I didn't like kissing girls.

SEVEN

Friday I'm exhausted. I didn't sleep at all last night. I kept having dreams about kissing Eden. Sometimes I'd *like* it—and then I'd have to un-come out to my mom and Frank. Other times I'd open my eyes and it wasn't Eden at all, but Mason. Wearing lip gloss.

The guys in gym class are organizing another game of touch football, so I opt for a slow jog around the track to try to clear my head. I've got to start thinking about the *Gumshoe* layout and look at the cover design again. The last of the writing and art should be submitted today.

Half the guys peel off their T-shirts, and I trip over my own feet. I stop, pretend to retie my Chucks, and check out who is on the skins side of shirts vs. skins. It's Brodie, last season's varsity quarterback, against Kellen, but Kellen has the Redneck on his defensive line—or maybe as his entire defensive line. Mason is on Brodie's team, staring down the Redneck with fire in his eyes, his glasses off, and his T-shirt is hanging from the waistband of his shorts. I stare for a moment. The morning sun paints his torso bronze, and I can't help but think of a sculpture of David and Goliath from Ms. Maude's art history slides.

I shake my head, hoping to erase the image like an Etch a Sketch. It doesn't work. This isn't just a passing bent thought. I have a crush on my best friend.

With all the distractions, it takes me twenty minutes to run a mile. Or maybe I ran two. I don't know. I lost count of the laps. I'm just finishing my shower when the others burst into the locker room with a thunderous roar of laughter, footsteps, and banging doors. I crank the water off, wrap a towel around my waist, and head to my locker—eyes on the tiles. I'm tying my Chucks when a pair of dirt-encrusted, steel-toed work boots fill my view.

"You work on the fag mag?" The Redneck towers over me.

"Uh, um?" *Fag mag? Where'd he get that?* Oh yeah, the male staff members are Michael, who's rumored to be gay; DeMarco, who doesn't play basketball; and me.

"The fag mag. Gum-on-my-shoe."

"Yeah, *Gumshoe*."

He juts his chin to one side, and I hear his vertebrae crack and pop.

I panic and grip the bench.

He doesn't chew me out for taking his sister to Shari's or eat me for breakfast, but rather grunts, "I wrote something."

"Cool," I choke out, and stand up. His Adam's apple is practically at my eye level.

"Taylor said I'd get extra credit if I submitted it." He shoves a piece of wrinkled notebook paper at me.

I take it. And hope he'll leave. Soon.

But he doesn't. He stands there like he's thinking, then says, "My sister said you're taking her to prom. That the truth?"

I nod, hoping he's not the overprotective type.

"You, like, her boyfriend or something?"

I don't know how to answer this, so I say, "Or something."

He cocks his head.

"Nothing serious," I explain. "Friends."

He nods once, then gestures to the notebook paper in my hand. "Don't show it to nobody."

I'm about to agree but realize I can't—in order to submit it, the other Gumshoes will have to read it. "Wait, Red—" I start to say, but I stop before I say *neck* instead of *Nick*.

He turns in slow motion, like I'd imagine a grizzly bear would if catching a whiff of blueberry pancakes.

"I'll, um, have to show it to the *Gumshoe* staff. Is . . . Is that okay?"

"Yeah, but no one else."

"Got it," I say, and slide the paper into my pocket.

Unsucceeding
By Anon

It doesn't take much to fall behind.
A spelling test, a book report,
A teacher who holds you back a grade.

A small step not taken and you've fallen short,
Fallen on your face. You've lost the game
Before you even stepped onto the field.

But work hard at what you're good at
Block every receiver, every punch,
Every blow to your self-esteem.

And it still isn't good enough.
Because you know deep inside
That you've failed at the American dream.

EIGHT

"So now that you have a date . . . ," Mason says, sliding into the seat next to me at our end of the cafeteria table. He has on a plaid button-down over a white tee, the sleeves of the former rolled up. "Suit or a tux?"

"Tux," I say, closing the file with my English paper on my computer. "And a real tie. Not a clip-on."

Mason laughs. "Yeah, Londa wears a clip-on at work."

Londa waits tables at some pseudofancy Italian restaurant, which is why she's almost always busy when my mom asks her to babysit my sisters.

Mason gestures at my computer and I give it to him. He opens a browser window and types *prom looks for guys* in the search box. A picture of a really cute guy in a well-fitting white shirt appears onscreen.

A shock of attraction jolts me. My fingers itch to

reach over and cover the screen so no one else can see it—and see right through me. Not that looking at a cute guy constitutes inappropriate computer use on school property, a suspension-worthy offense, but he is H. O. T.

Mason glances at me, a teasing smile tugging at his lips. "Buy a tux?" he asks the screen after reading the copy. "What planet are they from?" He clicks an arrow, paging through a slideshow of prom dos and don'ts.

The boys aren't as cute, so I start to calm down. Until a picture of Darren Criss—the dark-haired dreamboat of *Glee* fame—pops up. He's wearing a pair of chunky black glasses and a suit and looking a lot like Mason. "Yeah," I tell Mason and reach for my computer. "Classic. And renting."

If he notices me noticing him and any resemblance to Darren Criss, he pretends not to. "What do you want?" He jerks his chin at the lunch line.

"Pizza. And a Heath Bar," I say, standing up again.

"No, I'll get it," Mason says.

I hand him my caf card.

He takes it, his fingers brushing mine.

I watch him walk away, his jeans slung low on his hips and the pockets hugging his backside just right. My mind curves into the gutter, and I imagine sliding my fingers into one of those pockets.

No. No. No.

This has got to stop.

I shouldn't be crushing on him. Friend crushes always end in with a broken heart, if not a broken friendship. I should totally be crushing on someone else, like Darren Criss, for example, or Brodie Hamilton—every girl in school has fallen in love with him at some point in time. *How about Kellen?* He'd look good in a tux, even one with a clip-on tie.

Anyone but Mason.

When I walk into art, I see Eden sitting on a desk talking to Challis and a cluster of art-geek girls, one of whom is coloring her fingernails with a black Sharpie. I pretend not to notice them, figuring it'd be for the better, considering the beans I spilled to Eden yesterday. It doesn't work. I hear my name and turn around.

"Jamie asked me to prom!" Eden announces. "And we went on a date yesterday too."

"But he's—" Challis begins, then drops her voice to a whisper as she continues her sentence.

I can't hear what she's saying, but my mind fills in the blank. And my lungs fill with dread. *No,* I think, as if telepathy is a viable option. *I'm not out at school.*

The girls' heads bend together and bobble as they whisper. Sharpie girl's smile widens with each juicy bit of gossip.

After a minute Eden says, "Mason? Really? But he's going with Bahti."

The dread spreads outward from my lungs, and my arms go cold.

"They should so go to prom togeth—" Sharpie girl says.

Um. No.

"Ssh-zip!" Challis interrupts, zipping her lips and motioning toward me.

The conversation ends with an awkward silence, Eden and Challis each giving the Sharpie girl a reproachful look. She shrugs them off, mouthing the words, *It's true.*

Forget cold. My face flames as anger churns to life in my gut. *WTF?* I feel like shouting at her. *Mason and I are not going to prom together. It's not true—it's all in that marker-sniffing head of yours!* I clench my jaw shut and march past them, not looking in their direction. I put my things down next to DeMarco and slide into a chair. I catch a pencil as it rolls off the table and anchor it with my cell phone.

"Hey," DeMarco says, as if noticing that I'm not in my usual seat. "Deadline's today."

"Yeah," I reply, glad to talk about *Gumshoe* and glad to be away from girls.

If he notices that I'm steaming, he doesn't let on. "You read Juliet Polmanski's piece?"

I nod as Ms. Maude dims the lights and starts in on the race to the art-history finish line. Jackson Pollock

55

splashes up on the screen. I send her a silent thank-you because we aren't working on our portraits today. I can't focus on drawing right now.

I can't focus on anything. Not clearly, anyway. I tell myself that I don't want to know what Eden told Challis and her groupies, or on what planet that girl got the idea that Mason and I should go to prom together, or how the hell my social life is any of their business. I wonder how my crush became public knowledge when I hardly acknowledge it myself. I haven't told a soul. And I don't plan on it. Mason's my best friend, and I'd never do anything to hurt him—not that rumors that you're gay physically hurt, but they're pretty lethal when you're straight. I take a deep breath and vow to never trust a girl with any personal information—not even if I need her to be my prom date—*ever again*. I exhale, slump in the chair, and close my eyes. Exhausted.

The bell rings at the end of class, jolting me awake.

"See you later," DeMarco says to me, and nods at Eden.

She's standing in front of me as if she's waiting to talk to me.

I ignore her and scramble for my stuff. I reach for my phone and pencils, and my arm brushes my computer. It slides a few inches closer to the edge of the table. I grab it, but miss my papers and a folder of assignments. They fall to the floor, fanning out.

Eden bends to pick them up at the same time I do.

Conk.

"Ouch!" I rub my head where it hit hers, even though it messes up my hair.

But Eden doesn't seem hurt. She retrieves a wrinkled paper from under a chair then stands there reading it. "Nick?" she asks, her voice a whisper.

The Redneck's poem. I snatch the page from her hand. "You didn't see that."

"You're not going to publish this, are you?"

"He submitted it," I say.

"I just don't think it's a good idea. It's really personal."

"Look, Eden, I gotta go," I snap, not wanting to get into the details. Then I grab my stuff and shoot out of the classroom faster than if it were on fire.

"Jamie!" someone calls after me.

I don't want to talk to Eden, or anyone else for that matter, so I pretend not to hear. But that doesn't last long, because Challis's legs are as long as mine. She catches up in an instant.

"I've got it!" she says, breathless.

"Got what?" I ask.

"The graphic short! For *Gumshoe*!"

Relief douses me in the face. Challis isn't here to ask me about the art-geek girl whisperfest. "Oh, yeah."

Challis holds out a folder with translucent marker paper spilling out on three sides.

I shift my stuff so I have a free hand to take it from her. "Thanks."

"I hope you like it," she says, a twinge of mischief in her voice.

But I can't promise her I will.

The Love Dare
by Challis Carmine

SPENCER SCHOOL
est. 1909

SHOWERS

TEE HEE HEE!

I HATE THIS SCHOOL!

ANOTHER BAD DAY, SON?

I DON'T KNOW WHY I CAN'T JUST GO TO CENTRAL.

I WENT TO CENTRAL. AND LOOK WHERE IT GOT ME.

OH, DAD, YOU'RE NOT SO BAD.

HI. I'M JUSTIN.

TONY.

I'M HAVING A PARTY— FOR MY BIRTHDAY. I SENT INVITES TO EVERYONE IN OUR GRADE, BUT—

BUT NOT ME. IT'S OKAY.

JUST BECAUSE I DIDN'T HAVE YOUR EMAIL.

HERE.

TAK
TAK
TAK

friend

YOU MADE IT!

YEAH. NICE PARTY.

SWWSSH

GASP

?

OVER HERE, COME ON.

NiNE

I love it.

I hate her.

But I love it—how she turned a mean prank upside down, how on the very last page there was one blip of color in the heart above the boys' hands. I'm already imagining it as the only color in the whole magazine— even if I have to color that heart red in every copy. I stare at the hearts on the page, each saying so much with so little, each bringing a little hope to my own heart.

But first I tell myself, I have to get the other Gumshoes to agree with it. Seven pages is a lot of space, longer than our best short stories. Then I have to get it past Dr. Taylor—an English teacher—when it's mostly art, and a comic at that.

Who am I kidding? That's not what I'm worried about. I'm worried about what everyone will think— specifically, what everyone will think about me when I tell them I want it included in *Gumshoe*. I might as well march down Capitol Boulevard waving a rainbow flag.

I hate her.

I hate having to bring this to the meeting. I hate that I like it. I hate that I told her I'd fight to get it in.

Oh God, what have I done?

I signed myself up to champion *Gumshoe*'s first gay comic. *Damn it.*

TEN

Lia's stack of submissions isn't as tall as we had hoped, even with the contributions from Challis and the Redneck, plus the poem I found in my locker, which I snuck in at the bottom. She sorts the pieces into piles, and when she gets down to the comic, she adds it to my pile of drawings.

"It's a short story," I say. "Give it to Michael."

With that, Lia hands a pile of submissions to each of us. I watch as Michael opens Challis's folder and peers inside. He turns the pages right side up and begins reading.

I pretend that opening InDesign on my computer takes intense concentration. I angle the screen up and slouch down behind it. Dr. Taylor catches my eye for a second but then goes back to grading papers.

The silence in the room makes the rustle of turning pages deafening, and the dull taps of my fingers on my keyboard sound like footsteps in an empty hall. So when

Michael puts the folder on the table, it sounds like a clap of thunder. I jolt in my seat before I remember to play it cool.

"Crap," he says.

"What?" Lia and Holland ask in unison.

"We finally have a graphic short—but it's not very good."

My mouth drops in disbelief.

"Bummer," DeMarco says. "Let me see."

Michael pushes the folder across the desk to him. DeMarco reads the first page, passes it to Holland. Holland passes it to me, and I take it. I scan each frame slowly, as if I haven't seen it before, and then pass it to Lia.

When we finish, Michael collects the pages again. "It might just be me, but there's no plot. Right?"

This is when we all look at one another.

DeMarco shrugs. "Maybe it'll sell copies. Manga's popular."

Holland stifles a giggle. "It's a little fluffy, but gay boys are popular."

I sink even lower behind my computer, wishing I had a larger screen.

Michael shakes his head.

"What do you think, Jamie?" DeMarco asks.

"It's a love story," I say casually. "It's supposed to end happily ever after." I've read enough princess-meets-Prince-Charming picture books to my sisters to know this is fact.

"*Romeo and Juliet* is a love story," Lia says to prove me wrong.

"A morbid one."

"At least something happens."

"Yeah, they both die. Real exciting." I loop my finger in the air, then wonder if I should be looping it by my ear. I'm not a literary buff—I read only what's assigned—and I'm arguing the literary merits of a gay comic? *There's something seriously wrong with my brain.*

"It's called conflict," Lia informs me.

"There's conflict," I jab a finger at Challis's drawings. "This girl bullies the boys into kissing."

"But, yuck, that's what they *wanted* to do."

"Not in front of everyone. Not like that," I snap back, and realize that words aren't coming from some logical explanation I learned in English class. They're coming from my heart.

And maybe Michael can tell, because he cuts Lia off. "But if it were about a boy and a girl, there would be no story."

"But there *is* a story!" I say. "It's about two people finding each other."

Michael sighs like I missed his point.

"And it's a story about being picked on," I say. "It's about feeling different from everyone else. *Everyone* feels that way." At least I think everyone feels that way. *I feel that way.*

The others are silent, as if they aren't convinced.

So I continue, the words tumbling out as they short-circuit my brain, "It's not about being gay or straight. It's about finding an ally in a sea of bullies, finding love in a storm of hatred."

Holland nods.

Michael shakes his head.

DeMarco shrugs.

Dr. Taylor comes over and helps himself to the comic. I watch his face as he reads.

"Yeah," Lia says. "And there's another problem."

"A problem?" I ask.

"Yeah," Michael says. "We're not in the most open-minded school district. People might get upset."

"All it takes is one parent complaining and we could lose funding," Dr. Taylor says.

"And *Gumshoe* is toast," Michael adds.

"We just resurrected *Gumshoe* from the graveyard," Lia says. "It'd be a shame to dig it a deeper grave."

"Yeah," DeMarco agrees. "This is gonna be my magazine next year. We got to keep it around."

I look at Dr. Taylor, hope he'll jump in and say something about freedom of speech—about gay rights, about banned books, about anything!

But he's nodding right along.

And so is Lia.

"But it *is* good!" I say. "And it shows diversity.

Represents students in our school."

"I dunno," Holland says. "Maybe people would like it."

"People *would* like it," Lia repeats, "if the characters weren't gay for each other."

"That d-doesn't—" I sputter, my anger rising.

"It *does* matter. If it were a boy and a girl, it'd be fine," Lia says as if she solved our problem.

"Fluff," Holland says.

"And we're back to no plot," Michael reminds them.

"No," Dr. Taylor says. "It's not within our purview to change anything about the story."

Thank you, Dr. Taylor.

"It's either in or it's out," he continues.

"We should vote," Michael says.

I close my mouth so I don't look like a carp and choke down the lump in my throat. Challis is going to kill me. I said I'd get it in. And more than that, I want it in. I want someone, somewhere, to not feel alone and lost just because they read that story, and feel okay about coming out despite the odds stacked against them.

Dr. Taylor takes a sheet of paper and starts ripping it into squares. "Majority this time," he instructs, because we often go with a unanimous decision. Then he passes out the squares.

I write *IN*, fold it up, and pass it back. I want a million squares of paper. I want to write *IN* on all of them.

I want proof that I didn't let Challis down, proof I voted for what's right, proof we didn't censor her story.

Dr. Taylor collects the papers. Then he opens one and reads it. *"No."*

Another, mine this time. *"In."*

Then another no.

And a third.

"Yes."

Probably Holland.

Dr. Taylor reaches for the last one and opens it. "And the last one is a"—he pauses—"a no."

Double damn it.

ELEVEN

I practically run into Eden in the hall on the way to my locker. Practically, because I hear her voice before we collide. I stop in my tracks. I don't want to talk to her. Not now. Not after that craptastic *Gumshoe* meeting. Not after her stupid friends were gossiping about Mason and me going to prom together. Not after she read her brother's supposedly anonymous poem. Not after I told her I am gay.

"Thanks, Mr. Farnsworth. I'll get it done. I promise," she says, walking backward out of a classroom.

I step back so she doesn't bump into me.

"Jamie!" she says. "Do you have your car?"

"Yeah. Why?"

"I need a ride. My dad's gonna kill me if I'm late for Bible study."

That sounds a little ironic, but I go along with it. "Sure."

On the way out to the parking lot, Eden explains about her English paper—that Nick wrote one with the same thesis and how she couldn't turn hers in. "I started a second paper, but I didn't finish it. And it was due today!"

"Did you tell your teacher what happened?"

"Not exactly. If he thinks Nick is cheating—or we're cheating—we could get in a lot of trouble."

"Is he?" I ask.

Eden's green eyes grow wide behind her glasses, as if I just accused the Pope of having an affair. "No. He'd never do that. Wait. He saw my notes! I was watching TV, working on my paper . . ."

I watch as anger clouds her face, but then it passes, replaced with frustration.

"He's such a snoop. Why can't he leave my stuff alone?"

"My sisters are the same way," I say.

She swipes at tear with the heel of her hand. "I can't get Nick in trouble. His grades are in the crapper—you read his poem—and if Dad gets a call from any of his teachers, something's gonna hit the fan."

Nick used to be a year ahead of us in school, but in sixth grade he was held back. That couldn't have been easy for Eden. "Hey," I say gently, and put my arm around her shoulders. It feels a little weird at first, but then she sags into my side and it feels all right. We walk the rest of the way to my car like that. I unlock the passenger-side door of my once-blue car. I drop my arm and Eden climbs in.

"Where to?" I ask.

"Church of God, on Boise Ave."

I start the car and back out of the parking space. I turn on the radio, hum along to Joe Walsh, and try to ignore the question burning in my gut.

Eden toys with the crank that opens and closes the window.

"It's ancient, I know," I say about my car.

She opens her window all the way and turns her face into the breeze.

"Eden?" I ask, trying not to sound pissed. "Did you tell your friends what I said?"

"What did you say?" she asks.

I almost say never mind. But I want to know if she told Challis that I'm gay, because Challis seemed to know.

"I didn't say it—not exactly. You asked if I didn't like kissing girls."

"Oh," Eden says. "That."

"But did you?"

"What the frick, Jamie? I didn't tell them that!"

I want to believe her, but I don't. I need more. Proof. "But I heard you. In art."

"I wasn't outing you." She goes quiet and then mumbles, "I was, um, bragging."

"Bragging?" I ask.

"That you asked me to prom. Major braggage."

"Um."

"They practically squeed their pants!"

"About me?" I still don't get it. "But Challis is a lesbian?"

"Jamie, Jamie, Jamie," Eden says. "That doesn't matter. If there's one thing that girls—gay or straight—like, it's gay boys."

"That doesn't make sense," I tell her. "The very definition of *gay boy* is that they like boys."

Eden sighs as if I'm the stupid one. "We like you. And all the squeeably cute gay guys like you—both fictional and in real life."

"But you said you didn't tell them I'm gay!"

"It doesn't matter. They've got good gaydar."

Really good gaydar, I think. I'm pretty invisible. I never wear nice clothes, just my ringer T-shirts and jeans, slightly baggy and a bit boring. I've never been in drama club. The closest I've ever been to a Broadway musical was playing the trumpet in the orchestra for *The Music Man.*

"And even if you were straight, they'd do a slash pairing of you and somebody anyway," Eden says.

"Who?" I ask. The art-geek girls are always 'shipping people.

But she doesn't answer. I steal a glance at her and she shakes her head. "I can't say."

"Eden?" I ask, my voice low on the first syllable, like

my mom does when I'm in trouble.

"Okay. Well, I voted for J/Ellen."

"Me and Kellen Zabala?" I ask, deciphering the code. *Not bad.* I was just telling myself that Kellen is totally crush-worthy.

"Uh-huh." Then, "Turn in here," she says about the church.

I do and pull up to the walkway.

She gets out, then leans her head in the open window. "The pairings. They're stupid. Don't let them bother you."

On my way home, I giggle about the idea that Kellen and I have slashed together, as if we were as famous (and fictional) as Spock and Kirk, Sirius and Remus, Spike and Angel. Really? Kellen and me? That'd make for some pretty epic fiction—I might even read that book—if only we weren't real people.

Thank God it wasn't Mason. Ja/Son.

TWELVE

I'm groggy on Saturday morning—Mason, Gabe, and I watched both the seven o'clock and the nine o'clock shows at the three-dollar theater, followed by a round of video games—but I pull myself out of bed anyway. I've got to get *Gumshoe* done this weekend so we can work on edits next week. It goes to press on Friday. I put on yesterday's jeans and a clean shirt.

Mom is in the kitchen, watching the coffeepot as if it were the television.

"Something good on?" I ask.

"I'm just praying for a cup before the girls wake up."

"Frank gone already?"

"Uh-huh," Mom says.

"Can I borrow your office key?" I ask, meaning the one to her office downtown. It's the perfect place to work on projects. There are scanners and printers and Wi-Fi. And no two-year-olds.

* * *

I buy a cup of coffee—okay, a caramel mocha—and a muffin—okay, two—from Flying M on the corner. I love that place. They always have an art show on one wall and a funky gift shop in the corner, but the VALENTINES FOR AIDS posters are my favorite. They do an art auction every year to raise money, and the posters are created by local graphic designers—done in shades of red and pink. *Someday,* I tell myself, *my poster will be on that wall.*

At the office, I set up in the little room in the back. The one that will be mine this summer when I work here. Sure, it's stacked to the ceiling with rolls of blueprints and the desk is actually a flat file, but I have what I need: a scanner from the last decade. (My mom's firm used to photograph their projects on 4 x 5 film and scan the negatives with this monster.) It's perfect for scanning artwork.

I start with the male nude, then the stack of new stuff I chose yesterday. It's slow going, so I turn on the old radio. The scanner hums and clunks along to the classic rock while I eat breakfast. By eleven, I have everything in Photoshop and I'm turning my color scans into black-and-white masterpieces by adjusting the curves. I try not to think of Challis's drawings, or how they wouldn't need any adjustments, being straight pen and ink.

By one, I have the poems—including Nick O'Shea's—and flash pieces typeset, some all alone, others clustered in groups. I leave most of the artwork big, bleeding off the edges of the pages, and mirroring content in the shorter works.

I move my production studio to the sandwich shop down the street. I order a turkey sub and bottomless soda. I chunk through the short stories. We have six, each spread out over three or more pages. I slide the pages around, work them so that each one ends with a drawing or painting. I move in a set of seven blank pages and imagine *The Love Dare* among the sonnets. Then I hear Michael say, "But there's no plot," and hit the delete key.

Back at my mom's office, I print everything out, trim the crop marks, and make a dummy. I lose myself in the details of the typography—Goudy 10/13—for the rest of the afternoon, as if keeping busy will keep Challis's story from creeping into my consciousness. The red pen I'm marking the pages with doesn't help. It reminds me of how I wanted to color in the hearts in the last frame.

A poem catches my eye. A word, actually: *homophobia*. Instead of just looking at the letters and lines of type, I read it. It's about the words we don't say, or wouldn't say, in a perfect world. It brings me back to Mason with his AP French class and his bilingual family. And Challis's comic.

Screw it.

I pull out the comic. Put the first page on the scanner and hit return. A clunk and whir, and it pops up on the monitor. I repeat the process until I have all seven and save. By five, I have two dummies: one with Challis's comic and one without.

At Night I Dream
Anonymous

At night I dream that we live in a David Levithan novel,
a world set to music and lit like Broadway—
each moment deep, magical, and underscored by
the simple and the profound, like a Beatles' song.

Here, in my dreams, we love whom we love,
blinded not by the color of their skin,
worried not by the details of their gender,
nor about the book in which they find their god.

Here we speak a thousand languages,
understanding the nuances without having to ask.
And yet we have forgotten the word for hate,
and with it anger, hostility, and homophobia.

But in the morning, I wake to a bleating alarm clock
and the banter of bilingual breakfast conversations—
none deeper than the contents of the fridge—
and I pray for a passport back to dreamland.

And yet woven into the lilt and trill is a nuance
spoken not out loud—even though we have
two languages and a thousand words and ways
to say it—simply, deeply, profoundly. I love you.

THIRTEEN

I'm triple-checking the office door to make sure it's locked behind me when my cell rings.

The screen says EDEN. I answer, "Your number's in my phone?"

"Yeah," she says.

I wait for an explanation.

"I messed with it in art. When you were asleep."

"But—" I start to protest that we weren't even sitting next to each other yesterday. It's no use. This is Eden. "Never mind. What's up?"

"Want to do something?"

"Sure," I agree.

"Pick me up?"

"When?"

"Whenever."

I go directly from my mom's office to Eden's. The Redneck's truck is in the driveway when I pull up. I park in the street. I take a minute to check my hair in the rear-view mirror before I ring the doorbell.

A very large man opens the door and stands there, fitting in the frame like a puzzle piece. I see where the Redneck got his build and, at the same time, I wonder why Eden's so short. She has curves, so she isn't small everywhere, but she comes up only to my chin.

"Hello, Mr. O'Shea?" It sounds like a question, but really, it's an answer. An answer to why Eden wanted me to come over—part of her plot to be able to go to prom.

"Yes?" he prompts, as if asking me what I am selling.

"Is Eden home?"

He jerks in surprise, his head brushing the doorframe. When he recovers, he inspects me, tilting his head as he looks at my ears (which aren't pierced), and then up and down twice as if checking to see if I had somehow sprouted breasts. When he looks certain that I am male, he says, "I believe she is."

I do my best to smile.

He steps back and invites me in.

Nick is slouched on a plaid sofa in the living room. The TV is on, playing *America's Funniest Home Videos*.

"Eden!" Mr. O'Shea bellows in the direction of the staircase.

On the screen some guy gets hit in the balls with a baseball bat and I can't help but wince. Nick, on the other hand, lets out an evil-villain chuckle. He seems to notice me for the first time and looks my way.

I nod hello in his direction.

Nick mouths the words *fag mag*.

Eden bounces down the stairs in a skirt and blouse, a cardigan sweater buttoned over the latter. She looks like something straight out of the 1950s. "Hi, James," she says coyly. "How are you?"

"Fine, thank you," I reply.

Mr. O'Shea's eyes volley between us as if he's a referee waiting for us to slip up.

I don't dare. "My mother is expecting us," I say, even though she isn't.

Eden's eyebrows pop up.

"For dinner," I continue, partly because I think this will impress Mr. O'Shea, but also because I'm out of cash after the coffee, muffins, turkey sub, and soda I bought today.

"Oh," her father says. "You two have a nice time."

"We will, Daddy," Eden coos.

"Home by nine," he says, more to me than to her.

"Oh, goody! Thank you, Daddy!" Eden hugs him and says good-bye.

I open the passenger-side door for her, walk around, and slide in. "Thanks for the warning," I say.

"About my dad?" she asks. "He's a big teddy bear if you're on his good side."

"A teddy bear with a shotgun," I answer.

"No shotgun. He likes you."

"Because I'm a guy, I suppose."

"Bingo! If I'm out with you, well, they're pretty sure they won't find me sitting in a tree with a girl from church camp."

"And Nick?"

Eden laughs. "They don't worry about him. He's yardstick straight."

That wasn't what I was asking. "Not that. Does Nick have a bullet with my name on it?"

"No. Not a bullet, exactly."

"Comforting."

"I tried to talk him into retracting his submission to *Gumshoe*."

"You what?" I ask. "He didn't want anyone to know he wrote it."

"Um, yeah." Eden studies her fingernails. "He kinda said."

"You explained that it wasn't my fault, right? That you saw it by accident."

"Yeah, but, well . . ." She pokes at a cuticle. "He's still kinda pissed."

"Great," I say. "The last thing I need is the Redneck mad at me."

"Sorry."

I'd like to say that when I walk into my house with a girl who is dressed suspiciously like she is on a date, that she doesn't get the once-over. But she does. My mom looks at Eden first, and then at me. The twins hide behind Mom's legs, sans their usual shrieks.

I introduce Eden.

"Eden?" my mom clarifies, as if she was hoping for a "Steven" or an "Adam" or anything but a girl.

"Yeah," Eden says. "Like the garden."

Mom nods. "Nice to meet you."

I point to one wide-eyed twin. "This is Elisabeth, or Ann Marie. I can't tell them apart when they aren't talking."

Eden sinks to her haunches so she's at twin eye level. "Hey."

"C'mon, girls," Mom coaxes. "Say hi to Jamie's friend."

"Hi," the one that must be Elisabeth says. She steps around Mom and sits on her haunches too, her diapered rear sticking out.

"Hi," Eden echoes.

I sit on the floor and pull Ann Marie onto my lap. She lets out a peal of giggles and a slobbery strand of drool as I inform Eden as to which twin is which.

"So," Mom says. "Are you two on your way somewhere?"

I shake my head. "I thought we might have dinner here," I say.

"Oh, um, okay," Mom says. "There's probably something in the freezer."

Like I was expecting anything else.

Eden watches as I pull out frozen pizzas. I let her choose the toppings, and then I put two in the oven. We open cans of soda and sit at the table.

Eden asks about Challis's graphic short story—apparently Challis hadn't shared the details with anyone. "You've read it, haven't you?"

I nod.

"So. Is it über-magnificent-amazing?"

"Pretty much."

"You don't, by any chance, have it?" Eden asks.

And warning bells ring between my eardrums, an echo of Eden reading her brother's poem when she shouldn't have. "Maybe," I drawl. "But if Challis kept it secret—"

"She would have shown it to me," Eden reasons. "If Ms. Maude hadn't started in on her slides."

"I don't know," I say. "I don't want to give Challis any more reasons to hate me."

"Puh-leeze," Eden whines.

"Okay," I say as if I'm giving in. "I'll give it back to Challis; then she can show you."

"No fair."

"Fair," I say, and soon we are bickering like kinder-garteners.

"So you'll take it to Game Den tonight?" Eden puts down her deal breaker.

"Game Den?" I ask. I've been once or twice, but mostly I play video games at Mason's.

"Yeah. Everyone's gonna be there. But my dad doesn't let me go—especially not with Challis and crew."

"We're going to Game Den?" I ask, but I know the answer.

Eden nods. "My treat."

"You huge-Hoover-vacuum-suck at killing zombies." Eden slides her hand into mine as we leave Game Den, where we met up with Challis and the art-geek girls for two hours of video game entertainment. We're walking across the parking lot in search of nourishment because Challis is hungry.

"Hey," I protest, even though I do suck. "I saved you from a stomper or two."

"Only because you got in the way."

"We gotta go," one of the girls says. "See you in school?"

Challis pouts but gives the group of them hugs. Eden does the same. I just say good night. After they leave, I stop at my car and pull Challis's folder with her comic out of my backpack. I give it back to her. "I'm sorry," I say.

Her face crumples. "Rejected?" she asks.

"Yeah, but I'm going to try again. I got a scan of it." I attempt to sound positive.

"You think they'll change their minds?"

"Maybe. Some of the staff really liked it—I know I did." I tell her, not mentioning why they rejected it.

"You'll talk to them?" Challis asks, a flicker of hope in her blue eyes.

"I will. Monday."

She tucks the folder under her arm and leads us in the direction of Mexican fast food. Eden buys a round of sodas, plus a plate of nachos for the three of us to share.

"Wow, thanks!" Challis and I say, practically in unison.

"No problem," Eden says while she pays. "The least I can do for my two best friends."

Challis and I exchange glances as if to ask, *We're her best friends?*

I shrug and take the paper cups off the counter. I hand one to Challis and she leads the way to the fountain machine. Like a gentleman, I let her go first. She starts with Mountain Dew and proceeds down the line of levers until her cup is full.

My stomach feels queasy just thinking about the taste of that. I go for a regular old Pepsi before we choose a booth by the window.

Eden soon joins us with a plate piled high with chips, cheese, and toppings.

We dig in.

"May I read your story?" Eden asks Challis. "I heard

it was über-maginificent-amazing."

Challis shoots me a look, as if she is blaming me for Eden's interest.

I hold my hands up like a traffic cop.

"Okay, okay," Challis agrees. "You can read it. Just no greasy fingers."

Eden beams, wipes her hands on her napkin, and then holds them out for inspection.

Challis nods.

Eden then opens the folder as if the contents were holier than the Gutenberg Bible and starts to read.

I can tell where she is in the story by the sounds she makes. "Oh no" when Tony is teased; "aw" when he talks to his dad; and a squeal followed by "OMG. They're sooo cute!" at the end. After which she bounces up and down like she needs a visit the little girls' room.

"Awesomesauce!" she announces. "It's really, really good, Challis."

I think I see a gloss of near tears in Challis's eyes.

But she just smiles and says, "Thank you."

Eden turns to me. "Did it get rejected because of the LGBTQueness?"

I process the alphabet soup of her question and admit to half the reason it got rejected. "Sorta. Yeah."

Challis reaches over and takes the folder back, a muffled string of choice vocabulary spilling from her lips.

"I'm gonna try again," I say.

"Thanks," she says weakly, as if she thinks I'm powerless.

"But it's sooo good," Eden whines. "Challis, you're so amazingly talented. . . ." She trails off, thinking. "We could start, like, a petition or something!"

Challis gives me another one of her I-blame-you-for-bringing-this-up looks.

But Eden keeps on babbling, ticking things off on her fingers, "The GSA students, the Mathletes, the Japanese club—" She stops when Challis touches her hand. A blush rises to her cheeks.

"Thanks," Challis says. "But it's okay."

On the way home, Eden points me to a shortcut to her neighborhood. I follow her directions, turning left and right when she tells me to until I recognize her street.

Eden points to a cheery yellow house with lots of lights on. "You know Lia Marcus?" she asks, but doesn't wait for an answer. "She lives there."

"Oh," I say, glancing over at the house.

"We used to be best friends," Eden tells me. "Sleepovers-every-weekend, finish-each-other's-sentences best friends."

"Yeah?"

"We'd walk to each other's houses and watch soap operas every afternoon."

"Not anymore?" I look over at her. I've noticed that even though she tries to fit in with Challis's friends, she always seems to be on the outskirts.

She stares out the window at the porch lights of passing houses. "Not since I came out."

My gut feels like I swallowed an ice cube. "Ouch."

"Yeah. At first she pretended to be cool with it—kinda *So you like girls, who cares?*—but I could tell it bothered her because she wouldn't change her clothes in front of me."

"People are weird like that," I say. "If you like girls in general, they think you like them in particular."

"Ew!" Eden says. "That squicks me out. She was my best friend."

I might not be on the honor roll, but I get her gist: Kissing your best friend sometimes has the "ew" factor of kissing a sibling. I think of Mason and his slow-motion smile, the shape of his lips. Too bad I didn't get that brand of squick.

". . . making excuses not to sleep over," Eden says.

I scramble to catch up on what I might have missed.

"And inviting lots of friends when we slept at her house—as if she didn't want to be alone with me."

"I'm sorry," I say.

"I saved her the trouble of breaking it off. I stopped returning her calls. It was just too humiliating."

"Humiliating?"

"To have someone pretend to be your friend when they really don't want to be."

The ice cube feeling spreads to my chest as I imagine how awful that must have been. I read about friends fading away in one of those self-help books for gay teens that Frank bought me in ninth grade, but I never knew the people involved. Now, knowing about Eden and Lia, it all feels more real. More like it could happen to me.

FOURTEEN

Monday, the Redneck parks his truck next to my car in the student parking lot. I take my time getting my phone and car keys in all the right pockets, but he doesn't leave. He stands there with a scowl etched across his forehead.

So I take a deep breath and say, "Hey, Nick."

"'S'up, Fagmag?"

I wince at the sting of my new nickname. "Can't believe it's Monday already."

"You weren't supposed to show it to anyone," he says, the words coming out in one long grunt.

"Sorry about that. I dropped my books. Eden picked it up."

"That's what she said."

"It got in," I tell him, trying to cheer him up. "You'll get that extra credit from Taylor."

He doesn't cheer up, just changes the topic. "I know what you two are doing."

Crap.

"And if you think that pretending to be unfagged is helping my sister see straight, you got another thing coming."

Huh? I didn't understand a word of that.

"Got that, Fagmag?" he asks about my non-answer.

"Got it, Nick," I say, even though I don't. "No problem."

He stops to tie his boot and I walk faster. There's a reason I've been running a mile in gym class. It might come in handy someday. Soon.

That afternoon, at the *Gumshoe* meeting, I proceed with my carefully planned tactics. I show DeMarco, Lia, Holland, and Michael how the dummy with Challis's graphic short has more variety and more visual interest. Holland nods right along.

"I don't know, Jamie. Maybe we shouldn't do a comic. We didn't have one last year, and we won the award anyway," DeMarco reasons.

"But it looks amazing—adds visual variety," I say, purposely ignoring their previous comments about the story being fluffy and plotless.

"It's not how it looks from a distance, Jamie," Lia

says. "It's the characters—the gay characters. Kissing. It's, like, wrong in so many—"

Michael stops her. "It's not about making judgments; it's about the future of *Gumshoe*. We got funding from the school, from taxpayers. They won't like this story and we don't need it—it's just not that great."

"A thousand dollars," DeMarco says. "I looked it up."

Forget gaining ground—I'm losing this battle. I see it all over Holland's face. She's about to wave a white flag, surrender to the masses. And I should have known; Eden told me about Lia's not-exactly-accepting behavior last night.

"My parents are on the PTO," Lia says, "and they won't—"

I scramble for footing, try to find the right words. They fail me and I say, "Parents don't read high school literary magazines."

"True," Lia agrees. "But they don't have to read to see this!" She jabs her finger at the page where the boys are kissing.

This is when Dr. Taylor steps in. "Thank you, Jamie, for bringing this point up again. It was worth discussing. But I'm afraid the discussion is over."

The others pack up their things and file out of the classroom. I watch them go, feeling like a wounded soldier left on the battlefield. Stupid. I can't even think of the right thing to say. Even when I'm right.

Michael turns and gives me one last look, his hand on the doorframe. He takes a noisy breath, exhales. "Look, Jamie. I'm sorry."

"I thought . . . ," I start, but hesitate. "I thought you were, well . . ."

"Yeah, I know. I was in the GSA, so everyone, um, assumed things."

"You're in the GSA?" I echo, perking up a little.

"Was. To support my sister. But it wasn't worth the hassle."

I give him a questioning look.

"It was her club. She started it. When she graduated, I told her I'd go. But after a while, it got to be too much—the rumors, I mean."

I nod. I get it. I believed those rumors. But there's something I still don't get. "But if you're a straight ally, why don't you want Challis's story in *Gumshoe*?"

"C'mon, Jamie. It's not worth it. Take out the fact that it's about two boys, and the story falls flat."

"But it is about two boys," I say.

"But it doesn't mean it's good."

"I like it. I think it's brave."

"Okay, so you like it," Michael says. "But it doesn't mean it's worth the trouble. I've seen the hatred—parents storming the school board meetings, waving signs, quoting Leviticus—that's what happened when Nell started the GSA."

We were in junior high when this was going on—not that I remember it clearly. I do remember my mom getting upset, talking about sending me to Boise High and not Lincoln. I didn't understand why, exactly. Just that Mason was going to Lincoln and, damn it, that's where I wanted to go.

Michael takes an audible breath. "It was horrible. Scary. I don't want to go through that again. Not for some girl's fan art."

"I remember," I say. "But why can't we fight for this, too?"

"Because it's fluff, Jamie. It's not worth it."

"It isn't fluff. It's a love story—about two people like your sister. Doesn't your sister deserve a love story? Doesn't everyone?" *Don't I?*

"Yes," Michael says, his face looking tired as he sniffles. "Just not in *Gumshoe*, okay?"

I get the feeling this isn't going anywhere and I don't argue.

FIFTEEN

Tuesday starts off badly. Challis is waiting for me in the student parking lot before school. "I couldn't talk them into it," I say.

"Homophobic twerps," she mumbles, and then asks, "That was the reason, right?"

"They thought parents might not like it, among other reasons."

"Other reasons?"

"Well, someone said it was fluff."

"Fluff?" Challis asks. "It's not fluff."

"That's what I said, but he wouldn't budge."

"He? You mean Michael, not DeMarco, right?" Her jaw pops open. "Michael-who-won't-come-to-the-GSA-because-some-jerk-called-him-queer?"

Crap.

"Tell Michael I don't do fluff!"

I want to tell her to tell him herself, but I don't. "He

didn't want to lose funding."

Challis barks out a laugh. "Funding? This is more like censorship!"

I nod.

She must see my face just then, because she stops and says, "Thanks, Jamie. I know you did what you could."

I manage a smile.

And, awkwardly, Challis gives me a hug.

After school I still feel awful. I feel like I let Challis down, and for some reason, she's someone I didn't want to let down. Maybe because I put her on a pedestal, admired her because she was everything I couldn't be—out at school and in the GSA. I couldn't imagine how much guts that would take.

I have tons of friends at school, and honestly, it's a calculated move. I never say no to anyone who offers me friendship, from football players to band geeks, cheerleaders to brainiacs. Even though I was voted most likely to have the most Facebook friends, I still feel like I don't fit in: I'm one of the guys, but I'm not into girls; I'd hang out with girls, but I don't understand them.

My mom says that's why students created GSAs—that they are a place to fit in, no matter what brand of different you are. But walking through that door—room 302—at 3:30 on a Thursday would be like getting a tattoo on my forehead. It wouldn't ever wash off. My little secret would be out in the world and I could never take it back.

Challis's comic is under my skin, itching like poison ivy. If I told my mom, she'd call Dr. Taylor or Principal Chambers and make a big fuss. And the last thing I need is a big gay fuss.

I have half a thought to talk to Mason about it because he's logical with a clear-cut sense of right and wrong, and he'd see that censoring Challis's story was wrong. But talking to him about this might lead to talking to him about other things—like me.

I call the one person I can talk to.

We meet in the park a few blocks from her house. "Challis understands," Eden tells me, twisting the chains of her swing to face me.

"I guess," I agree. "But it's the principle of it all. Her comic should be in *Gumshoe.*"

"It should be. But that isn't how the world works. We should be able to get married in the state where we live."

It takes me a minute to catch up. She didn't mean "we" as in us, but "we" as in all same-sex couples. I adjust my backside in the pinch-y rubber swing.

"You'll see it more when you're out," she says. "Or is that why you're in the closet?"

"I'm out," I say defensively.

Her eyebrows go up.

"To my mom," I admit, and dig the toes of my

sneakers into the wood chips.

"Cool," she says. "No wonder she looked at me cross-eyed."

"Yeah. I don't have a lot of friends who are girls."

"Aw." Eden reaches over and grabs the chain of my swing. We twist to face each other.

"That makes me feel special."

I smile as a wave of shyness passes over me.

"You're, like, totally cute, Jamie. And you haven't had *any* girlfriends?"

My cheeks warm at the compliment. "One," I say. "In kindergarten. Before I knew girls had cooties."

"Before you knew what gay was?" Eden prompts.

"Yeah," I say. "I didn't figure that out until junior high."

"I hated junior high."

I nod sympathetically, and then tell her about the day that I began to think that I might be gay. "In eighth grade," I begin, "we had a substitute teacher for a whole week. He was barely out of college—like, twenty-two, tops. Mr. Middlebrook. The girls went into insta-flirt mode the second he walked into the room—I swear the wind from their batting eyelashes blew his necktie up over one shoulder." I laugh, thinking this would be a great *Gumshoe* story.

"He called my name, looked at me, and smiled. And that moment, I knew what the girls were feeling."

I remember that tumbling mix of awe and bashfulness, admiration, and the intense desire to crawl under my desk as if it were yesterday.

"Did you ever talk to him?" Eden asks.

"Oh, that's a funny story too. During class he caught Ashley Quincy texting and took her phone away."

Eden smiles. Ashley Quincy isn't her favorite person. No one popular is.

"And Ashley said, 'Come on, Gerrod. Give it back!' Turns out, he was her cousin. He told her to come back after school to pick it up. At that moment, I wished more than anything that I had a phone. Because I wanted to get caught texting, wanted to have Mr. Middlebrook take it away and ask me to come to his classroom to after school."

Eden laughs approvingly.

"Ashley pouted for a good ten minutes, until Mr. Middlebrook walked over, bent down, and whispered, 'Come on, Goober, it's not that bad.'"

"He called her Goober?" Eden asks.

"Yep. And Ashley smacked her hands down on her desk so hard, Mr. Middlebrook jumped. Then he went back to teaching algebra."

We sway side to side on our swings.

"Ashley started passing notes telling everything she knew about him: that he was allergic to hot dogs, puked on roller coasters, and listened to country music. I think she meant to turn the class against him, but the girls found this information fascinating—thought he sounded sweet, and not at all like any eighth-grade boy they knew."

"Sounds like it," Eden said. "Eighth-grade boys smell."

I laugh.

"So what'd you do?" Eden asks.

"I found a way to stay after school."

"You got in trouble?"

"Nope. I found a math problem he explained differently than our teacher had. And would you believe there was a line at his desk? All girls and me. All waiting for their cell phones—they had been texting in class. On purpose.

"He had the phones in his desk—all but Ashley's. Hers was in his jacket pocket and when he reached for it, all these notes spilled out. They were love notes. From girls."

Some kids burst out of a minivan and run across the grass.

"In his pockets?" she asks, watching the kids. "Like, girls put notes in his pockets?"

I nod. "'Cell phone?' he asked me. 'No,' I said. 'Math question.' Boy, did he look relieved. 'How do you put up with them?' he asked, pointing to the notes. I didn't really get that he was confiding in me, so I told him I thought they were crushing on him. And he shook his head and said, 'Double not interested.'"

"Gay," Eden concludes. "So now you're a math whiz? Gerrod Middlebrook inspired you."

"I aced algebra—learned how to really solve problems, not just answer the ones that were on the tests." I'm in AP Calculus, but I don't mention it.

"Cool," Eden says.

"He was the first gay man I ever met," I admit.

"But you knew you were gay?"

"Maybe not right away, but that was the week it started to click—kind of like algebra."

Eden and I sit in still silence. And I realize that I never told anyone that story before, even though it totally defines who I am and how I relate to people around me. It makes me feel close to her. I wonder if she feels the same way.

"Eden?" I ask.

"Yeah." She turns in her swing.

"Promise me you won't tell anyone."

"What? That you're gay? It's a little late for that." She says this with a laugh.

"Whaddaya mean?"

"Um, dot. Dot. Dot."

"Eden?"

"Everyone knows, Jamie. I don't have to tell them."

"Not everyone," I say, thinking of Mason.

"Almost everyone?"

"I haven't told Mason," I admit.

"Well, hurry up and tell him."

I shake my head. She doesn't understand. In fact, she's probably one of those people who thinks coming out is as easy as a circling a day on a calendar. But coming out to Mason? Not exactly my idea of a national holiday. It looms like a dentist appointment—a dentist appointment where I'd have eight cavities, need a palette expander, a root canal, and my wisdom teeth pulled.

"You're afraid he'll reject you," Eden says.

It isn't a question.

SIXTEEN

Wednesday, the *Gumshoe* staff has planned to meet in Dr. Taylor's classroom during lunch to go over edits.

"How's it going?" I ask Michael as I plunk my computer on a desk. He and I are the first ones here.

"Good." He inhales. "But the limo thing, well, I did the math. It's pretty expensive."

"Yeah?" I ask. I'd almost forgotten about the limo. And now that Michael and I have a cheese grater in the middle of our quasifriendship, the thought of spending an evening with him and Lia makes me feel like I just ate too much school pizza.

"We've got three couples. But splitting the cost four or five ways would be more affordable."

I nod in agreement, but Michael doesn't seem to notice.

He's counting off couples on his fingers. "Lia and I,

Holland and DeMarco, and you and Mason."

I fight back the crawl of a hot blush. "And Eden and Bahti," I say to correct his mistake.

"Eden and Bahti?" Michael repeats. And without missing a beat, "So we do have four couples—perfect!"

By the way he says this, I think he's still confused. But I give him props for not going all Lia on the idea of another same-sex couple. "I'm going with Eden, and Mason's going with Bahti."

"Oh, yeah," he says with a shrug. "Of course."

"So, should we pay you now, or on prom night?" I ask.

"Let me get you the number for four couples, then you can pay me back whenever."

"Cool." I smile as I open my laptop and feel a little forgiveness form in my chest. Michael isn't an awful person. We just disagreed. And I need to get over it.

I promised Mason we'd go get fitted for tuxedos after school, so we are inching along through mall traffic, trying to find a men's clothing store neither of us have been to before. He's humming the tune to "I Remember Clifford," the piece I'm playing in the concert next week, and drumming his fingers on the dash to keep the beat. I'd been a little late getting out of band, and he had been listening to us practice.

"What color is Bahti's dress?" I ask. During art today,

Eden had shown me a picture of a dress in a prom magazine. It was neon pink. Then she proceeded to tell me that I was required to wear the same color tie and cummerbund. Having seen my fair share of the color on account of my sisters, I protested. "No pink!"

Eden had exploded in a fit of giggles and nearly fell off her chair. "I'm kidding," she said when she finally caught her breath. "This isn't my dress. Mine's black with white trim."

"Cornflower," Mason says.

"Cornflower?" I ask. "What's cornflower?"

"Sort of blue sort of lavender—that's what she said."

"Not bad," I say, and repeat Eden's joke.

It follows us into the store, Mason pointing out pink things as we browse.

"Not bright enough," I tell him about a shiny vest.

"How about this?" he asks, pointing to a Boise State orange tuxedo. "I bet we can order one in pink."

The thing is so hideous it has me running back to the rows of safe black jackets. I find a salesman and ask which ones are rentals.

"Prom?" he asks.

"Yeah. I want something, um—" My brain freezes. He's classically handsome—square jaw, blue-jean eyes. And very well dressed. "Um, traditional. Black and white."

The sales guy juts his chin at Mason, who is still

checking out the orange tux. "Good choice. Your date will look fab in color, but it'll just wash you out."

"Um, yeah, no. He's not my date." *More like, I wish he was my date.*

The salesman lowers his voice. "Too bad."

I look back at Mason. He has the orange jacket on over his black They Might Be Giants T-shirt and is tugging at the lapels. He tilts his head and does a bad Elvis impression in the mirror. He looks ridiculous.

"He sure is cute," the salesman says with a tsk.

My head jerks in his direction and back to Mason. And, yes, in his own geek-in-black-plastic-glasses way, he *is* cute. I feel a now-familiar tug at my heart. "Yeah."

"So," sales guy says. "Let's get you measured."

His fingers touch my shoulders as he holds a tape measure to the seams of my shirt, then they brush my skin as he measures my neck and arms, and by the time he's measuring the outside seam of my jeans I find myself humming "I Remember Clifford" to divert my attention from the process. Then I shrug a black jacket over my shoulders and the sales guy smooths it into place. He checks the length of the sleeves and nods as if he's satisfied.

I look in the mirror. Smile so my teeth show—perfectly straight and still strange to me, even though it has been two years since I got my braces off. The jacket looks good. I button it, then unbutton it. I put on a serious face and say to myself, "Bond, James Bond."

Mason appears in the mirror behind me. He has on a white jacket this time and a blue bowtie flopping over his T-shirt collar. He draws a fake pistol from the waistband of his jeans and aims it at me in the mirror.

I reach out, grab his wrist.

And he bursts out laughing and wriggles free. "Very 007."

"Like you can talk?" I tell him, and sing, "You ain't nothin' but a hound dawg . . ."

He puffs up his chest, straightens his jacket in the mirror, and ignores me. "I think I look good in cornflower."

I stare at his reflection. He could wear any color with that jacket and look amazing. The crisp white fabric makes his shoulders look broader, his skin glow like warm honey, and his curls shine inky indigo. Sales guy was right. He is cute. Dreamy even.

Even if I shouldn't be thinking about it.

SEVENTEEN

I am armed with a sixteen-ounce caramel mocha when I show up at my mom's office on Thursday afternoon. I am eager to put *Gumshoe* to bed—i.e., getting the files ready for the printer—tomorrow at four p.m.

But first, I have to give it a good long look. The group of us has been editing onscreen, and with how puny my laptop is, we could have missed a comma, an apostrophe, or a dozen. I don't want to hear about that from Dr. Taylor, so I'm printing a copy and inspecting it under the fluorescent lights.

"Hey there," Mom greets me. She has a pencil behind one ear and a roll of blueprints under one arm. "You look ready to work."

"Gonna finish it tonight if it kills me."

"The back office is all yours. Let me know if you need the big table, okay?"

I nod. Mom doesn't usually let me do school stuff here during office hours, but today is an exception. "Thanks."

I plug in my computer, connect to the network, and select print. The printer hums to life in the next room and I hear the first page spit out. The cover, with its painting of a koi pond populated by tangerine-colored fish, is vivid, whereas the image on the back—a photo of a girl sitting on a pedestrian bridge over the Boise River—is more subdued. The paint on the bridge had faded in the sun, almost matching her copper-colored curls. Both the fish and the girl had been voted favorites, but the fish won out because of the title of the piece, "Decoys." It went with our detective theme. And, in the end, the fish made a better cover.

I run my finger over the date and price. Four dollars. That alone is depressing. A year's worth of killing ourselves for four dollars—four thousand dollars if we sold them all. But we probably wouldn't. I think we sold about three hundred last year. Then we used some to apply for the award, and donated a bunch to other schools' libraries. That was why we needed funding from the school. From taxpayers. *Gumshoe* wasn't making a profit at four bucks a pop. *Why isn't it five dollars? Or ten?*

It takes me two hours to proofread every page and another half hour to make the changes. Mom comes in and looks at the pages spread out in front of me. "It looks great, honey."

"Thanks."

She gives my shoulders a squeeze. "I'm proud of you."

"Enough," I say, teasing.

"Never," she replies, and hugs me again. "Lock the door when you leave."

I click print again. While I wait, I put the marked-up pages in the recycling bin under the desk. From the shadows, a black-and-white sketch catches my attention. I pull the paper out from under the pages I just put in the bin.

It's a page of Challis's short—the one with the party invitation in the envelope and the little heart floating up. My heart feels warm in my ribs, like I am standing in a sunny window, as I read over the speech bubbles:

"But not me. It's okay."

"Just because I didn't have your email. Here."

Then, like algebra with Mr. Middlebrook, pieces of a plan begin to fall into place in my mind. I click into InDesign, find the pages from an old document, and copy them into my new one. After which, the file has an odd number of pages, something that doesn't work when you're laying out a magazine. And I know who can help

me even them back up again. Scrolling through my con-
tacts on my cell phone, I find Eden's number.

"Jamie!" she answers. "Did you get my corsage?"

"Yeah," I say absentmindedly, even though I didn't.
And prom is Saturday.

"Can you get a phone number for me?" I ask.

"Sure," she agrees before I tell her whose number I'm
looking for.

Then, after I tell her, she asks, "What's this about?
Prom stuff?"

"Sorta," I answer. "I want to ask her something."

EICHTEEN

Prom day is finally here. I have showered, shaved, and found a matching pair of black socks. I'm working on buttoning the starchy shirt when one of the twins bangs on my bedroom door. The accompanying yelps tell me it's Ann Marie.

I bend down to twin level, and then open the door. "Hi, Annie M."

She's wearing a tutu, a red Supergirl cape, and one of Mom's high-heeled shoes. A purse swings in the crook of her arm. The other shoe is abandoned in the hallway. She flings her arms around my neck and that's when I see my mom aiming her smartphone at us, obviously making a video.

"Ooff!" I say, and let Ann Marie knock me over.

She lands safely on my chest and crawls up me on all fours, losing her shoe. She kisses my face with a-little-too-wet kisses as Mom towers over us with the phone.

"Where's Elisabeth?" I ask.

"Waiting to make her entrance," Mom says. "We're playing dress up, in honor of prom."

"I noticed," I say, sitting back up and cradling Ann Marie like a baby. She screeches and wiggles to an upright position on my lap.

"Elisabeth," I call through the open door.

She doesn't quite get the concept of making an entrance but rather runs down the hall with her arms flapping like she's about to take off.

"Whoa," I tell her. "I want to see how pretty you look."

She screeches to a halt and stands still, her fingers twitching with the effort. She has on a purple satin dress-up gown over rainbow leg warmers and a pillowcase cape. A rhinestone tiara slides down her forehead and lands on her nose like sunglasses.

"Wow!" I say. "You look like a prom queen!" I hold out my free arm for a hug. She takes off her tiara and runs to me. Holding them both, I notice that Ann Marie is working up a pout. "And," I tell her, "you look like a superhero princess."

"And you need to finish getting dressed," Mom says. She puts down her phone and helps me into my vest and jacket. I have the clip-on rent-a-tie, but I also bought a real bow tie. Mom sees it and exclaims, "Very classy!"

"Not that I know how to tie it." I figured if I couldn't

tie it, I'd wear it loose and pretend it was on purpose. The casual look. To go with my footwear. Converse. Of course.

"Let me," she says.

So I sit on the edge of my bed and watch Mom's face frown with concentration as her fingers work the loops and knot. At last she smiles, satisfied. Her eyes go a little misty and she kisses my cheek. "You look just like your father."

I guess I do, but I haven't seen him in years, so my memories are faded at the edges.

"We were your age when we met," she says. "And he was the most beautiful thing I had ever seen."

I press my hand over hers for a moment. "And Frank?" I ask. *Frank isn't beautiful.*

She shrugs. "Frank's a good man. But he's not your father—nothing ever quite compares to the first time you fall in love."

I feel a blush creep up my neck. I study the creases on my slacks, the hole in my sock.

"You know . . ." She changes the topic. "By the time you were born, he'd filled out across the shoulders. His face changed too—lost that boyish look you have."

So I wasn't going to be a beanpole all my life? *Good to know.*

But then she switches back to their love life or, well, lack of one after yours truly. "What was I supposed to do with a baby in a third-floor walk-up? In San Jose?"

I know the rest of the story. She moved back home to live with her mom and work for this amazing architecture firm. My grandfather had just passed away, and my grandmother needed a little more noise around the house. And a baby fixes that. We still live in the same house, a Cape Cod nowhere near Cape Cod. And my grandmother turned into a snowbird, bought a mobile home, and married a retired truck driver named Stan. They come visit every summer when life on the road gets a little too quiet.

"Jamie, you look so darn grown-up," Mom says, and pats my knee.

"Aw, Mom," I tell her. "Don't get all nostalgic on me. You need to get some footage of me and my ladies in waiting."

She dabs at the corner of her eye with her sleeve.

After I've put on my Chucks and done my hair to a polished, messy perfection, I pose for pictures with the twins in the living room. The doorbell rings.

"I get," Elisabeth says, and with boost and a little help with the deadbolt, she does.

Mason steps inside, wearing a white jacket over black pants and looking a little like he just dropped from heaven.

I go to open my mouth to say something but find it's already hanging open.

He looks down at Elisabeth and the corner of his lips twitch up into a smile. By the time he sees Ann Marie's getup, it's an all-out grin.

"They dressed up for prom," Mom explains, as if Mason isn't already well versed in the oddities of life with two-year-olds.

"Very fancy," Mason tells the girls. He smiles again as they twirl around to show him their capes. He looks amazing—his black glasses all Buddy-Holly-retro-cool with the white jacket and blue bow tie. His smile is bright and imperfect, but perfect in its own way. He takes Elisabeth's tiny hands in his and together they spin in a circle.

He pauses when Ann Marie clamors to join in, but I'm the one who feels dizzy, like my heart isn't pumping enough oxygen to my brain. *Or maybe this is what falling in love feels like?* I shake the thought away because I'll never make it through the night with that idea running laps around my mind. *He looks nice,* I tell myself, because that is a thought I can deal with. *Like Darren Criss.*

Minutes tick by, and I become aware that I haven't said a word—not even hello.

Mason stops spinning and comes into focus again. "Looks good," he says, and nods at my tux. "The sneakers are so you, Jamie."

"Yeah," I manage. "You too. But not sneakers, I mean, the flower corn—cornflower, um, tie." I'm babbling. And

I can't stop. Infatuation has hijacked my vocal chords. "Blue, but not."

"Totally," Mason agrees, as if something I said made sense.

"The color thing. And real shoes," I continue, trying—and failing—to speak in full sentences.

Mom saves me by asking to take our picture outside on the steps. Mason throws an arm over my shoulder just as Mom says, "Cheese." I grin like an idiot as her phone makes its little shutter sound. She takes another picture, and I find myself hanging on to Mason for a moment too long. He smells like Speed Stick, shampoo, and all I've ever wanted.

"Let me take one," Mason says, sliding out from under my arm. "You and your mom."

"Oh, no," Mom protests, patting at her frizzy hair.

"You look great," Mason assures her, and snaps a photo.

I drive to Michael's house, where the limo driver will meet us. The plan is to pick up the girls in style, stopping just long enough for parents to snap a few photos, then go to dinner downtown before prom. The limo pulls up in front of Eden's house, and I get out. Being more than three feet from Mason, I feel my head clear as if I just took the right allergy medication. *Thank God. I might be able to form a sentence.*

Before I reach the door, it opens. Eden sticks her head out. Her strawberry-blonde hair is piled up on her head with falling-out-on-purpose ringlets on either side of her face. She beckons with one finger.

I step closer.

"I know kissing me would be like kissing a dead skunk, so I won't ask you to do that."

"Um," I say. Not what I expected. But then again, maybe I should stop expecting things from Eden. "Thanks."

"But, puh-leeze," she begs in a mock whisper, "put your arm around me when my parents take pictures."

"Sure," I agree.

"My dad's on the verge of a meltdown," she says quietly. And, not giving me a chance to ask for clarification, she shouts, "Jamie's here!"

The O'Shea clan—minus the time bomb in question—comes outside. I nod hello to Nick and he does the same. He looks less like a Neanderthal in a black suit. I am introduced to Eden's grandparents, Nana and Poppa, as Eden's new beau. Nick chuckles at this.

The three older O'Sheas all have phones or cameras. But no shotguns. Eden's mother positions Eden and me on the steps, then in the yard. I obey like a trained seal, then worry that I'm not convincing anyone of anything. So I wrap an arm around Eden and whisper, "Skunk stew or skunk sausage?"

And Eden bursts out laughing—making the photos look like we were the gayest straight couple on planet hetero.

But when a shadow the size of a Mac truck falls over us, our grins retreat.

"Only to the school-sponsored after-party," her father bellows at me. "And home by zero one-hundred."

A twisted, clown-in-a-horror-movie smile crosses Nick's face.

"Yes, sir," I say, even though I'm picturing Cinderella's coach turning back into a pumpkin. I make a mental note to ask Eden what time zero one hundred is.

"Oh, thank you, Daddy!" Eden says, and flings her arms around him as if he just granted her a wish.

Each stop is step and repeat. The limo pulls up at Bahti's house, then Holland's, then Lia's. Each time, we wait for parents to take pictures of the couple. Lia's parents insist on taking photos of all of us. They seem happy to see Eden, even if Lia doesn't hide her surprise/disgust well. Eden and I ham it up, pretending that nothing is wrong. Mason raises his eyebrows at us, which makes me blush through my freckles.

Finally we arrive at the restaurant. I'm starving and help myself to the breadbasket while scanning the menu for something not too expensive. I pass over the burger—it seems too casual for prom—and choose a chicken dish.

Eden says she's going to get the same thing.

"Order whatever you want," I whisper to her.

"I was in the mood for skunk sausage, and I don't see it on the menu," Eden says with a straight face. But it doesn't last long.

"I think it's a special," I say. "With apricot couscous and asparagus spears."

Eden buries her giggles in her napkin.

I laugh at my own joke but stop when I catch Mason watching us flirt. He looks ready to kick me one in the shin.

I mouth, *What's wrong?*

He shakes his head, his curls taking a moment to catch up with the motion.

For a nanosecond I think he might be jealous, but then I remember. Prom was my idea, and he's here because of me—babbling, incoherent, I-have-a-best-friend-crush-on-him me. I smile sympathetically and offer, "I know it's not McCall."

"It's all right," he says.

My heart pings in my chest, and I suddenly want to make him the happiest person on earth. So I pick up my water glass, and around the table everyone does the same.

"To friends!" I say.

Glasses clink and droplets of condensation sizzle in the candle flames.

"To friends," Mason echoes, his eyes on mine.

NINETEEN

Three hours later, the bass is thumping its way through a hip-hop song and I have long lost Eden to her crowd of squealing, giggling friends. Challis and the art-geek girls stole her away with compliments on her dress and whispers of gossip.

The words of the song are muffled by the persistent beat, and I can't help but move to it, even though I'm dancing with no one in particular. I look up to see Bahti do a 180 in Mason's arms—her little backside keeping the beat against his fly. Facing me, she raises her arms up, taking handfuls of thick hair with them. Then she lets go and her hair falls, brushing Mason's face as her hair tumbles to her shoulders. She leans back against his chest and turns her head so it's nestled under his chin as their hips grind to the bass.

I try not to stare.

Bahti reaches back, puts her hands on Mason's hips,

and slides them down along the satin stripes on his pants.

I can't help it.

All the parties in Kellen's backyard, the keggers in Brodie's basement, and I've never seen Mason pay so much attention to a girl. Not like this, anyway.

The thump of the music echoes in my ribs. Where my heart used to be.

He's looking down at her. And she's smiling her million-watt smile back at him. I see it now. How perfect they are for each other. My straight-A best friend and the third runner-up for valedictorian—somehow prettier now that she's wearing makeup and a form-fitting, thigh-skimming dress. It's like they've been waiting for the drama of high school to end so their real lives could begin.

But, wait. *What the—?*

Bahti reaches for me. Her fingers are in mine, pulling me in to make a sandwich. The bass still thumping, the three of us move as one—the sound tugging at our hips and knees. Mason and I bounce lower and lower, Bahti a narrow pillar between us. His knees brush mine and he flashes me a grin, then—for a moment—it's like we are dancing together. Just us. The disco ball trailing little squares of light over his shoulders and the music freeing up our hearts and letting them beat for each other.

Until the song fades and another begins.

"Phew," Bahti says, and piles her hair on top of her

head. "I need something cool to drink."

"Me too," Mason agrees. They head toward the tables, and I let them go, pretending to be absorbed in the new song while I regain my composure.

"There you are, dahling!" Eden says when she finds me.

"Ah, my love," I respond in my own fake British accent. "I thought you left me for Lord von Skunk."

"Leave you?" She cozies up to me and we start to dance. "Never."

"Not even for the fair Lady Carmine?" I ask.

Eden's mouth drops open.

And I know I'm onto something.

But Lia, of all people, cuts in by tapping me on the shoulder. "May I have this dance?" she asks, in an equally silly British accent that sounds, well, practiced.

Eden and I stop dancing, our arms falling limp at our sides.

I look at Eden.

And she looks at me, surprised, and maybe a little hopeful.

Until Lia glowers at me.

I feel my eyebrows wrinkle. I sort of shake my head, but neither girl seems to notice. If anyone in this room needs three minutes to talk, it's them. Not me.

Lia puts her hands on my shoulders. I look at her dress—it reminds me of a princess costume in my sisters' dress-up box—and wonder if I could get away without touching it. But she puts her hands on my shoulders like we're dancing, so I feel like a dork with mine by my sides. Carefully, I hold her by the waist and resist the urge to squirm away.

"So, how's prom going, Jamie?"

"Good," I say.

"When Michael and I invited you to share a limo, it never occurred to me that you'd bring *her*."

"I know you used to be friends." I shrug and pull a dumb guy move. "So why not?"

"Why not?" Lia squeaks.

I wait.

"For your information, we aren't friends anymore."

"Too bad," I say. And in defense of my prom date choice, I continue. "Because Eden's really nice. Funny, too."

Lia rolls her eyes and sighs as if I'm stupid.

"What? There's nothing wrong with Eden," I say to push her buttons.

"Um," Lia says. "I don't know if you know this, but she's a total lesbo."

"Yeah," I snap, "I know. And the word is *lesbian*."

Her mouth pops open as she inhales sharply. "The comic. The smutty comic in *Gum*—" Lia's eyes scan my face. "I get it now. You're both bearding it," she says as if the words taste like bile.

Her words slap my cheek, but my urge to fight gives

way to my lizard brain. I choose flight and let go of her waist faster than if her dress were on fire. Then I nearly run to the men's restroom, my heart pounding like a snare drum. But the room reeks like wretched-up spaghetti, and my stomach heaves at the stench. I spin around, push the door open, and head back out into the hall—holding my stomach and gasping for air.

I go through another door and find myself in a little lounge, sort of like a waiting room at the doctor's office. I sink into a chair and lean my head back so I can breathe better. I take a few deep breaths—calming yoga ones—with my eyes closed.

The door swishes open.

"Um, Jamie?" a voice asks.

I open my eyes to see Challis peering down at me.

"It doesn't matter to me," she says. "But do you know you're in the ladies' room?"

"The what?"

"The lay-dees' room," she says slowly, gesturing with an outstretched arm.

I follow with my eyes as it sweeps around the lounge: mirror, loveseat, chair, table with a box of Kleenex.

Is this what the ladies' room looks like? I wonder. I haven't seen one since I was five and had to go in with my mom. I have no choice but to believe Challis, even though there isn't a toilet or sink in sight. "Sorry," I mumble, and stand up.

I'm reaching for the door handle when she says, "Jamie, you look really nice tonight."

I stop. Turn and look at her. I mean, really look.

Her short, blond hair is sort of tousled, and she has on a sky blue sundress. It's cotton, and not shiny. And kind of plain. She has on a pair of ballet flats with scuffs on the toes.

"So do you," I say, because it looks like prom clothes weren't exactly in her budget. "Blue brings out your eyes." And it does.

"Thanks," she says.

"You're welcome," I say, and make my exit, but in the hallway I have a thought. So I turn around and go back into the ladies' room. (This time I *do* see Helvetica girl in her triangle dress.)

I look around the lounge, but Challis isn't there. Spying a door I didn't see before, I stick my head in.

Challis is sitting on the counter among the sinks, her long legs drawn up under her chin and one ballet flat dangling from her toes. A cigarette hangs from her lips, and her other shoe has fallen to the floor.

"Yeah?" she asks. Bored.

I step forward, so I don't have to shout. "I thought, um, that maybe you could ask Eden to dance." Because there's no way Eden would ask her, and Challis has more balls than the football team.

Challis laughs, cigarette smoke sliding from her nose.

"I don't do closet cases."

I don't know what I thought she would say. *But that wasn't it.* My lips open in an imitation of a goldfish. "Oh."

"Jamie," she says softly. "They just break your heart."

A run of goose bumps fire up my arms, cold as snow. I shiver. And turn to leave.

But the door opens in a flood of pastel satin, a roar of giggles and shrieks. Soon I am surrounded by a storm cloud of perfume and half a dozen girls I hardly know.

"Hey, Jamie," one coos, swooping in on me like a Kansas twister.

"You're in the wrong room," another pouts, while a third reaches up to straighten my bow tie.

"Yeah." I blush. "There are no comfy chairs in the guys'—"

But they aren't listening. They're smoothing my perfectly messy hair, touching my lapels.

I'm beginning to feel naked despite my clothes.

And Challis is laughing—a Wicked Witch of the West cackle—as I duck away from an air kiss and run for cover.

"Save me," I tell Eden when I find her at the refreshment table.

"From what?"

"I just got mauled by a pack of girls in the ladies' room."

Eden covers her mouth as if that will stop the giggles from escaping her lips. When she gets it under control, we find a quiet corner and sit on the floor. She rests her head on my shoulder and slips her hand into mine. We listen to the music and watch people dance.

My brain drifts back to what Challis said. *Was she warning me? Saying something about me? Or just saying she wouldn't dance with Eden because she wasn't really out with her family?* So I tell Eden, "Somebody said something to me."

"Lia?" she asks.

"No, somebody else. But I did talk to Lia."

"And?"

"Um, yeah. I kinda bailed on her."

"Been there, done that," she says. "Sorry."

"I can't believe she hates you so much."

Eden shrugs and her hand moves in mine. "Can we talk about something else?"

"Sorry," I apologize, and follow it with what I had started to say. "Why wouldn't someone go out with someone who's in the closet?"

"Where'd you find that question, under a rock?"

"Eden," I whine. "What does she mean?"

"Challis," Eden guesses. "My words or hers?"

"Um, both?"

"Challis likes girls who are out. It's, like, if you're going out with someone who's still in the closet, the whole relationship has to be in the closet too. I'd be okay with that. I understand. But Challis doesn't have much patience."

"So I'm not worth the time of day," I conclude. "That's what she's saying."

"If no one knows you're gay, yeah."

I feel the goose bumps on my arms again, and ask, "I'm the heartbreaker?"

"Huh?" Eden asks.

I tell her what Challis said.

"I think the only heart you're breaking is your own."

I immediately think of Mason—Mason dancing with Bahti to be exact. The empty feeling in my ribs comes back, mixed with jealousy. *Is that what a broken heart feels like?*

"Eden?" I ask.

"Yeah?"

"Does someone not liking you back break your heart?"

She looks at me. "You mean me or you?"

I try to smile. It feels like a wince.

She nods as if she understands. "It hurts. But more like a bruise. Not so much broken."

"Oh," I say.

"Sometimes," she says, "the first step to telling someone you like them is to come out to them."

"Yeah," I agree. "But it's not like I can tell this person

I like him. He's straight."

"But could you come out to him? I mean, in case he isn't."

I play along, because art-geek girls think everyone is gay. "Maybe."

"Good," Eden says, and squeezes my hand. "So you're gonna tell Mason?"

"Yeah." I feel my fingers wrap tighter around hers, as if the mere mention of the subject scares me. "I'll tell him."

Eden squeezes my hand back and says, "Sometimes I wish things weren't so complex."

"Like, so I wouldn't have to come out? Yeah."

"Like, if people didn't care, if love was love."

"Love is love," I say, more to myself than to Eden, as I scan the room for Mason. He and Bahti are back on the dance floor, swaying to a slow song and deep in conversation. I don't know which hurts more: his arms around her or that they seem really interested in each other.

"Do you ever want to be like them?" Eden nods in their direction.

"You mean straight?"

"It just looks so easy. One dress, one tux. Just the way things *should* be."

"I dunno, maybe. I never really thought about it like that." I see where Eden is coming from. She'd been raised by people who thought that a couple was supposed to be a man and a woman, not two of one variety.

We're quiet for what feels like an hour. I watch the other couples at the dance. Sure, they are all Eden's "right" genders, wearing all the "right" clothes, but I don't want to be them. Not in my heart. *I want to be me, not them.*

"I think about it all the time," Eden says, interrupting my thoughts. "My parents, they want me to . . ." Her voice fades away, and she rubs her thumb over the back of my hand.

"That must be really difficult—to not fit their expectations," I say. "I'm lucky. My mom is so great about everything."

"Your stepdad too?"

I groan. "He's my biggest fan. He threw me a party when I came out. And he wants to go to Pride next month."

I feel Eden's shoulder shake with laughter against mine. "I've so got to meet this guy."

"Please, no."

"Aw, I could use a little male support. My dad and Nick aren't exactly throwing me parties."

"If it helps," I tell her, "I'm totally cool with you exactly how you are."

"Aw," she says sarcastically, but her fingers tightening around mine give her true thoughts away.

"But if you want to pretend to be like them"—I nod

at the straight couples on the dance floor—"we can."

Eden stands up and I do too.

"May I?" I ask with a little bow.

"Why, certainly, dahling," she says.

But after I fold her into my arms and she rests her head on my chest, the silliness melts away. We sway to the music. I close my eyes, content.

It feels nice to hold someone—to be half of a whole—like them, I admit to myself. I half expect my next thought to be, *But she's a girl!* But it isn't. I'm glad it's Eden. I like her. And more than that, I like having someone to talk to about being different.

Technically, prom ends at midnight, but around eleven o'clock, Brodie and Ashley stop by the little cluster of chairs where Bahti, Mason, Eden, and I are sitting. Ashley is wearing her prom queen tiara, and Brodie, a purple sash. The girls sit up a little straighter, as if Brodie and Ashley are the king and queen of England, not of prom.

"Viveros," Brodie says as a greeting. "After-party, my house."

"Sweet," Mason says, holding out his fist for a bump.

Brodie gives him one with the arm that Ashley isn't hanging off of. "You too, Peterson."

"Wouldn't miss it," I promise, even though I owe it to Eden to take her to the school- and father-sanctioned after-party. There's no way that I'm going to not abide by Mr. O'Shea's only request. I'll just go to Brodie's after that.

When Brodie and Ashley are out of earshot, Bahti lets out a little squeal. "We just got invited to Brodie Hamilton's, la!"

"Yeah," Mason says as if it happens all the time, because, well, it does.

But not to brainiac girls like Bahti Rajagopolan. Girls like her aren't on Brodie's radar, nor are they in Ashley Quincy's social circle.

"Should we get going?" Mason asks.

"Yes, yes, yes," Bahti says, jumping up.

"No," Eden protests. "I want to stay to the end."

"We need to talk to Michael," I tell them both. "He's going to drive us to the school."

"The school?" Bahti asks, as if I just said "Brazil."

"Yeah, for the after-party."

"But we just got invited to Brodie Hamilton's!"

"We'll go to Brodie's," Mason explains. "After the school party."

"And after I go home," Eden adds sadly. "I have to be home by one."

Bahti's eyebrows furrow. She is not liking this plan.

"School party?" Mason asks her. "Then Brodie's. Promise."

"Okay, sure," Bahti says.

"After the last dance," Eden says, grabbing my hands

and pulling me to my feet. "I love this song!"

It's "Kiss Me Slowly" by Parachute, and I have to agree.

The last dance is slow and romantic, and Eden is cuddled up against my chest. She feels small and vulnerable, the top of her head coming up only to my chin. I hold her, wonder what it feels like to dance with someone special—someone more than just friends. Does it make you feel strong, like you're protecting them from the world? Or is your heart so far out on your sleeve that you're vulnerable, incapable of any action but hanging on for dear life?

TWENTY

The school-sanctioned after-party wasn't well attended, so there was plenty of food—appetizers, pizza, and every variety of cupcake known to man. I ate five.

Which is why I turned down the beer Brodie offered me when Mason, Bahti, and I walked into his kitchen. Beer and cupcakes somehow didn't go together. Or maybe it was the image of the rainbow sprinkles making a reappearance in that did me in. "You got soda or something?" I ask.

"Sure, man," Brodie says, and hands the Solo cup to Mason instead. He opens a cooler.

I choose a can. "Thanks."

"So, you driving people home?" Brodie asks me.

"Yeah, I guess."

Brodie holds out a fist for a bump, then gives me one of those half-handshake-half-hug deals. "You're the best, Jamie."

I raise the soda can in a mock toast—because I know he's thinking what I'm thinking. *No more Jordan Polmanskis.*

Mason taps his cup to my can. "Yeah," he says. "Jamie's awesome."

"And dateless?" Brodie asks, looking around. His gaze stops on Bahti.

"She turned into a pumpkin," Mason explains for me.

"Too bad." Brodie says this with half a grin and a little sarcasm. He's looking at Bahti like guys look at girls—adding up her pieces and parts as if to determine her score.

She notices and blushes.

"Can I get you something?" he asks her, ignoring us completely.

"Sure, a beer would be great, la."

I glance at Mason, see if he's noticed the obvious flirting that was going on between his date and Lincoln High's star quarterback. No, Mason's attention is on the deck-turned-dance-floor just past a set of French doors where some couples are still in formalwear and others are in street clothes, and all are dancing like they've been drinking.

Once Bahti has her drink, she follows Mason outside. Since I no longer have a dance partner, I stay inside and mingle. I get called in to ref a drinking game and then pulled away to argue the band geek vs. dorkestra hierarchy at Lincoln with three orchestra girls and DeMarco.

"Band geeks are the original," I explain. "Orchestra dorks are simply copying our amazingly uncool status."

"See!" Holland, a violinist, says to the others. "That makes the dorkestras dorkier."

"Dorkier," DeMarco, our first chair trombone, says. "Not geekier."

"Yeah, something like that," I agree, not pointing out that none of them actually register on either scale, seeing that they are at Brodie Hamilton's post-prom party.

"But what about marching band?" someone asks.

"Geekier," I say, because I've been a card-carrying member for the past three years.

"Totally, the uniforms are so—"

I don't hear the rest of Holland's sentence. Not with Kellen making an, um, appearance. He's shirtless but wearing a bowtie.

"What happened to you?" Holland asks.

"Spilled my beer," Kellen says, holding up an empty plastic cup as proof.

"Bummer," DeMarco says.

"And the girls are watching *Magic Mike.* So I did my best Chippendales impersonation."

"How'd I miss that?" Holland asks what I'm thinking.

"They're still watching. Downstairs," Kellen answers, referring to the big screen setup in Brodie's basement.

Then he ambles toward the kitchen, bare broad shoulders and all.

"Channing Tatum!" Holland says, jumping up. "Let's go!"

The girls stand up, but neither DeMarco nor I move a muscle.

"You go," DeMarco says to her.

Holland catches my eye and jerks her chin toward the cellar door as if to say, *Come on.*

I shake my head.

Holland and her friends disappear.

"As much as I'd like to be in a dark room with a dozen horny, drunk girls," DeMarco whispers, "I don't wanna know how badly I don't measure up."

"I hear you," I say.

Instead DeMarco and I head to the kitchen in search of more drinks. We both get fresh sodas and munch on pretzels with Brodie and Kellen, while complaining about the upcoming exams.

When I go to find Mason and Bahti, it's after three. I'm getting tired and don't want to fall asleep at the wheel—that'd pretty much cancel out my designated-driver status. The music on the back deck had been turned down due to the hour, and the dance floor had dwindled from mosh pit to country club. The remaining couples slow dance under the strings of white Christmas lights, some of them locked at the lips. I didn't see Mason and Bahti, so I pan the fenced-in yard from the apple trees to the fire pit. No luck.

Until I see them.

Kissing.

My body runs cold as my heart stops pushing warm blood to my extremities.

His wide, tan hands are cradling her face—his thumbs on her delicate cheekbones, fingers in her hair.

Oh God.

Their lips move over each other's.

I shouldn't be watching this.

There's tongue involved.

I can't look away.

She presses closer, wrinkling his tuxedo jacket—that she's wearing.

His thumbs slide toward her ears, deepening the kiss.

All of a sudden I want to look away.

Want to run, hide.

Cry.

I study the laces on my Converse, how they've gone gray near the eyelets. I wonder how much string I'll need to tie up the hole in my heart. Because, even though I know Mason doesn't like me like I like him, I haven't had proof before tonight. And, if I am honest with myself, I don't just like him. Or have a Darren-Criss-look-alike crush on him. No. This is more than a bruise. There's some major breakage. I love him.

When I look up, Bahti notices me standing there.

Mason turns, sees me.

"Hey," I manage. "I was thinking of, um, uh, leaving."

Bahti runs the back of her hand over her moist lips. "So soon?"

"It's three in the morning!" I snap, my voice cracking on "three."

"Past someone's bedtime?" she asks, equally bitchy.

"Easy," Mason says slowly. "We can go."

Bahti shoots him a look.

"Or we can walk," he replies with a shrug.

"Okay, okay," Bahti says. "Let me find my shoes."

And when she's busy, Mason mouths the word *sorry*, nodding his head in Bahti's direction.

Is he apologizing for Bahti's attitude? Or for making out with her?

TWENTY-ONE

It's Monday, and the *Gumshoe* proofs are here: a color print of the cover, and a stapled dummy of the inside—that's black-and-white. Deaf to the bustle in the hall around me, I thumb through it, turn to the subject of my moment of insanity. It's there. Complete with the new title page we designed at the last minute.

"Everything okay?" the printers' rep asks me. We are standing outside the main office and the second bell just rang. The noise fades as if someone turned down the volume.

"Yeah," I assure her. It's not her fault I sent her these files and not, well, the ones I was supposed to send.

"Okay, so look everything over and have your adviser sign here." She points to a sheet of paper labeled PROOF APPROVAL.

My stomach spins as if I just stepped off a Tilt-A-Whirl. "Does Dr. Taylor have to sign this?"

"It gives us the go-ahead to print the magazine. It's a contract."

"I'm eighteen," I tell her. "So I can sign it, right?"

She isn't expecting this question. "I think Dr. Taylor signed off on it last year, but maybe just because it was new. So whatever your editor says, okay?"

Crap. I'm not the editor, either. *Damn it. Why didn't I think of this?*

"I've got the cover on press Thursday. Last job of the day—I wanted you to come press check. So four thirtyish?"

"Yeah!" I say, psyched about seeing my work on an honest-to-goodness sheet-fed offset printing press.

"Call me if you have any changes—or if we're ready to print—and I'll come get the proofs." She smiles at me.

I pull my lips into a smile and nod. The gesture brings back the tilt-o-swirl feeling—or maybe it's because I am holding in my hand proof that I am an idiot.

I duck into the bathroom, find a stall, and lock myself in. I set the rolled-up color proof on end and open the dummy. I sit on the toilet and spread the pages on my lap. With a car key, I pry open the staples and then ease out the offending pages.

They're only coming out now so that they can be in there later—without Michael and Lia censoring them. I can't let them do it. *Gumshoe* isn't theirs and only theirs. It belongs to all of us, the football players and the marching band, the chess club and the cheerleading squad, the brainiacs and the dorkestra. Even the art-geek girls, and maybe especially the art-geek girls because they each submitted something.

I page through the proof and feel a little distant. Maybe because I haven't see it in a few days, or maybe because it seems to have a life all its own, as if the artwork grew roots and the poems grew branches with little *e* and *o* leaves. And, even as the designer, I can't smother it. Can't stop it from growing. Can't force it to be something it isn't. *Gumshoe* just has to be. Even if it drags me kicking and screaming from the safety of my closet.

My eyes catch on a poem that Kellen submitted months ago—before Hailey Beth Johnson became his other half. Holland insisted we put it in. And Lia had whispered, "Proof he's single." It was about breaking up with his previous girlfriend after she had made out with some other guy. I read it and wonder how he could walk away when he still loved her. Wonder if I'd ever get over Mason and Bahti and that kiss.

Evidence removed, I press the staples closed again with the flat edge of my key. I slide the pages between the screen and keyboard of my computer and head back to the office for a late pass to my last morning class before lunch.

A Million Things
by Kellen Zabala

It was a bonfire summer night.
It was a million stars in her eyes.
It was her skin warm on mine,
the taste of lemonade on her lips.

Then it wasn't a text on my phone.
It wasn't sweet nothings in my ear.
It wasn't her hand warm in mine,
but the taste of his beer on her lips.

It was a bitter winter's night.
It was a million sorry excuses.
It was the end of our relationship,
the taste of our last kiss on my lips.

It wasn't that I couldn't forgive.
It wasn't that I was jealous.
It wasn't that I didn't love her,
but the taste of his beer on her lips.

TWENTY-TWO

"We should go to McCall," Mason says over school pizza and french fries. He has his geektastic day planner open and his glasses in his hair as if he's seventeen going on forty-two.

I thought I'd talked him out of this. We went to prom instead.

"Just for the day—your mom won't kill you if it's just for the day," he says. "We won't set foot in Frank's precious condo."

"But when? We have exams coming up."

I watch Mason's lips as he says a single word. "Friday."

Mesmerized, I fall speechless. When I recover, I ask, "Friday? This week, Friday?"

Mason taps the day on his calendar as if it's already planned.

Thursday is the senior prank and Friday is senior skip

day, so I tell him, "No one will want to go, not after being up all night with the prank."

"Not everyone," Mason says. "Just us."

And the way he says it, with his voice soft and his brown eyes both molasses and serious at the same time, has my heart expanding like a balloon filling with air; one dub beats louder than the others. "Okay," I say, not because my brain thinks it's a good idea, but because my heart tells me to.

Mason flashes me a grin and flips his glasses down onto his nose.

I catch myself before I fall off my chair, then hold my ground. "If it's just for the day and not in Frank's condo, my mom will be cool with it."

"But we're not going to tell her," Mason says. "Remember?"

I nod, even though I thought we weren't telling them because of the overnight aspect, and the possible kegger. *But now?* I'm not sure I get it.

"It'll be our thing," Mason says. "A trial run on getting out of here."

And I like the sound of that.

We hash out the plan over a plate-size puddle of ketchup and the rest of our fries. It's pretty simple, really: A) Tell our parents that we won't be going to school because it's senior skip day. B) Say that Gabe and Londa invited us out on a friend's boat and we'll be out at Lucky Peak—and yes, we'll have life jackets, and no, there won't be any beer. This is the perfect lie. Because if they find wet towels, a cooler of soda and sandwiches, and sand in my car—it'll all be explainable. And Gabe and Londa will totally back us up—except for the fact that Gabe will be working at the garage and Londa will be buried nose-deep in schoolwork.

I'm calm, cool, and collected at the *Gumshoe* meeting after school, but then again, I have removed the evidence from the proofs. No one suspects a thing. Michael even thanks me for all of my hard work while Holland gushes over the layout and DeMarco points out my illustrations of a pipe, magnifying glass, and footprint that I've put in the short stories to indicate time skips. "Looks awesome," he says.

"Yes, Jamie," Dr. Taylor says, handing me the signed proof approval sheet. "It looks good. Lincoln High will be proud."

I smile weakly, knowing that after I put the offending pages back in, he'll probably have something else to say to me.

"Jamie," Lia calls to me as I scoot toward the door, hoping to leave the meeting before I meet my end.

Damn it.

"Wait up," she says. "I've got prom pictures."

So I turn and walk back to where she and Holland are sitting.

She has a stack of prints in her hand and she lays them out on a desk as if they are tarot cards. "Oh my God," she says to Holland. "DeMarco looks sooo cute in this one!"

I peek at the picture. He does look cute, even upside down.

"You are so lucky that DeMarco is tall. I mean, you got to wear those amazing heels and everything," Lia gushes. "I mean, with a shorter guy . . ." Her voice drops to a whisper and then silence, as if the rest of her sentence was too horrible to mention.

"I know!" Holland says, taking the cute DeMarco photo from Lia.

I don't get it. *What does she know?* But I don't ask. Nope. I am too busy salivating at the next photo. I mean, trying not to salivate.

"I always thought Mason Viveros was such a dork," Lia says, turning the photo of Mason toward Holland. "But he dresses up nice."

I have to stop myself from grabbing it. I stuff my hands in my pockets.

"Brainiac, maybe," Holland says. "Did you know he has the second-highest class rank?"

Huh?

"Bahti is so pretty," Lia says, ignoring Holland and

talking about the next photo. "She should wear makeup more often."

"God," Holland says. "She looks great in that dress. I could never wear that—I am way too fat."

Holland isn't fat.

"Yeah, me neither," Lia agrees, flipping to another photo.

Eden is in it and Lia doesn't make a comment; she just adds the photo to a small stack off to one side. When she's through sorting, she takes the stack with my friends' pictures in it and presses it into my hands, as if she wants me to destroy the evidence that she ever went anywhere with Eden. I figure it's for the best. Because after she sees *Gumshoe*, I'm sure the pictures of me will be used for target practice.

Stopping by my locker, I pull a picture of Mason and me from the pile. We're smiling at the camera with our arms around each other's shoulders. He looks happy and I look dazed. I hang it in my locker—proof that we were once friends. Because after *Gumshoe* is printed-folded-stapled-trimmed with those pages in the centerfold; and after Mason opens it and reads Challis's comic about the boys falling in love he'll look at me. And wonder. Wonder why I put it in—I'm sure no one will conceal that fact—and he'll know all about me and my secret. The secret I'm not sure I can tell him because I'm afraid he'll drift out of my life, leaving me with only pixilated memories.

TWENTY-THREE

It's after midnight on a school night and I can't sleep. Rain is pounding on the roof, and I'd like to think that is what is keeping me up, but it isn't. My smooth move with *Gumshoe* is gnawing a hole in my stomach and turning me into an insomniac, not to mention lying to my parents about my upcoming whereabouts on Friday, the recent Mason-kissing-Bahti tragedy, or Mason forgetting to tell me that he *is* the runner-up to the valedictorian.

A ping sounds from my window, and I nearly tumble from my desk chair.

Tap, tap.

I peer out into the rain, where a shivering figure hugs himself, standing among the rosebushes—his dark hair plastered to his head and his glasses reflecting squares of light from my window.

I pull on a T-shirt before I race downstairs, jump the baby gate, and open the door.

Mason steps into the foyer without a word. He stands there, dripping rainwater like tears on the tile, until it occurs to me to fetch him a towel. He rubs his face, then his hair, then attempts to dry his glasses. But the moisture smears across the lenses, eliciting a swear word, said—to my surprise—in Spanish.

I lead the way through the dark house and up to my room. Mason sits cross-legged on the floor, the damp towel around his shoulders like a blanket.

". . . comes into mine and Gabe's room," Mason begins midsentence. "Starts goin' through our stuff, saying we lost the keys to his truck."

I sit on the floor too, lean in, and try to catch up.

". . . starts asking me about my prom picture. Who the girl is and if she's Latina."

I think he's talking about his dad. And the pictures I gave him—the ones where Lia and Holland commented on how pretty Bahti looked. I figured he'd like those.

"I say no. And he acts all offended—asks me 'What? You too good for Latina girls?'"

"What'd you say?"

"Nothin'. I just let him go on. Told me all about his conquistador days. About how when he was my age he had a baby already—like that's something to be proud of!" He's talking about Clara and his father's other family—the one in Mexico that he went to visit that summer in junior high.

"I sorta lost it," Mason admits, wiping his nose on the towel. "Told him I wasn't like that. Never wanted to be like that. Never wanted to be him."

I wince.

"Said it in Spanish. So he'd be sure to understand."

Holy crap.

"He slapped me so hard I saw stars." Mason hugs his knees, gives into the tears. "Damn it! He hit me! Hasn't done that since I was a kid."

"Sucks," I say.

"I almost hit him back. I'm taller. Bigger." Mason's lip quivers, he leans forward, hides his face in his hands. "I almost hit my own father, Jamie."

I don't know what to say, so I just scoot closer and put my hand on his arm, even though I want to wrap my arms around him, hold him until everything feels okay again, protect him from his father and everything that is wrong in the world.

I think of Eden and how I *can* hold her through a million Parachute songs, how I can thread my fingers into hers for support, how she can kiss my cheek and leave a mark, and it's all okay. And we're just friends. But I've known Mason longer—since elementary school—and I can't do any of those things just because we're both male. So I just touch his arm, even though I want to do so much more.

He rests his head on my collarbone as if it's too heavy to hold up alone.

We stay like that until he's all cried out. Then I offer him a pair of pajama bottoms, a dry T-shirt, and a sleeping bag on the floor. I send Londa a text, so someone knows where Mason is and that he is all right.

I lay awake for a long time, listening to Mason breathe. Slow and even, peaceful. And so unlike his relationship with his father—filled with obligatory questions and one-word answers, the first asked in Spanish, the reply in English, "Fine." When it goes any deeper than that, Mason pretends he doesn't understand—even though he can translate the entire exchange to me at lunch the next day. They're exactly alike. Mason and his dad, stubborn as goat heads—those weeds with thumbtack-sharp seeds that live for seven years without water—neither one giving ground.

TWENTY-FOUR

After school on Thursday, I stop in the band room to pick up my trumpet. The end-of-year concert is coming up, and I need to practice outside of class. I consider practicing at home, but since I have to be at the printer in an hour, I decide to stay here instead. I pull out the sheet music for "I Remember Clifford" and start to play.

I'm lost in the music, in the sweet sadness of the song, so I don't see her right away. I look up, and Eden makes a loop with her finger to indicate that I should continue, but I stop playing. "Hey."

"Hey," she says back. "I was, um, wondering if you could drive me to church."

"Now?" I ask.

"In a few," she says with a shrug. "Keep playing."

"Cool. I have somewhere to be at four thirty. I'll drop you off on the way."

160

I go back to my music and wonder why Eden seems different. It isn't her clothes or her glasses or even her red-gold hair. She looks the same. But there's something about how she asked me the very same favor as she did two weeks ago. I figure it out. It's *how* she asked. She asked nicely, as if I might say no. And the timing? It's not last-minute. She'd have time to walk, maybe even catch the city bus. Again, maybe in case I said no. I finish the song, and start to pack up my music and my trumpet.

"That's a great piece," she says. "Not all oompah oompah like the band usually plays."

This makes me think of German guys in lederhosen, and I laugh. "It's jazz. That's why."

"I just might like jazz," she says.

"Well, you're in good company." I gather my things.

Eden falls in step beside me as we walk down the hall. "I haven't seen much of you this week."

"Yeah. It's been just art class, hasn't it?" *Rhetorical. I know.* "I've been busy. We've got this concert, then my AP exam. And my stepdad is out of town—which means I'm promoted to lawn boy."

"So it's not me?" she asks.

"What? No."

"I mean, since prom is over and everything."

"No," I say again. "We're still friends."

But she doesn't answer.

Huh? I *thought* we were friends. I turn my head and

bend down so I can see her face. "I wasn't just using you for a prom date."

She stops walking, and I see her smile for a second, but she frowns again.

"What?"

She swipes a finger under her glasses. "I'm so stupid. I dunno, Nick said—I thought—"

I wait, because I hate when I can't get the words out and people interrupt me.

"I thought that maybe—since prom was over—you didn't want to, um, hang out anymore."

"I'd love to hang out," I say.

"You would?"

"On one condition," I tell her in mock sincerity.

"What's that?"

"You teach me how to kill zombies. I want to kick Mason's butt."

"Dunno," she says, suppressing a smile. "That might take a while." Now the smile is out. "'Cause you suck eggs."

"Duh," I tell her. "That's why I need you."

"You need me?"

"*Need* you," I say, and slip my empty hand into hers.

At the printer, they treat me like an important client. The secretary asks me if I want something to drink and gets me a glass of ice-cold water from a watercooler. I wait in their conference room and look at all the cool things they have printed: pocket folders with silver ink, die-cut holiday cards, annual reports with glossy covers.

Then the pressman walks in holding an oversize sheet of paper with the *Gumshoe* covers on it. He has a five-o'clock shadow, green eyes, and ink stains under his fingernails and down the front of his T-shirt. I wonder if all pressmen are this buff—from lugging around pallets of paper or something.

". . . it's a work an' turn," he's telling me as he puts the paper on this table under bright lights. "It's running this way through the press." He motions to the paper vertically.

My brain scrambles to process the information.

"So we can make adjustments to the cover and not affect the back."

"Great," I say, and step over to study the artwork. I've spelled *Gumshoe* and *Lincoln High School* correctly. I sound out *literary* and *magazine* to make sure those are right too. *Phew.* I tilt my head to one side and try to see the fish and the girl on the bridge through the glare of the lights. Finally I find an angle where I can see them, but the fish don't seem as bright as they were on the proofs. But I'm not sure how to say this. There seems to be a secret language printers use: offset and litho and CMYK and dot gain. I know a little about it but not what to say now. Besides, I don't want to hurt cute press guy's feelings. I pretend to study the page more.

"Sorry I'm late," the rep says, stepping into the conference room. "Running proofs to people in this traffic is enough to drive me crazy."

"No problem," I say.

"Your proofs! They're still in the back!" she says, and buzzes out of the room.

When she returns, she spreads out the rolled-up paper next to the press sheet. "Looks like we'll want to bump up the colors, don't you think?"

She read my mind.

"Yeah," I say. "So it looks more like this." I tap the fish on the proof.

"Sure thing," the pressman says with a grin. "You want to come on back and I'll show you how it all works?"

I restrain myself from bouncing on my toes. "Of course."

He leads me down a hall that smells like solvent and through double doors into a massive room with a concrete floor. The sound of machinery is deafening, and the smell is even stronger.

"That's the Heidelberg!" he shouts, pointing to a printing press as large as my living room—okay, bigger. It's thrumming like an airplane engine, and paper is shooting out the end closest to us. Printed sheets are stacked waist high on palettes all around us.

"Over here is the bindery," the pressman says. "Cutter, stitcher."

An older guy is feeding thick stacks of paper into a guillotine. It beeps before the blade comes down, slicing the paper neat and clean and square.

"Your magazine's gonna be over here," he says about the stitcher—the only quiet machine in the room. It's off. There are pages of a book lying over metal bars that loop around the room like modern art. "The signatures will fall into the saddle, and *boop, boop,* they'll be stapled together."

I nod. *Maybe the secret language of printers isn't so technical after all.*

"An' we're in the back on the little press. Love this thing. Nice, tight registration. Four stations—haven't got your aqueous going yet. Just runnin' makeready."

I nod again, even though I didn't understand a word. I peek into the press and see my fish and my girl. There's a two-inch stack of them. *Wow.*

The pressman puts my sheet on his light table, arranging some weights so the little color boxes printed in the margins line up with a row of buttons on the table. "These control the colors," he explains as he presses them. "And we'll see if that helps!"

He hits another button, and the press lets out a warning buzzer before it hums to life.

Soon more *Gumshoe* covers are stacking up at our end. After a few, the pressman reaches in and pulls one out. He puts it on the light table.

It's more vibrant than the last one, but he seems concerned. He gets out a machine and takes readings from the little squares of color. "Spectrophotometer," he explains.

I don't attempt to repeat that one and watch as he presses more buttons, prints more covers, and pulls out another sheet.

This time the koi are sunset orange, the river a shiny blue-black below the bridge. I gasp a little. It's perfect.

"You like?" he asks me, a smile on his unshaven face.

"Yeah, it looks great!"

"Then all I need is your John Hancock." He hands me a red Sharpie and gestures at the perfect press sheet.

I must look confused.

"Sign it anywhere. I'll match all the others to this one."

I sign it in the middle, careful not to smudge the wet ink.

TWENTY-FIVE

It has been decided that the sculpture of Abraham Lincoln in the quad will be, ahem, amended into the shape of a giant phallus.

I have no clue how.

This was Brodie's idea. And because it was Brodie's idea (or maybe because he offered to be the model), the senior class agreed that old Abe should be a dick for our senior prank.

"Whoa, man," Mason says, surveying the contents in the bed of the Redneck's two-tone pickup by the light of a streetlamp. "This is crazy!"

"Go out," Brodie tells him, making a throwing motion with a roll of toilet paper.

Mason and three others fan out over the dark school lawn, and with his magic arm, Brodie lands a roll of Costco-special single-ply in each of their arms.

Mason raises his in triumph, then bends his knees and

sends it sailing, a ribbon of white trailing through the night sky.

I'm still trying to absorb the fact that it's midnight and I'm at school—and not with good intentions—when Brodie presses a roll into my chest and I take it.

I find my target, a maple tree not far from Abe. And wonder if I should have Googled "how to TP a high school" before attempting this feat. First I loosen the end and reel out a few squares to get it started, and then, in a Brodie-inspired throw, I let it fly. *Not bad*. I run to retrieve the rest of my roll, rinse and repeat.

When the quad looks like a Halloween hit-and-run, Brodie summons us back into a huddle. I put my hands on my knees, breathing a bit harder than the others—maybe because of adrenaline or maybe because of Mason's giddy smile and his shoulder brushing mine.

"Good work, team!" Brodie says in what must be his quarterback voice. "They've got the chalk around back," he says. "And the drinks." He winks when he says this, and I wonder what's wink-worthy.

But when Kellen tosses me a bottle of red Gatorade, I catch it.

Mason gets a blue one, and I'm so glad mine is a tolerable flavor that I don't miss the lack of a click when I unscrew the top. I raise it to my lips and chug half the bottle.

"Dude," Kellen says. "Slow down."

I peer at him around the end of my raised bottle.

He holds up a bottle of his own. It's glass and reminds me of an ad campaign—I feel my eyes go wide and I struggle to put on a poker face as my brain processes the typography: Absolut.

Vodka.

In the Gatorade.

This wasn't my first drink. Mason's dad had given us beers at a barbecue on the Fourth of July after sophomore year—said not to tell our moms, that this was a guy thing. He passed them out ceremoniously, unscrewing the top and pressing a bit of lime to the lip. Gabe first, then Mason, then me.

Eager to repress my now-pretty-clear sexual orientation and eager to impress one of the manliest guys I knew—Mr. V—I took it, poked the lime wedge into the bottle, and took a sip.

My poker face wasn't working that day either. My facial features screwed up so tight it was like I bit into the lime directly—and that it was marinated in lighter fluid.

"Aw, Jamie." Mr. V cuffed my shoulder. "This is the *light* stuff."

"That's why it tastes like piss," Gabe whispered as we clinked our bottles together in a wind-chime-like song.

I choked down that bottle of beer while wondering how I'd ever manage to become an adult. I mean, I had a stepdad and I knew the rate at which beer was consumed (three to five bottles per football game, a pitcher per base-ball game), but I wasn't sure I was ready to enter the adult world, or at least, the beer-drinking one. Because I just didn't like beer. It was bubbly like ginger ale but bitter and watery like some sort of cruel joke.

But Gatorade and vodka—that was passable; it tasted like Hawaiian Punch. And with all those electrolytes, it might even cure its own hangover. *Genius.*

"Chalk or Abe?" Brodie asks me.

"Huh?" I ask.

"Chalk the gym wall or turn Abe into a dick?" he clarifies.

I'm about to say chalk, because, um, the penis thing is—

When Mason interrupts, "Design the sculpture, Jamie."

I shoot him a look.

"Jamie's awesome at art," he recommends.

"Chalk is art," I protest. But no one hears me. "Typography . . . ," I try.

So I unload bales of Pink Panther insulation from Nick's truck. Kellen has a tape gun, Brodie has scissors and a box of garbage bags. I don't get it. So I just watch. First the insulation goes on, pink side out, until Abe is obscured in a column of pink.

"Tape," Brodie says to me.

I grab the gun and follow his instructions, starting at

Abe's feet, and I wrap the clear packing tape around and around the insulation like stripes on a barber's pole. I try to concentrate, really I do. But every time I loop the north side, I have to reach around Brodie, who was holding the stuff in place. First, his worn-out Nikes, then his bulging calves covered in blond, curled hairs.

My next pass was at thigh level and I didn't want to, well, bump anything. The next one I aim at waist level, and as I reach around Brodie, he says, "I think this is working!"

But Kellen, who has a little distance from the project and can probably see it better isn't so sure. "Maybe. But maybe not."

I spiral the tape up, tear it off.

Brodie steps back to get a better look. "Awesome!" he shouts. "That's an effin' huge dick!"

"It doesn't look like a dick," Kellen says.

"Yeah, it does," Brodie counters. "You've just never seen one that big."

I stifle a nervous laugh as I step back to stand beside them. I flutter my T-shirt off my chest in an attempt to cool down; I'm burning up even though the night air has a chill.

"It looks like Abe Lincoln wrapped in insulation," Kellen says.

And this is when Brodie looks over at me. And even though it's dark, and the moonlight a cool blue, I think he can tell that my face is Pink-Panther-insulation-pink. "It, um—" I start, feeling even hotter than before.

"Somebody's drunk," Kellen says to Brodie.

"It doesn't look like a dick," I finish.

And Brodie's face falls.

"Yet," I add, and pick up the tape gun.

Brodie stops directing the operation, stands out of the way while I work. I wrangle the column of insulation in with more rounds of tape and then have Kellen add another layer around Abe's top hat and secure it in place.

An audience gathers: Challis, the Redneck, Michael, Holland, Ashley Quincy, and Hailey Beth Johnston.

"That's my dick," Brodie announces. "True to scale."

This gets the girls giggling and Challis gagging.

"Man, if that's your cock," the Redneck says, "I feel sorry for your girlfriend."

Brodie takes this as a compliment, and Ashley turns cherry red.

But it wasn't meant as a compliment, and the Redneck tells him so. "The head's all deformed."

Kellen and I step back from our work—well, he steps and I totter.

"It still don't look like a dick," he tells me.

He's right. There's a tuft of pink fluff sprouting from a corner of Abe's hat like a cancerous growth.

"I can't reach that part," I defend my work.

"And the chicks like big head," the Redneck suggests.

"Not me," Challis chirps.

But I doubt her vote counts.

So Kellen adds more stuffing to Abe's head and hat area, and I tape it down in a generous manner.

"It's still got a disease," the Redneck advises.

I roll my eyes at Kellen.

"And it kinda needs a slit," Kellen whispers.

My face bushes hot.

"Get on my shoulders," Kellen says, crouching down like he's on the line of scrimmage.

I just stare at him. This isn't a football game and I don't have a ball. Just a tape gun.

"Climb onto my shoulders, dude. So you can reach."

"Oh," I say, then silently wish I had a crush on Kellen and his shoulders—which I was about to sit on. *Sit on!*

I'm not a cheerleader and not used to climbing on people. So I put the tape gun down, for safety purposes—not wanting to knock Kellen unconscious with it. Then I swing one leg over Kellen's back, and he shifts under me. I grab at his head for balance, get my other leg in place.

He stands without a grunt, as if my weight were simply the first rep, easy as pie on his massive quads.

I gulp down a wave of nausea as my perspective on the world changes and my stomach lurches. "Tape gun," I say instead.

"Tape gun, Brodes," Kellen echoes, pulling Brodie from a lively conversation about the details of his dick.

From my perch on Kellen's shoulders, which are most certain to win awards for steadiness, I sculpt the top end of our sculpture to a dome of perfection.

"Sweet," Brodie calls up.

"Now it looks like *my* cock," the Redneck informs us. He has an audience—the others, Mason included, have returned from chalking the gym wall and have formed a half circle around the masterpiece.

"Naw, man. It's mine," Brodie counters.

"Looks like mine," the Redneck says. "Right, babe?" He nudges the girl next to him, who shoots him a look of daggers.

"I modeled for it," Brodie says.

For a minute I think they both might just whip them out.

Kellen reaches up for the tape gun and then bends his knees so I can slide down.

My Chucks hit the ground and then, surprisingly, my ass does too. Which triggers a giggle fit that sloshes the contents of my stomach. I grab Kellen's outstretched hand and let him pull me to my feet. Now standing, I look up. See Kellen's beautiful, square-jawed face, messed-up hair, and a giant phallus almost growing from his head, and burst into another fit of laughter.

"You okay, Jamie?" Mason asks.

I stagger a few feet. Nod.

The motion doesn't help the dizzying concoction of

thoughts, vodka, and red Gatorade.

Mason touches my shoulder.

I clutch my stomach, trying to stop the spin.

"Jamie," Brodie's voice swims toward me. "You gotta put the condom on."

This is so out of context—and so far in the gutter—that everyone joins in laughing.

But my stomach isn't game. It spins like a carnival ride. And I lose an epic battle to keep the contents inside. Mason sees what is happening and jumps back just before my stomach heaves and a fountain of liquid gushes out, sickeningly sweet and bitter at the same time.

"You should probably sit down," Mason says, steering me away from the damp spot I made in the grass. He sits next to me, close enough that I can feel the heat coming off his skin contrast with the cool night air.

I watch Kellen and Brodie wrap my masterpiece in a condom of immense proportions made from clear plastic bags and packing tape.

"Dude, you need to lay off the booze," Mason says.

"I didn't know," I protest.

"Just joshing you, Jamie," he says, and drapes an arm over my shoulder. His hand rests on the back of my neck, his thumb on my bare skin.

"You don't think I'm a total wuss?" I ask, keenly aware of his touch.

"Nah," he says, and moves his thumb across my skin

in the slightest caress.

I attempt to ask a second question, but his touch and my thoughts swirl together in a dizzy, drunken mess, and I imagine we're dancing to "Kiss Me Slowly," his arms around my neck, my arms around him. I real-life lean closer to him, catch his eyes with my own.

He doesn't back away.

I have half a buzzed thought to kiss him before I snap back to reality. *God, I so shouldn't drink alcohol. It makes me crazy.* Mason is not gay—he very clearly said so. Okay, not *said,* but kissed a girl. With tongue. He does not want to kiss me.

Mason looks away, or rather, up.

I follow his gaze and find Challis standing over us, one eyebrow arched.

Mason's hand falls from my neck as if we were really up to something.

Challis sits and hands me a half-empty bottle of water. I take it but give her a questioning look.

"It's water," she says.

I unscrew the cap and drink.

"You didn't drive here, did you?" she asks.

"Nah," I say. I didn't want my car at school if the cops showed up. "My car's at Mason's. We walked."

"We're gonna crash at my place," Mason says.

Challis's eyebrows shoot up.

"Let's just say my mom has no clue I'm here." I give

her a look to explain that she's reading way too much into this.

"No, I—" She starts to apologize, then stops. "You shouldn't be driving tonight. That's all."

"Yeah," I agree. Then together we say, "No more Jordan Polmaskis."

Challis takes out a pack of cigarettes. She shakes one out and offers us one, but Mason and I shake our heads.

The finishing touch to the sculpture is a single sticker, classically black-and-white by design, reading: *Just wear it.*

My giggle fit strikes again when Brodie won't let Kellen put additional stickers on the sculpture. "It's a work of art," he says. "It only needs one plaque—art speaks for itself."

"But—" Kellen says, a sticker without a backing in his hands.

"Here," Brodie says, and takes it from him. Then, with a mischievous grin, he reaches around and slaps the sticker across Kellen's ass. It lands on one pocket, the condom shape pointing suggestively at its target.

Kellen's face flickers with annoyance, but he's too much of a man to be scared off with a little gay reference.

I burst out laughing.

"I love you, man," Brodie tells Kellen.

"And that"—Kellen points at Abe-the-condom-covered phallus—"looks like you, dude, not your dick."

177

"I can't believe we're doing all of this and we're not going to be at school tomorrow," Challis tells me. "We won't see everyone's reactions."

I fold up my knees and wrap my arms them. It's suddenly cold.

"Yeah," Mason says. "I'd like to see Mr. Purdy's face when he sees Abe."

"Totally," Challis agrees.

"Eden will tell us," I say.

"Eden's going to school on senior skip day?" Challis asks.

"Yeah, her parents. Hey, you wanna be in the pictures?" I ask, pointing to the gathering crowd.

"Why not?" she asks with a smile. She stands up, puts her cigarette between her lips, and offers me both hands.

I take them and she pulls me to my feet.

The three of us join the crowd around the pink, condom-ed sculpture. We lean into the frame while Hailey Beth takes a photo.

"Jamie!" Kellen shouts. "Get in the middle, man. This is your work of art." He tugs me front and center and wraps a beefy arm across my shoulders.

TWENTY-SIX

"Wake up, sunshine," someone says, shaking my shoulder. "Road trip!"

I roll over and look up. Mason is peering down at me because I'm lying on the floor of his and Gabe's room in a sleeping bag. I flop one arm over my eyes. "I've got a headache."

"Too much Gatorade?" he asks. "Or not enough?"

So much for the concoction curing its own hangover. "Thanks for the warning."

"I didn't see the vodka either," he says. "But you puked it up—so you're gonna be fine."

"Yeah," I say. "Right."

"You remember everything, don't you?" he asks.

"Yeah, Abe's a dick," I say, because I know that part is true. Deciphering what happened between us, however, is a little less clear, and more likely to be fiction—a product of the vodka and my overactive imagination.

"Brodie, man," Mason says.

"There's a reason he's class president," I say, and slide out of the sleeping bag.

Mason offers to fill my gas tank and I let him. He also buys us a bag of breakfast sandwiches and cups of orange juice at the fast-food place. Then we are on the road, first driving west across town, then north through bare, rocky canyons. We leave the desert and sagebrush behind as we pass the tree line. It's been forever since I've been to Frank's condo—probably since Ann Marie suddenly decided she didn't like her car seat and started screaming the whole way. It's relatively quiet in my Honda, the radio playing softly over the sound of the engine, my best friend beside me—the way road trips are in the movies or, at least, without toddlers.

I promise myself I won't weird out around Mason. I won't let my mind wander to the fit of his shirt, the amazing of his smile, the zap of heat when his fingers brush against mine. I send up a silent thank-you that he isn't wearing that tux—that was a problem. I couldn't even form a damn sentence, I was so infatuated. But I am not going to go there today. Mason needs a break from school, work, and his family and the general craziness of senior year, and I'm his best friend—not some brainless zombie with a crush on him.

I point to the odometer as it changes from 149,999 to

150,000, and Mason leans over the console to see.

"Seven, six, five . . ." He counts off the tenths of a mile as we pass the airport and the cabin with a tree growing through the roof.

"Three, two, one!" we chant together, and the nines blink to zeros.

"Where to?" I ask as the little lakeside town materializes around us.

"Ponderosa State Park," Mason says.

We start with a hike to the lookout, where we sit on the rocks and watch the boats go by on the lake below. We snap a few photos, then walk back down to the water's edge. We jump from rock to rock, edging our way out into the lake without getting wet. I dip my fingers in and jerk them out again, wondering how it isn't still ice, or maybe snow, like on the surrounding mountains.

For lunch we sit at a picnic table near the water and unpack the little cooler Mason brought: sodas, hoagie rolls, cheese, a container of cold cuts, another of macaroni salad, a can of chile peppers—his favorite—plus a selection of cookies.

"Looks great," I tell him, knowing if I packed lunch it'd be two PB&Js and half of a two-liter bottle of soda from the back of the fridge.

Mason smiles at the compliment and hands me a plate.

"Plates?" I ask, and then see the napkins. And silverware! Not to mention the can opener that he's using for the peppers. "You went all out."

I assemble a sandwich, careful to use a fork and not my fingers.

Mason spears an olive-green pepper with a knife and offers it to me. It reminds me of a slug, but I let him put it on my sandwich anyway. They aren't very spicy.

He serves himself a plate of food, pops open a soda, and starts to eat without saying a word.

"This is really good."

Mason shrugs. "I figured we'd be out doing stuff. Get hungry."

"Yeah. This is nice. Thanks."

"Just me and you," he says.

I pause with my soda halfway to my lips. *What does that mean?* It's always me and him. *Right?* "Totally."

"I mean, Eden's nice and all, but . . . ," Mason says.

Oh. I get it. Eden. I wait for him to say more, maybe tell me what he thinks of her.

He doesn't.

"You two should shoot zombies sometime; she's pretty good," I say.

"I dunno," Mason says. "She kinda gets on my nerves."

I know the feeling. "Yeah," I say. "But she's all right— if you ignore the annoying stuff."

This makes Mason smile. "So you're not, um?"

"Me and Eden?" I choke on pepper juice and start to cough. Tears well in my eyes, and I try to cough the tickle from my throat. I down the rest of my drink before it goes away.

When I recover, Mason raises his eyebrows as if to tell me to get back to the point.

"We're just friends. She's a lesbian."

"You sure?" he asks.

And I hope to God that wasn't supposed to be a secret! I don't think it was. *Was it?* "Pretty sure. But don't tell anyone. I don't know if I was supposed to say that."

"Don't worry. I won't."

And from the tone of his voice, I am certain Eden's maybe-secret is safe. Mason's like that—if he says he's going to do something, it's as good as done. He keeps secrets as well as he holds grudges. I think about my own secret. And how I haven't been guarding it as much as I have in the past. Eden and the art-geek girls know, and probably the *Gumshoe* staff too. And last night, well, my guard was way down.

I look at Mason and watch him eat. I wonder if he knows that I'm gay, and if he's just waiting for me to tell him.

We have never talked about gay things: not celebrities, not gay marriage, not the fact that 10 percent of people we know are probably bent. Each silent year that goes by makes it harder and harder to bring up. So now, four years in the closet later, the topic has become a huge rainbow elephant in the room. And I'm afraid of getting trampled.

College is looming, exciting and unknown at the end of August, and the thought of it has my stomach vaguely queasy. It's a huge change. I'll be moving out of the house where I've lived my whole life. I won't see my mom every day, won't have to put up with Frank's enthusiasm, mow the lawn, or watch my sisters. I should be excited, but part of me is nauseous. The only Alka-Seltzer in the situation is Mason. I need to come out to him, need to face the elephant, and stare it down. But first, I need some guts. I need to know that Mason will be okay with me—the whole me—because I can't imagine my life without him. The idea of having him with me calms the worst of the fear bubbling inside me, but when I think of coming out to him, it all comes boiling back.

I avoid the topic and ask, "So what about Bahti?"

"What about her?" Mason replies.

"Um, you—" *Were kissing her!* "You seemed to hit it off at prom."

"Yeah," he says. "She can *dance*."

"That's not all. I mean, if I recall," I pry.

"Oh, that." He looks down at his sandwich and stuffs the last bite in his mouth.

I wait while he chews.

"Whatever," he says. "We were a both little buzzed."

"So you're not going out or something?"

"No," he says, and laughs—an I-can't-believe-you-just-said-that laugh. "I don't date in high school."

"Too much drama, I know," I say. "But high school's almost over."

"So I should date someone who's going to Berkeley when I'm going to WSU?" he asks. "Talk about long-distance drama."

"Maybe not her, but someone," I say. "Take a break from the books."

"Yeah, like you're taking advantage of your chick-magnet status?" he challenges me.

"What?"

Mason laughs. "Uh, yeah."

"I am not a chick magnet."

"Okay, let me rephrase that, a stalker-girl magnet."

"I'm hardly the one all the girls want. Lia and Holland were gushing over you after prom," I retort, shifting the focus away from me and wanting an answer I wasn't getting out of him.

"Yeah, right. They think I'm a nerd."

"They do not." I leave out what they did call him for the sake of my argument. "They said you cleaned up nice."

"Sorry, Jamie," Mason says with a shrug. "I don't need a summer fling. I'm working full-time mowing lawns for Sal, then I'm outta here."

"Sorry, Jamie"? What does that mean? "You don't need to apologize to me."

"Don't worry about me, okay?"

I'm not worried. I'm crazy about you. And if you had a girlfriend, it'd be a whole lot easier to turn off the crazy.

"Hey," he says after a while. "We should get going." Then he starts putting things back into the cooler.

"Sure." I didn't think we needed to be anywhere any-time soon, yet I follow along. I wipe off the plates with a napkin and slide them into a ziplock bag. He eats the last chile pepper like someone might eat a single strand of spaghetti, tilting his head back and slurping it down.

When we're back in my car and driving into town, Mason points me to the marina parking lot. I pull in but don't cut the engine.

"The marina?" I ask.

He doesn't answer but flips open his cell as if check-ing the time. Then he gets out of the car.

I hurry to put it in first and set the parking brake. I wiggle the keys from the ignition and open my door. "Mace?" I ask.

"Could you open the trunk?" he asks.

I get out and unlock it.

Mason sheds his long-sleeve shirt and tosses it in the trunk. He has a T-shirt underneath—white and new.

And even though I had told myself I wouldn't drool over Mason, I admit I like the way it looks. See, Mason and Gabe share the same closet. The new clothes usually start life on Gabe's side and migrate to Mason's after they've shrunk or Gabe outgrew them. And the spotless, white, still-has-creases-from-being-folded T-shirt? It makes Mason's skin look darker and his smile brighter.

Then he unzips his backpack and pulls out a pair of shorts.

He's already wearing shorts, so I am completely lost—which must show on my face because Mason can't keep a straight face any longer.

"You are so bad at surprises, Jamie," he says, and starts laughing.

"A surprise?" I ask. "What *kind* of surprise?"

"Duh! A marina kind!"

This makes no sense.

He puts his bag and cell phone in the trunk and shuts it.

"A marina surprise?" I ask, following him inside.

At the counter he tells the woman, "Jet Ski rental under Viveros."

I'm still processing this as she smiles and says, "Yes, I have your paperwork right here. Have you rented from us before?"

"No. First time."

"Well, welcome!" she says before delving into the

page of details, how much it costs, and how we need to watch a short movie about safety.

And it sinks in. Mason rented a Jet Ski and we are going to take it out on the lake. Which is very cool, but at the same time, very expensive.

Mason nudges me. "You excited yet?"

"Yeah," I say. "For a second there, I thought you were going to pull a Frank and rent a canoe."

"And paddle in circles all day?" Mason asks, remembering the day Frank took us canoeing. "Never again."

We watch the video. And after I change into the shorts Mason brought for me, and we both ditch our socks and sneakers, the marina employee hands each of us a life jacket. We zip and buckle as we follow her out the door to the dock.

Stopping at a red Jet Ski, she says, "Here you go! Full tank. It's yours for an hour."

Mason steps onto it and straddles the seat. Waves splash over his bare feet.

"Put your hand through here," the woman says about the strap that is attached to the key. "You won't want to swim after it. Plus, there's a little clock so you can tell the time."

"Great," Mason says to her, his wrist through the strap. Then to me, "Climb aboard."

Which sounded like a great invitation. *Right?* But climbing onto a small, bobbing watercraft from a small, bobbing dock without grabbing on to one's rather cute best friend's arm, shoulder, or waist is harder than it sounds. Especially when said watercraft sinks under your weight and you get wet up to your ankles in freezing-cold lake water. I stifle a yelp.

"Have fun, boys!" the woman says as she gives the Jet Ski a little shove so we move away from the dock.

Mason steers it out of the bay and we putt along like we're in a golf cart. I put my hands behind me, wrapping my fingers around the sides of the seat so I won't topple off into the lake if a wave comes our way.

Then, as if the last of the NO WAKE signs is a checkered flag, Mason guns the engine. The Jet Ski lunges forward and I shoot backward. I catch myself before I splash into the lake. Glad to have an excuse, I wrap my arms around Mason and hang on tight.

"Slow down!" I shout in his ear as I grip his life jacket.

"Why?" His question is torn to shreds by the wind.

"You're going too fast!"

So Mason slows down. Not golf-cart slow, but to something more tolerable, like a Volkswagen bus. And I slowly peel my arms from around him. The buckles of his life jacket have etched squares in my skin. "Better?" he asks.

"Yes."

He slows down even more, taking a route along the

shore like we are on a tour. "You gave me the Heimlich maneuver there."

"Sorry. I didn't want to fall in."

"It's witch-tit cold!" he agrees. Then, after a few more minutes of scenery and watching other boats, he asks, "Can we go fast again?"

This time, I wrap my arms around his waist and get good grip before he guns the motor. But I still close my eyes when he crosses through the wake of a big boat and we shoot into the air. I think I count the seconds before we land—and my heart is pounding triple time.

"You see that?" Mason asks, cranking the handlebars and aiming back toward the wake. The Jet Ski slides into a steep turn, and the cold lake water splashes up our legs.

"No. I had my eyes closed."

He slows the Jet Ski, turns to look at me. His eyes are sad and serious. "Jamie, this is supposed to be fun."

I shrug. "I'm just not used to it." A half truth. The rest of which is I'm scared out of my skull of landing in the lake—my body instantly becoming frozen fish food.

"It's probably because you're not driving," he reasons. We slow even more, and he cuts the engine. "Switch with me."

I don't know what bothers me more: that we might drop the key into the water and have to swim after it, that I might fall in, or that Mason and I will, um, brush against each other in such a way that renders me speechless.

Okay, well, that one wouldn't be too bad.

I step onto one running board and he steps on the other. The Jet Ski wobbles, reminding me of a soon-to-capsize canoe. When I sit down, Mason sits behind me, close enough that I can feel how warm he is compared to my own damp skin. My brain empties of all other thoughts.

". . . the throttle, and that's the gas." Mason is reaching around me and pointing to things on the handlebars.

Oh, God, he's explaining something. And I missed it.

"Got it?"

"Yeah," I say, although the only throttle I'm familiar with is on a lawn mower.

He pulls the strap from his wrist and hands me the key. His arm brushes mine, and I close my fingers too soon. They close on air. My heart leaps at the thought of dropping the key.

"Here," Mason says, pressing it into my fingers and practically closing them over it.

I get the strap over my wrist and the key in the ignition. Then I ease the Jet Ski forward, putter it up to golf cart, and once I get the hang of the steering, I go to Volkswagen bus.

"Good job," Mason says with a reassuring squeeze.

So I push it a little faster and a little faster still. The choppy waves are slapping up under us, slamming the Jet Ski up and down. My muscles jerk and twist with the motion and my stomach lurches.

"There you go. A little faster and you won't feel those."

I squeeze for more gas and it rockets ahead. The wind whips my face, but the choppy ride smooths out as we skim over the surface.

"Awesome!" Mason shouts in my ear. "Woo-hoo, Jamie!"

I let a whoop fly into the wind.

And I'm pretty sure I feel Mason hug me tighter.

TWENTY-SEVEN

"It's good to go outside your comfort zone," Mason says, getting all philosophical on me as we lie in the grass at the edge of a little beach, letting the sun dry our clothes.

"Yeah," I agree. "That was friggin' awesome!"

"I told you. McCall's great without Frank."

"No canoe," I say.

"And just us."

My skin goes cold, as if I weren't sprawled on the warm ground in the warm sun. *He said this earlier, in relation to Eden.* But now I'm not sure I understand. I want to ask him to translate, but don't know how. "You're going all nostalgic on me," I accuse instead. "It's not like we won't see each other at college." WSU and the University of Idaho are only eight miles apart.

"Not nostalgic," Mason says, turning his head to

look at me. His glasses are resting on his chest, drying like the rest of us.

I study his bare face, his chocolate eyes, and boy-long lashes. His straight nose and his lips, dusky pink, shapely and—I so wish I was Bahti and he was buzzed—kissable.

It's hopeless.

I'm hopeless.

I roll over onto my stomach, prop my chin on my hand. I lean closer, watch a smile tug the corners of his lips up. *I imagine this is an invitation, imagine closing the gap between his lips and mine.* My head spins, dizzy from lack of oxygen, and I remember to breathe. I pull back, gulp down a breath.

". . . things change. New place. New friends," Mason says.

And *damn it.* I missed something. *Again.* Something important. "Sure," I say.

"It's not like I'm *not* looking forward to college. I need to get away, out from under my father's thumb, but I—I don't want to lose you in the process."

It seems like he says this in slow motion, because a million thoughts pop into my head in the time it takes for the words to form on his lips, starting with, *You lose me all the time—I get lost in my fantasies for seconds, minutes, hell, I don't know. And I'm so glad I didn't come out to you—then I might lose you for good. And God, I love you. You won't ever lose me.*

I don't say any of those things. "We won't lose each other. I'm taking my Honda to college, and if you want a ride back to Boise, you're gonna have to call me."

"And if your Honda needs an oil change, you'll have to call me."

"I can change the oil," I say, lying through my teeth.

"Yeah, right." Mason laughs. "And I can play the trumpet."

"Can too."

He gives me a shove, and his glasses slide off his chest and land in the grass. "Like, when?"

I shrug. "Dunno."

"You're such a dork," Mason says. "You probably never change the oil in your car."

"And you're a brainiac," I retaliate, not wanting to admit that he's right.

"Am not," he says, moving his glasses out of the way.

And I know I'm in for it.

I duck from his reach as he aims to mess up my hair, and I get a good shove in. He falls onto his back in the grass, momentarily defeated, but he recovers and rolls back my way. I hold him off, my long arms an advantage. "What is it, Mason? A four-point-two GPA?" I tease.

"Hell, no," he says, twisting out of my grip and pressing me back into the grass with a shoulder in my ribs.

"Four-point-five?" I taunt, his weight heavy on my ribcage.

A flicker of recognition crosses his face. His rather close face.

I know I'm onto something. "It is, isn't it?"

Mason sits up, no longer wrestling.

"Impressive," I say.

"Boatload of work," he says.

"So you're runner-up."

"Yeah," he says.

"Who's valedictorian anyway?"

"Juliet."

"No way!" I say. "She doesn't talk. How can she possibly give a speech?"

"She better give a speech," he says.

"Oh my God, if she doesn't, you'll have to." I sit up.

"She'll do it," he says, more convinced this time.

"It was the best of times," I say, holding my fist like a microphone and pretending to give a speech. "It was the worst of times—"

"It was the age of wisdom, it was the age of foolishness," Mason continues.

"And now that we are all headed our separate ways," I say in my microphone voice, deviating from Dickens because I don't know the next line.

"We had everything before us," he says.

"Freedom, college, the future . . ."

"The whole effin' world!" Mason says with a whoop. He jumps to his feet, then reaches down for my hands and pulls me up.

I'm barely standing when he bounds down the beach and into the water.

I follow like an excited puppy on a leash, dizzy and dancing like the sunlight and shadows over Mason's white T-shirt. Until the cold of the lake water grabs my ankles and pain rockets up my legs. "Holy—" I exclaim.

Mason's in up to the hem of his shorts, still whooping and splashing.

I'm swearing at the water.

And, when a wave splashes higher, I switch to praying. Which Mason finds funny. He wades back to me, holding an arm over his stomach as if to hold the laugh in. "I love you, man," he says, propping himself up on my shoulder.

The heat radiates from his hand, down my body. And I half expect the lake to begin to boil.

The pine trees swallow up the last shred of daylight as we leave McCall and begin the trip back to Boise. We'd spent the evening lingering over burgers and fries, drinking refills, and talking about all the stuff we've done over the years—from replacing Londa's hamsters with toads we found in the sprinkler box to floating the river in inner tubes and freezing our behinds off while the rest of me blistered with sunburn (Mason got a tan) to watching all the Jason Bourne movies in a row when Brodie was all bummed about losing the homecoming game—so it's later than it should be. We're crossing the vast spread of valley floor when the radio station goes to static. Mason adjusts the dial only to find eerie silence.

"Do, do, do, doo," I sing what I imagine the theme to *The Twilight Zone* might be.

"Ha-ha," Mason says, and turns the stereo off.

A huge pair of headlights illuminates the interior of the car as an eighteen-wheeler comes up behind us.

Mason turns in his seat, looks over his shoulder. "He's really moving."

I scan the road ahead as the headlights get bigger, brighter. There are a few cars in the other lane, driving toward me, so there's no way the rig can pass. I flip the rearview mirror to dim, but it doesn't help. It's as bright as noon in August in here. I can't see a thing.

Mason stays turned in his seat, as if he wants to watch the end of the world barreling down upon us.

I want to get out of the way, so when I see what might be a driveway, or maybe a cross street, I flick my blinker on and hope I'm right. The blinker *ca-chink-ca-chink-ca-chinks* a rapid rhythm that matches my pulse—like we're both on meth.

"Huh?" Mason asks.

It doesn't look like much, maybe an old ranch road, and I slow as much as I dare—eliciting an earsplitting blast from the truck. I pull over onto the gravel and the truck roars past, its horn still bellowing. The cars I saw earlier pass by us, their taillights red blurs.

We sit there until the sound fades, leaving us alone with the manic *ca-chink-ca-chink* of the blinker. I turn it off, hoping to signal to my pulse that it's okay to return to normal.

"That the blinker?" Mason asks.

"On crack," I reply with a laugh that diffuses the tension in my muscles.

Mason turns on the radio. A whisper of static, then nothing. This bothers him. I don't know why.

I look in the rearview mirror. It's clear and I want to pull back out on the road.

But Mason barks, "Put the flashers on."

I push the button as he gets out of the car. The emergency lights come on with a vengeance, machine gun *rat-a-tat-tatting* into the now empty night.

"Pop the hood!" Mason shouts.

Reading his lips, I do as he says.

The headlights hit Mason's white T-shirt and give him an angel-like glow and highlight the shapes of his muscles underneath. He fiddles with the latch and the hood rises, blocking my view.

So I climb out and join him. I peer under the hood too, at the jumble of hoses, moving parts, and wires. I can't tell one thing from the next, and it isn't the disco lighting—I don't know crap about cars.

"Electrical," Mason says. "Maybe the battery."

And, as if the car hears him, the headlights dim notice-ably, flicker like candles, and go out. The engine sputters and dies. A cold prickle works its way up my arms as the darkness edges in around us. But Mason is all business. He takes his cell phone out and peers at the battery in the square of light.

I wince when he leans over and rubs at the battery with the hem of his new T-shirt, leaving ink-black smudges.

"See if it starts," he says.

I climb back inside, put the key in place, and turn. Two clicks, faint as the ticking of a clock, answer me. I let go. Try again.

Tick.

"No go?" Mason asks.

I open the door.

". . . or a new starter motor." He's in the middle of a sentence. "Maybe an alternator."

I feel it coming, a wall-of-cold-water feeling. Dread. None of these things can be found on the side of a high-way in the-middle-of-nowhere Idaho in the middle of the night.

"Damn it," I say, the anger in my voice surprising me.

"You got triple A?" Mason asks quietly.

"No. Why would I?" I ask. I know the answer. But I lash out at him just the same. "I never go anywhere!"

"Flares?" he asks doubtfully.

"No!" I shout. My voice echoes as if to repeat just how alone we are. *How screwed.*

"Geez, Jamie," Mason says. "Chill."

That does it. Lights the fuse, hot in my gut. Pushes out the last of the cold dread and ignites the anger inside me. "This was your idea. Your goddamn stupid idea! McCall. What's so goddamn special about it? What's wrong with Lucky Peak? Lake Lowell? They're a whole lot closer!"

"I just—" Mason begins. He takes off his glasses, rubs the heel of his hand into one eye socket. At the same time, his cell phone lights up, illuminating a black smudge on his cheek. "I wanted—"

"What?" I shout. "To break the rules? To screw the hell up?"

"I thought . . . ," his voice trails off.

"You thought what, Einstein? That this would be fun? That getting stuck on some two-lane highway to nowhere would be fun?" I'm being an asshole and I know it.

"Never mind!" He stomps around to the passenger side, reaches in for something, and slams the door.

"Argh!" I shout at the trees. I feel the anger leaving my body with the guttural sound, so I growl out more frustration. At Mason. At my stupid-ass car. At the world.

And when I'm done, I feel like crying. But I gulp it back. There's no way. No way I'm going to let Mason see me do that. He's leaning on the remnants of a split-rail fence, his shoulders hunched and his back to me.

I collapse in the driver's seat. Weary now, and cold. And wishing for a bed.

After a while, the passenger-side door opens and Mason pokes his head inside. "There's nothing we can do until morning. I called Londa, told her to tell Mom what happened."

"You told your sister?" The last thing I need is to get in trouble right before graduation. "Your mom will call my mom!" As I say it, I know it's the right thing to do. I should call her.

Mason doesn't hear me. He reaches over, takes the keys from the ignition. Soon he's opening the trunk and rifling through our backpacks. When he returns, he has on a long-sleeve shirt. He tosses one to me. "Come on, let's go."

I'm still angry. Angry that I let him get me into this mess. I leave the shirt where it fell on the stick shift.

He waits.

A car passes and then fades into the vastness of the valley.

Finally Mason shuts the door without a word. I hear his sneakers on the gravel as he leaves, walking on the shoulder back toward town. *To my stepfather's condo*, I bet. That's where he wanted to stay all along. That's why we're here.

TWENTY-EIGHT

McCall. McCall. McCall. That's all I've heard since before prom. I repeat the word as I walk along the dark shoulder of the highway, half curse and half prayer. Curse that I'm here at all, and prayer that I make it into town without getting run over by a trucker or eaten by a bear.

I thought I'd catch up with Mason, but no. I've walked a good three miles along the empty shoulder—jogging even, hoping to catch him. I'm in town and I haven't seen him. A neon sign blinks CLOSED. The gas station, plastered in signs for Coke and beer, glows like a lighthouse. And sitting on the curb, eating something wrapped in paper, is Mason.

My heart sighs with relief. I walk over. Sit down.

He hands me a gas-station burrito, half eaten. A peace offering. I peel back the black-smudged paper and take a bite. It's still warm, spicy.

"Said the auto-parts store is open on Saturdays," Mason says, gesturing at the clerk inside. "I've got my debit card."

"Yeah," I say, and hand him the burrito. "Thanks."

It's way after midnight when we turn the hidden spare key in the lock of the condo door. I flip on the lights, see Mason clearly. A smudge of grease is on his cheek, his hands darkened to a grimy gray. Not to mention his T-shirt, with a series of Rorschach-esque blots along the lower half.

"You want to snag the shower?" I ask him.

He laughs a little through his nose in agreement.

"Not that you don't rock the greasy mechanic look," I say, knowing that's what he hates most about working in his dad's garage—the grime that never really washes off. I show him the way through the master bedroom to the bathroom.

Immediately he starts pulling off his long-sleeve shirt. As I close the door, I see him tug his T-shirt off, the muscles in his shoulders rippling and, in the mirror, his flat stomach and defined pecs sweaty with perfection.

I sigh. I kick off my shoes, take off my damp, slightly sandy clothes, and lie down on the bed in my boxers. I rest my head on my arms. *Pew.* I need to take a shower too. Not now, *obviously.* But in a few. After I call my mom and tell her that I got myself into a complete and utter mess.

But I don't call my mom, because soon my eyelids refuse to open, and my arms and legs won't budge. The white noise of the shower in the next room lulls my brain to sleep.

I jolt awake from a dream so real my lips feel bruised from all the kissing—we were at school. All kissing our significant others in the hall by our lockers: Eden and Challis, Brodie and Kellen. *Whoa, I so didn't see that one coming.* Me and . . . this is when I woke up.

But I press my eyes closed—will myself to fall back asleep because I want to know who it is. *Really* want to know. I roll on my side. *Who is he?* I reach to adjust my pillow, and my fingers brush warm skin. I jerk my hand away.

My eyes open in surprise, as if my dream and reality just collided.

Mason.

Mason in bed with me? I wonder. Then I remember where we are. In Frank's condo. Frank's one-bedroom condo. AKA Frank's one-bed condo.

My eyes adjust to the darkness, and the neighbor's porch light coming in around the edges of the blinds reveal Mason's form next to me. He's lying on his side facing me, his hair a dark puddle on the pillowcase. His right hand is resting in the space between us, his fingers curled toward his palm.

I slide my hand back over and touch his wrist.

He doesn't stir.

I move my fingers up so they rest on his palm and it looks as if we are holding hands. My sleepy brain begins to concoct a fantasy: *We're walking on the Greenbelt on a crisp, cool morning, our fingers woven together, our hands palm to palm.*

I force myself awake and shake off the idea.

I shouldn't be doing this.

It's so wrong in so many ways.

I begin to move my hand, but his fingers close around mine.

"Don't," he says quietly.

Surprised, I catapult backward and out of bed.

"You're awake?" I ask, catching myself against the wall.

"No," he mumbles into his pillow as he rolls over.

"Okay," I say, and hope that he's talking in his sleep—hoping he won't remember this in the morning. I inch closer again and pluck my pillow from the bed. I fold my arms around it and hug it to my chest as I walk into the living room. My heart can't handle sleeping with Mason.

The second time I wake up, it's to the beeping of the microwave, practically in my ear. Because I'm now on the couch, only half covered by throw blanket.

"Hey," Mason says, putting a steaming cup of

something on a coaster. "I made you tea. There's nothing else in the cupboards."

I sit up and let the blanket pool in my lap. I'm not surprised. This was Frank's bachelor pad before he married my mom. He was on the ski patrol and spent the weekends here in the winter. Summers he'd spend in Boise, working as a contractor. That's why there was only one bedroom. Which was why we didn't come up here much—a family of five in a place built for one, maybe two. We didn't fit.

I take the mug of tea and let it warm my hands. It feels good. "Sorry I got angry at you last night," I say, remembering, but not mentioning, the handholding.

"Sorry I made you come up here," Mason says. He wraps his fingers around his own mug. He stares into it instead of looking at me. "I had this vision—it'd be so perfect, so fun. Something I'd always remember. Just you and me. You know?"

The *why* to why we're here. The words wallop me in the gut, forcing a lump of guilt into my throat. *Why did I have to be such an asshole? Why don't I change the oil in my car?*

This meant so much to him, and I ruined it.

"I had fun," I say. "Jet Skiing was great."

"Yeah?" Mason asks, his eyes tracing a path up my bare torso to my face.

"Yeah," I agree.

He rewards me with half of a smile, and says, "Nice boxers."

I look down because I forgot what underwear I put on twenty-four hours ago. They're blue with yellow smiley faces on them, the fabric crisp and the colors garish because I don't wear them very often. My face warms. I hurry to put down my mug and say, "I should probably get dressed."

Mason's lips fold in like he's holding back a grin.

Blanket and all, I dash to the bedroom. But being alone and away from him doesn't cool my heated face. Instead I see the bed. He has straightened the sheets and blanket. There's a pillow on the side where he slept. I tug on my jeans and tell myself to calm down. *Nothing happened in that bed.*

But something did happen. I was being stupid and holding Mason's hand, and he said, "Don't."

Don't do that?

Or don't let go?

TWENTY-NINE

We're paying for our breakfast burritos and bottles of soda at the gas station when Mason's cell rings. He answers it.

"*M'ijo. ¿Dónde carajo estás?*" his father's voice booms.

I shiver. It might be the cool morning air, but I doubt it.

"At the gas station," Mason answers, nodding for me to take the change from the cashier.

Although I hear Mr. Viveros as clearly as if he were standing right here—he's shouting—I don't understand a word of his rapid Spanish.

"You don't have to come get us," Mason says, probably to dilute the anger, and heads out the door. "We'll be there in fifteen minutes." He takes off across the parking lot, walking so fast I have to jog to catch up.

If we don't die first, I think, guessing that Mr. V found

my car. And my car is three or four miles down the road, meaning it will take a lot longer than fifteen minutes to get there.

Mason shoves his phone into one pocket and the Coke into the other. Then he breaks into a jog. I follow, my burrito like a hot baton in a relay race.

I'm sweaty and panting by the time we spot my car. And Mason's father. And his tow truck. I gasp for air. Hands on my knees I catch my breath and say, "The tow truck? Crap."

"Yeah," Mason agrees between breaths. "We'll never hear the end of this."

"More like I'll never be able to pay him back." I imagine the pump at the gas station and how quickly the dollar amount would blink from three digits to four to five, filling the tank of Mr. V's tow truck.

We straighten up, square our shoulders, and walk into the firestorm of Mr. V's angry accusations. I pick out enough words—insults Gabe taught me—to know that Mason is feeling like the gum stuck to the sole of my Converse.

"Sorry for all the trouble," he says through a tight jaw. "And thank you for coming to get Jamie's car."

I can tell that Mason's forced calm is throwing his father off his game. He looks a little confused.

"Yeah, Mr. V, thanks for saving my bacon," I add.

He scowls at me.

"Can I help get this loaded up?" Mason asks, jutting his chin at my car. The tow truck is positioned in front of it.

Mr. V grunts a response, and I don't make a move. Mason, though, gets to work unfurling the chain and crawling under my car to hook it to the axel.

After a very long, very silent drive back to Boise in the cab of the tow truck, I walk home from Mr. Viveros's garage because I can't bring myself to call my mom. I let myself into the blissful quiet of my house without the twins. There's a grocery list on the kitchen table, and with how stressed my mom is, it's a pretty good guess she's at the supermarket. Frank is, as usual, nowhere to be found. And I swear the calendar in the kitchen said he was home this weekend. *Whatever.*

So I turn the shower to hot. I step out of my smelly clothes and under the stream of water. When I'm finally clean, I pull on shorts and a tee and collapse onto my bed.

Mom knocks on my door. "Hey," she says through the open space. "How was your little vacation?"

"Good," I admit, sitting up and swinging my legs over the edge of my bed. "Until my car died and I ended up owing Mr. V for one helluva tow *and* an alternator."

"Karma sucks," she says, sitting next to me.

"You can say that again. Mason said he'd put the alternator in for me so I didn't run up a bill for labor on top of it all."

"Look, Jamie, I am trying really hard to let you be an adult and make your own decisions."

"Yeah, Mom. I know."

"But this one?" she says touching my knee. "Well, it wasn't your shining moment. In fact, it was pretty stupid."

I have half a thought that I should blame the whole fiasco on Mason. But I step up to the plate. "School's been stressful. We needed a break before exams."

"I get that, Jamie. That's why I said okay to senior skip day, why I was okay with you spending the night at Mason's. But lying to me about where you are? That's not okay."

"I'm sorry."

Mom reaches over and touches my cheek. "I was worried about you. Mrs. Viveros called me. You know the thoughts that run through my head when the phone rings at eleven thirty at night?"

I know how those calls make her jump—and that's when I'm home. *But what about when I'm not?*

"You should have called me, Jamie."

"I know."

"But you didn't?"

"I was— God, I felt so stupid."

"Karma," Mom says.

"Karma has my butt mowing lawns for Sal this summer," I tell her, guessing at what my punishment might be.

"Karma has you working for me this summer. You can mow lawns on weekends."

"I suppose you're going to tell me to get started?"

Mom stands ups and walks to the window. She peeks out through the blinds. "Yes, in fact, I am. The lawn could use it. Then maybe a little babysitting? Just while Frank and I grab dinner."

I smile. Weakly.

"And that movie I've been wanting to see . . . ," she adds.

THIRTY

Monday, Eden nearly tackles me in the hallway. "You should have been here!" she says.

"When?" I ask, pulling books from my locker. I notice
her brother lurking across the hall and I nod a curt hello.

"Friday!" Eden says.

"Hey, Eden," Nick says.

She shoots him an annoyed look that I'd never dare.

"You need a ride home tonight?" Nick asks. "Or are
you doing something gay after school?"

"No," she says. "I have Japanese club. And it isn't
gay."

"Yeah, it is," he mutters.

She glares at him until he shuffles away.

"Friday? It was senior skip day?" I say, getting back
to our conversation. "I was in McCall."

"But it was so cool—no one went to first period. We
were all out in the quad!"

I raise my eyebrows. This is überbad behavior as far as Eden goes.

"And Principal Chambers got on the loudspeaker—told us to go to class—but we watched the janitor unwrap Abe instead. There was a shipload of tape on that thing!"

"I know." I shut my locker and give the lock a spin.

"All my classes were study hall. I mean, since no one was here. And it was Day of Silence and all."

"Day of Silence?" I ask.

"Um, yeah," she says as if I'm stupid. "Nationally. You know, the GLSEN LGBT anti-bullying campaign?"

"Oh, yeah," I say.

"You'd know these things if you were in the GSA," she points out.

And at that moment, the noise in the hall seemed to die down, her voice sounding like she shouted it into a bullhorn by comparison. "Shh," I say.

"Why?" she whispers back.

"I don't want—you know."

"You mean you don't want to come out of the—" she starts.

But I reach over and press her lips shut.

"Cwosits ave wery wittle wentilashoon," she mumbles through my fingers.

"What?" I ask, moving my hand away.

"Closets have very little ventilation, Jamie."

"Very funny."

"I thought you were going to tell Mason when you went to McCall."

"Huh? No. Where'd you get that idea?"

Eden's own hand jumps to her lips. She shakes her head.

I roll my eyes.

"Well, I didn't. So I'd appreciate it if you—and your friends—wouldn't either," I explain as I remember what I *did* tell Mason. *That Eden was a lesbian.*

"Okay. Okay."

"But you are out, right?" I ask. "At school?"

"Yeah," she says. "Except that my parents keep pushing me back in."

"So doesn't make any sense," I say, half wondering how God divvied up the parents. My mom *wants* me to be out.

The bell rings.

Eden hooks her thumb in the direction of her first class. It's in the opposite direction from mine. "See you in art?" she asks.

"Uh-huh," I agree.

During announcements, Principal Chambers's no-nonsense voice rings out over the loudspeaker. "If any student has information about the writing on the gym wall or about the defacing of the statue of President Lincoln in the front quad, please report what you know to the front office.

Your name will be kept confidential."

I laugh. No one will turn anyone in. It'd be like raising your hand and saying, "I was there!"

I'm stretching my hamstrings on the edge of the track when I see the others spill out of the building. There's several Frisbees being tossed among them—probably another Brodie-inspired soccer-unit replacement. They fan out over the football field, except for Brodie, who stands in the end zone. When everyone appears to be in place, Brodie shouts, "Fifty alive!"

The group trips over themselves, trying to catch the disc before it hits the ground. Some end up sprawled on the grass, except Mason, who emerges unharmed with the Frisbee—and fifty points. I let out a whoop and he looks my way with an ear-to-ear grin. His glasses are off and he's wearing a threadbare Lincoln Lions tee, sunshine yellow and snug across the chest.

He gestures for me to join them.

I shake my head. Because there is no way I'd be able to catch a Frisbee with him smiling at me like that.

I finish my mile and take a shower. I'm dressed and almost out the locker room door when I hear the Redneck roll his neck behind me, his bones popping like far-off fireworks.

"Fagmag," Nick says. "You tell the principal I made Abe into a dick?"

"No," I say. "Why? You get called into Chambers's chambers?"

"Yeah." His fists planted on his hips, each as big as a dodgeball. "She knew I was there—like someone narced on me."

"Uh, maybe someone saw your truck there?" I take a guess. Or saw the photos on Facebook. *Crap.*

"You better not rat," he warns.

"Why would I rat?" I ask him. "I'd be in trouble too." *Idiot.*

He looks me up and down, maybe trying to decide if I'd tattle, or maybe to see if I'd make a nice lunch. "I know you messed with the fag mag," he tells me.

Messed with Gumshoe? *Double crap.* How does he know about that? Oh, yeah. Challis helped me with it. Challis and Eden are friends. And he's Eden's brother. "Yeah," I agree. "And since you didn't rat on me, I won't rat on you."

I watch his face as my words sink in. His face lights up real slow, as if it's on a dimmer switch. "Yeah, cool," he says.

And I hope he means it.

At first I think the whole school overheard Eden in the hall earlier this morning, because everyone is looking at me, saying "hey" or smiling as if I'm their new best friend. The I'm-pretty-sure-is-gay sophomore who wears tie-dye shirts cuffs me on the shoulder and says, "Cool," when he passes me in the hall. I do a 180 and watch him walk away. *Huh?*

I feel like a celebrity—albeit an outed one—until I see Brodie and Kellen in the cafeteria at lunch. Our table, which is normally pretty tame at the end where Mason and I sit, is teaming with students. And it's pretty clear that they are the celebrities, not me.

"Like, how did you get the idea?" a blond junior asks Brodie.

"Abe is kinda tall, you know," he replies. "And has a hat on his head."

The girl giggles, a *tee-hee-hee* sound escaping from around her blue-polished fingernails. The guys laugh. "Head," they repeat.

Mason plunks a stack of textbooks down, his day planner on top. "The average IQ around this place has gone into the crapper." He nods to indicate the newcomers.

"Heck," I say. "It just doubled, now that you're here."

His lips form a swearword that he doesn't say out loud. "I asked for that one."

"Sorry," I say.

"Whaddaya want?" He is asking about lunch.

"Pizza," I say, and hand him my caf card. "Fries."

"Save me a seat," he says, and escapes.

"Jamie!" Brodie shouts. "Now that man's an artiste!"

The blond girl's head swivels my direction. And soon the whole crowd is looking at me.

"He's the one that did all the work—taping and sculpting," Brodie explains out loud while his hands gesture the shaping of a very large penis.

My face heats up faster than a propane grill.

"Really?" the blond-and-blue girl asks, easing away from Brodie and closer to me. "That was a lot of work."

I force a smile.

"I'd, like, never have the guts to do something like that," she says, now so close I can smell her shampoo. "Are you gonna get suspended?"

My smile warps into a gape.

Her touch on my arm doesn't help.

I gulp in a lump of air, wonder if I *will* get suspended—it wasn't like we disassembled the principal's car and reassembled it on the roof like the class of 1977 was rumored to have done. And we didn't flood the basement in an attempt to make an indoor swimming pool (class of 1985), and we didn't photocopy hundreds of exams stolen from teacher's desks and briefcases and drop them down stairwells and off the roof (class of 1991). We just wrapped ol' Abe in a little insulation and covered him with a plastic bag in case it rained—and the chalk murals, they were gone too, thanks to a power washer. I say, "I hope not."

"Oh, but it'd be so cool. I mean, like, we could all

protest for you," she coos.

I wince, then decide that the best way to get rid of horny girls is to ignore them. I sit down in the seat closest to Mason's books. I open the first thing I lay my hands on and pretend I'm busy reading.

Only it isn't a book.

It's his day planner.

And I'm open to April. There with rows of tiny printed letters in each of the calendar squares—homework assignments, tests, and my band concert tomorrow night. I can read those. I can even read some of the Spanish. *Trabajo* on the days he has to work. But there are other notes. Not in either language. Like on this past Friday—the day we went to McCall—there's several sentences.

In French.

And even though I can't read them, I feel guilty. I snap the planner shut.

Blond-and-blue girl has moved on to drooling over Kellen, and Hailey Beth—his girlfriend—is doing her best to fend her off.

And so my fifteen minutes of fame faded into oblivion, no one noticing that I'm gay or even caring enough not to hit on me. I breathe a sigh of relief.

THIRTY-ONE

After school, I get a text from Mason.

Car is ready. Can I drive it?

I think about my clutch. And how Mason doesn't drive stick. And how my mother would kill me if someone else ended up in a fender bender on my already-very-expensive insurance. Then I figure that Mason can probably learn anything—especially about cars—in six seconds flat. And the garage is only a few miles away. He is my best friend. I text him back.

Sure.

Soon I hear a car pull into the driveway, purring as it idles. I look out my window and see my car—the once blue paint worn away at the edges, the bumper scratched, and the passenger side of the windshield marred by a spider-shaped scar from a rock chip repair gone bad. I guess Mason couldn't fix everything about it. I bound down the stairs and out the door, still in my bare feet.

Mason is putting the hood up, still wearing his gray shirt with his name embroidered over one pocket. I join him.

"New alternator." He points to the only shiny item under the hood. "The battery's past due but fine. And this belt here"—more pointing, this time at a bunch of whirring parts that must be the engine—"is pretty worn."

"Oh," I say. "Okay." It's kind of hard to see.

"So before we go up to Pullman, she's gonna need a new one."

"Moscow," I say, putting my college destination on the map.

"And I tuned her up."

"Wow," I say. "Thanks."

Mason shuts the hood and motions for me to climb in. My knees brush the dash and I scoot the seat back.

Now sitting in the passenger seat, Mason reaches over and flips up my sun visor. "This is an oil change sticker," he says, pointing to one of two new additions to my windshield.

"Oh," I say. "So that's what they look like?"

He ignores my sarcasm. "And when the odometer gets to 153,024, the oil needs to be changed."

"Okay."

"And your tires—they're at about half tread—should be rotated at about 159–160."

"You rotated my tires?" I ask, deducing the fact from the new sticker.

"Yeah," he says, a little Jamie-you're-being-stupid tone in his voice.

"You didn't have to," I say.

"Um, yeah. For when we drive her to Pullman," he says. "We gotta take good care of this baby."

I get an urge to grab him behind the ears, kiss him on the mouth.

But I don't.

I take in a long yoga breath of warm, purring-car air. Mason said "we"—as if my car now belonged to both of us. *And all the work he did?* Rotating the tires, tuning the engine, and changing the oil. It's an apology-thank-you-I-love-you-man all in one. This is my moment. *Say it. Come out.*

Now.

"Mason?" I ask, and tell myself I shouldn't look at him. I fix my eyes on the sun shining onto the corroded windshield. It's blinding, but better than watching Mason's face when I say what I'm going to say.

"Jamie?" he asks, as if my name were musical.

"I, uh—" I get the first word out, but stop when pain stabs me between my eyebrows. I close my eyes, and spots swirl under my lids. *Another yoga breath,* I promise myself. *Then I'll say it.*

I breathe in as slowly as possible, and when I get lightheaded, I let the air whoosh out. I gather my courage, open my eyes, and look at my best friend since third grade, and say, "Um, uh. Yeah. I— Um. Thank you?"

"No problem," Mason says. "I probably should have tuned her up before the trip—then we wouldn't have gotten stranded."

I didn't say it. "Next time," I say half to myself and half to him. "Before we leave in August."

"I can't effin' wait!"

But I can, or I have to, because I can't seem to get the words past my lips.

I chickened out. Maybe because I don't think I could handle anything less than complete acceptance, as if even the slightest hesitation on Mason's part would shatter me, break my fragile hold on sanity, and leave me in pieces on the threshold before I stepped out into the world. Or maybe because coming out to Mason will change everything in more ways than I can count, even his half-hugs and head rubs—obviously meant to ruin every good hair day and tease me about my vanity. And definitely because coming out is something I can't take back; coming out would be forever mine, for better or for worse.

THIRTY-TWO

Eden passes me a folded square of drawing paper. *You owe me a dollar.*

I look up at the very last art history slide: an illustration I'd seen on a book jacket in the school library. It's by Nick Gaetano, an actual, living artist. *Dang it.* I didn't think Ms. Maude would finish before the end of the year. And we have another week of class. I'm pulling out my wallet and looking for a dollar among the receipts when the lights flash on.

"We've got about twenty minutes," Ms. Maude announces. "So let's spend some time working on our self-portraits."

I hand Eden a dollar so soft it feels like fabric.

"So," she says, "now that I'm rich, let's go out. My treat."

"Sure," I say.

"After school?" she asks.

"Can't. Band concert's tonight."

"And you didn't tell me?"

"Come," I say. "We can do something after."

"You sure?"

"Yeah," I say, catching Ms. Maude looking in our direction with one eyebrow quirked as if to ask why we weren't getting to work. "Of course," I whisper. Then I go to the back of the room to retrieve my project from the shelves. I pick up a hand mirror from a basket Ms. Maude keeps for this assignment.

I open my pad of paper to my self-portrait. I have the profile drawn in, my carefully messy hair, my forehead, nose and lips, and chin down to my squarish Adam's apple. That was the easy part. The part where I'm looking at the viewer is harder.

I study my reflection. Smile. Frown. I turn my head, look back into the mirror, and laugh because I look like a total doof. I decide to face front and sketch my right eye. I start with the lids, then the iris and pupil. I sketch in a highlight, a few eyelashes, but not too many so I don't look like a girl. I shade in the shadows, the curve of the cornea.

Eden leans over. "Who are you doing again?"

"Maxime Quoilin," I say, and pull a printout about him from my papers.

I hand it to her and ask, "Why does Nick think I'd rat him out for the senior prank?"

Eden laughs. "Yeah, he got called into Chambers's chambers. Serves him right, too. I didn't sneak out to the senior prank."

"But why me? Like, a quarter of the class was there."

"In Nick-thinking?" Eden asks, putting my printout down. "I pretty much know how his simple mind works. A girl wouldn't do it—no guts. A brainiac like Mason wouldn't do it—too smart. And his football buddies like Brodie and Kellen wouldn't do it—no reason. And so, well, that leaves you."

"But I didn't turn him in and I'm not going to."

"Oh, I hear you. He's my brother. I have to live with logic like that." She picks up my drawing and taps her Copic pen on her lip as if she's thinking. "I still say Picasso."

"Why?"

"I dunno, something about the two yous—how I can see who you think you are and who you want to be. . . ." Her voice trails off.

"Don't go psychotherapist on me," I tell her, even though she might be writing my "artist statement" for me. I take a mental note: *Who I am. Who I want to be.*

"This one"—she points to the profile with her pen—"is all—"

I jerk my drawing away—out of reach of the ink.

"I'm not gonna draw on it, Jamie," she promises. "It's all confident, chin up, and the whole shebang. But the eye looking at you, he's not the same. He's worried, not sure of things."

I look at her. Look at my drawing, at the two versions of me. *My inside and my outside.* Look in the mirror. *Yeah,* I say to myself. Gumshoe *is being printed with a certain unapproved addition, I haven't told my best friend I'm gay, and the Redneck thinks I turned him in to Principal Chambers. Of course my inside looks worried.*

"But what's Picasso about that?" I ask.

"I dunno," Eden says. "Picasso's people always look like they're about to fall apart."

I manage to keep myself together all through the dress rehearsal and through dinner at McDonald's with DeMarco, Bahti, and the other band geeks. But as I tuck in my red shirt in front of the mirror in the boys' bathroom, I see it. The worry on my face.

Eden explained to me how the eyes say everything. Paging through her sketchbook, she pointed out the emotions of the characters in her drawings—a fine collection of manga-style same-sex couples.

I stopped her at a page picturing two girls, one tall and the other short with exaggerated curves. The tall one was bending down to kiss the other girl's forehead.

"You didn't see that."

"But it's good," I said. So good, I recognized that it was Eden and Challis.

She pretended my compliment didn't mean anything, and then she drew me a cheat sheet: happy, snarky, worried, frightened, embarrassed, in love, etc. It was like a chart you might give to an autistic child to help them learn emotions—a row of faces.

I tried to take an eraser to my drawing after that. But Eden wouldn't let me.

"Honesty is part of art," she said, holding my wrist. "It's good."

Honestly, I think to my reflection, *I look kinda gay in this.*

I'm wearing a red button-down shirt. It's crisp at the collar and cuffs, but sort of soft and sort of shiny in between. I've also got on my only pair of dress pants—black—a belt, and my Converse. My undershirt has a regular collar, not a V, and it shows. I consider taking it off but think that might be tacky, like John Travolta in the seventies.

The colored shirts are a tradition. Seniors wear colors—the girls' dresses and guys' shirts—and the rest of the band dresses in black. Why I agreed to red, I have no idea. Other than it was on the sale rack, my mother looked exhausted, and one of the twins was screaming.

I raise my chin, smile at my reflection, and pretend to be out and proud. It works.

For a minute, anyway.

Until I bump into Bahti backstage. Bahti in her

cornflower blue prom dress and makeup—a complete 180 from an hour ago—and looking like the girl Mason kissed.

She smiles her million-watt smile at me and says, "Good luck with your solo!"

"Thanks," I say.

"You'll do great," she says, as if I look as though I need encouragement.

I force my eyes from her lips, from the thought of where they had been. I pretend I see a tarnished spot on my trumpet and rub it on my sleeve.

"Really," she assures me as the underclassmen file out onto the stage.

I nod.

Together we seniors wait for our names and sections to be called: percussion first, then brass, then woodwinds.

Bahti touches my arm when it's my turn.

"Jamie Peterson, our first chair trumpet," Mrs. Templeton announces.

I walk out into the lights, playing a snippet of the Lions' fight song. When I get to center stage, I finish the note, spread my arms, and take a bow. The audience claps. Someone shouts my name, and I know Mason's out there.

I take my seat and check that I have my music on my stand. The concert runs smoothly, better than the dress rehearsal. And I get so into my solo that the music melts away my memories of the moment and leaves me with a natural high.

I'm driving to Shari's after the concert, and every time I look in the rearview mirror, I ask myself, *Why did I think this was a good idea?*

See, I told Eden we'd go out after the concert. And Mason was there, so I asked him to join us. But he said he didn't want to be a third wheel.

"You won't be," I said, even though he didn't make any sense, because Eden and I weren't together like that. "We can invite other people."

"Yeah," said Eden, chiming in.

"Good job, honey," my mom said after she made her way through the knot of people.

"Sounded great," Frank added.

"Thanks," I said, and let my mom kiss me, and then they were off to enjoy a rare evening alone. Londa was babysitting.

I turned back to Mason and tried to convince him that Eden wasn't *that* annoying (his real reason for declining). In a few minutes Eden had rounded up a few friends, mainly Holland, DeMarco, and Bahti. Bahti still wearing her prom dress.

"You don't mind if I come along, la?" she asked me.

And I said, "No, of course not."

Stupid. Stupid. Stupid.

So Eden's riding shotgun and the others are in the backseat. All buckled in. But there's only three seat belts—Bahti and Mason are wearing one.

I can see them in the rearview mirror, tangled and twisted together—she's sitting on his lap and their legs go one of his, one of hers, one of his, one of hers. And her skirt is, well, shorter than I remember.

Why did I think this was a good idea?

We all sit in a big round booth at the restaurant. We order slices of pie and sodas.

"This is so much fun!" Eden announces, like the sugar or the excitement of a night out makes it impossible for her to sit still.

"How did you manage this one?" I ask. "It's after nine on a school night."

"I told my dad it was intermission," she says with a giggle.

"So he thinks you're still at the concert?"

"He hasn't been to a high school band concert in twenty-five years. He won't know they aren't four hours long."

DeMarco laughs. "It practically was—I thought Mrs. Templeton would never shut up."

"All the sentimental speeches about us graduating," Bahti says. "I thought we'd never get out of there!"

"I thought girls liked that stuff," Mason says.

Bahti looks at him. "I felt a bit bad for her." She shrugs.

"I'm just glad she didn't talk for four hours," I say, taking a bite of my cherry pie.

"Shh," Eden whispers. "Don't tell my dad."

Holland's phone rings as if on cue—her parents checking in on her—and the conversation soon evolves into a competition of whose parents are weirder.

Mason, however, doesn't join in. He eats his piecrust with his fingers, and when I look at him, he's already looking at me.

"What?" I ask. "Pie on my chin?"

"No," he says. "That color. It looks good on you."

I look down at my red shirt and feel my face burn. It probably matches. "Um, thanks?"

He smiles for half a second as if he's the one who's embarrassed, but he recovers quickly. "My dad does the same thing!" he says to the others as if he had been listening to them all along.

What was that? I wonder. *Was he flirting? With me?*

I shake off the thought and chime in. "My stepdad does that too."

And even though Mr. V can be pretty old-fashioned at times, Eden's parents win the trophy.

I drop Bahti off first, partially because her house is down the street from Shari's, and partly because I want Mason to wear his own damn seat belt. Eden is next, and so on, until Mason and I are alone in the car. He's got the window open, catching the night air in his fingers. I think about attempting yesterday's non-conversation again, but the urge to reveal my biggest secret and lose my best friend has drained from my bloodstream. Instead I turn on the radio. We sing along to the Rolling Stones' "It's Only Rock 'n' Roll." I drive through our neighborhood, and when I stop on the street in front of Mason's house, I know I won't be digging down deep into my heart and spilling my guts all over the place.

THIRTY-THREE

I have a plan. It's simple and easy to follow. And even a B-average student like me can manage it. *I can do this,* I tell myself as I drive to Mason's house the next day. I know he's home because he sent me a got-out-of-jail text, meaning he's off work.

I have to do this. Gumshoe is due back from the printer tomorrow, and Mason will see it. Sure, he won't know the details of Challis's comic—not at first—but he will hear as soon as the rumors that aren't rumors start turning the mill. He'll learn about how it was voted out and how I put it in without permission. And that it's kind of a big deal. A big gay deal.

I am going to come out to Mason.

I park in the street and check my hair in the rearview mirror. I walk up the driveway past Mr. V's truck, and rap on the open screen door.

"Come in," Londa calls. Then, when I step inside,

she says, "Jamie! How are you?" She says this as if I am her favorite little brother, as if she'll bake me cookies and pour me a glass of milk.

"Busy," I say.

"Tell me about it," she says, making her point with a wooden spoon. The kitchen smells amazing—like onions and garlic and chicken. "Papers due, exams . . . I'm so ready for summer break."

"Yeah," I agree, and nod at Gabe who comes in to raid the fridge.

He holds up a can of Orange Crush.

I nod again, and he tosses it to me.

"You staying for supper?" Londa asks.

I shake my head. Just in case my little announcement doesn't go over well.

"Enchiladas *verdes*," she says to temp me. "I made them myself."

"Sounds delicious, but . . ." I can't think of a lie she'll believe.

"So you're staying?" She smiles.

I know better than to argue with Londa. She doesn't take no for an answer.

"He's in his room," she says, and nods in the direction of the hall.

As I walk the two yards from the kitchen to Mason and Gabe's bedroom door. I think about how I'm not good with words—spoken ones, anyway—and with two little words, to be precise. *I'm gay.* Who am I kidding? People always have to say that twice. So that's four words:

"I'm gay."

"What'd you say?"

"I'm gay."

Or in my case, seven, total. *"I'm gay. I love you."*

Mason is lying crossways on his twin bed, with his bare feet resting on the wall. His blue-black curls fall over the edge. He's reading a paperback copy of *Moby-Dick.* I say hi, and he looks at me upside down as I fidget in the doorway like a kid who forgot to take his Adderall. My orange soda is probably shaken to the point of combustion.

"Hey," he says, but doesn't get up. "Car still running?"

"Yes, like a dream." I start counting backward from ten to distract myself from what I came here to do.

Ten. Mason folds down a corner of a page in his book.

Nine. He looks at me. "You can sit if you want."

Eight. I sit on the floor and hug my knees to my chest.

Seven. He flips around so he's sitting cross-legged on the bed and facing me.

Six. "You look like you need a movie."

Five. I need so much more than that.

Four. "Popcorn," he adds. "A big tub of popcorn with lots of butter and salt."

Three. "Yeah," I say. Because junk food is supposed

to be really bad for you, and right now, I'd kind of rather be dying of a heart attack.

Two. "Awesome! I've got AP English lit tomorrow, but I'm all studied out."

One. I'm gonna say it. Two words and I'll be done.

"Boys! Dinner!"

Mason scrambles up and out the door. I unstick myself from my thoughts and stand up. In the dining room, I sit in the extra chair next to Mason and across from Londa. I put my orange soda next to my plate but don't dare open it. Mr. Viveros holds court at the head of the table and waits for Londa to stop fussing with the salad tongs. We join hands and bow our heads. Mrs. V's hand is as soft as Mason's is calloused. Mr. V prays in Spanish, and usually I can follow along with my high-school vocabulary, but I say my own prayer instead.

Thank you, God, for my second family and for Mason. Especially for Mason. And if you grant wonderful things to quasibelievers like me, all I ask for is this: Please don't let anything change when I come out to him. Amen.

And then we are passing plates, praising Londa's cooking, and eating. I listen as everyone shares stories of school and work and odd customer requests.

"She didn't know you don't buy risotto at the grocery store. It's a dish, not a type of rice," Mrs. V explains.

"He wanted one tire—for sixteen-inch rims. SUVs are

eighteen now, so it's not like we had a sixteen-incher just lying around," Mason says.

"So we put on his spare," Gabe adds.

"I hope he doesn't get a flat," Londa says.

"Not my problem," Mr. V says. "I tried to tell him it'd be best to order two."

I file that in the back of my head. *Always order two tires.* And *Risotto isn't rice.* I take a bite of cheese-smothered enchilada and find myself savoring it, as if I'm trying to remember the complex combination of flavors. I look at each person as I eat. Mr. V is eating slowly, his face serious, his stern-father-boss-business-owner expression etched into the wrinkles between his eyebrows. Gabe serves himself seconds, his biceps filling out the sleeves of his T-shirt as he puts the tray of enchiladas back on the table. Londa, the girl I probably would have fallen in love with if I liked girls, smiles at me—beautiful and perfect—and I feel a pang of longing under my heart. Mrs. V—her name is Jean—touches my arm before asking me to please pass the salad dressing. She sometimes jokes that she used to be a tiny little thing before she met Mexican food. I think I might even miss her corny joke. I pull my gaze away and glance at Mason. He's shoveling dinner into his mouth as if there might not be any tomorrow. He pauses and takes a drink of milk. A drop lingers on his lips and my heart aches. I know I'll miss that.

He catches me looking. "Too spicy?" he asks about

my half-eaten enchilada. His concern is genuine, because he can eat a whole bowl of the hottest salsa while I'm good with a few bites of *pico de gallo*. And I think my heart might split in two.

I shake my head and take another bite.

"Okay," he says as if he believes me. Then to his family, "Anyone know what's showing at the dollar theater?"

"Oh, yeah—only the next installment of the best spy thriller ever!" Gabe says.

"You already saw that," Londa tells him. "I know. We went together."

"And I didn't get to go?" Mason asks.

"You were at your girlfriend's house," Londa reminds him. Then makes air quotes when she says, "Studying."

This is news to me.

"For AP, and she's not my girlfriend," he retaliates.

"Yeah, yeah, yeah," Londa says as Mason attempts to inform her of his no-dating-in-high-school rule.

"Movie starts at seven fifteen," Gabe says.

"Same as last week," Londa says. "Big surprise."

"We should go," Gabe says to the two of us.

Mason looks at me.

And a little tiny part of me wants to burst into tears. *This wasn't how my plan was supposed to go.* I try to smile.

"Come on, Jamie, you look like you could use a break."

"Yeah," Gabe adds. "Senior year is rough sh—" He stops before he curses at the dinner table.

Mason presses his shoulder into mine. "Just us guys. Whaddaya say?"

"It's not like I want to see that movie again," Londa says.

"Yeah. I'll go," I agree, because sitting in the dark with bullets flying and things exploding will be so much better than sitting on the couch with my mom explaining how my confession riddled our friendship with bullet holes and the whole thing exploded in my face.

THIRTY-FOUR

I am so dead. One-thousand-copies-of-*Gumshoe*-with-um-a-little-addition-are-going-to-be-delivered-to-the-loading-dock-in-fifteen-minutes dead. And Michael is already pissed at me for a little "typo" on the posters that changed the price of *Gumshoe* by a dollar. He noticed it first thing this morning.

"Honest mistake," I told him as we hung up our green posters among the pink ones for the GSA's end-of-year party. "I forgot the price," I say, even though I didn't. It is part of my evil plan to take over the world one high school literary magazine at a time.

"So we make a little more money," Holland said, tearing a piece of masking tape off with her teeth. "That'll be great for next year's budget."

"But everyone knows it costs four dollars," Michael protested with a nasally huff.

"Not everyone." Holland tipped the top of her head toward me.

"Yeah, sorry about that," I said, taping another *Gumshoe* poster next to a GSA one as I read the copy. *GSA Party! Room 302. 3:15, Thursday. Everyone is welcome!*

But I'm sure that in fifteen minutes, I am really going to be sorry. Not for what I did—it needed to be done—but I am going to be sorry that people will be upset. At me.

Especially Mason. Because he'll figure it out. He'll figure me out. And pretend everything's okay. Even when it isn't. Even when he knows I am a big fat liar.

And a party at 3:15? *Out of the question.*

Even though the loading dock is in the shade and I'm only missing Mr. Purdy's class, my T-shirt has damp spots growing under each arm. I check my cell for the time and when I look up, I see a truck pulling into the parking lot. The printer's logo on the side is as tall as I am.

The truck backs up into place and the driver steps out. "Delivery for Lincoln High, attention James Peterson?" he asks, looking up at me.

I nod.

The driver climbs the stairs and unlatches the truck door. It rolls up. He maneuvers a stack of white boxes onto a dolly and then rolls his way over to me. I open the door. "Here okay?"

I'm not really sure where to put the evidence that

might get me expelled, so I say, "That's great."

He goes back for another load, and another. With each box a little pebble of guilt drops into my stomach. I count twenty boxes, and my stomach aches as if it's filled with twenty stones.

"That should be all," he says. "Sign here."

And again I am signing my name—as if the authorities need more proof that I'm the perp.

"Here's your samples," the driver says, and hands me a shrink-wrapped package with the koi fish shining through.

"Thanks," I say, gulping down a lump in my throat. "Have a nice day!"

"Sure thing," he says, and heads out.

I sit on the cool cement floor, my back against the boxes, and tear open the shrink-wrap. I run my fingers over the fish on the cover, and then I open to the table of contents. Slowly, I turn the pages, checking the commas and inspecting the images. They look good—there's plenty of contrast.

Then I'm there: at the comic book within a book. The cover that Challis drew that night I called her is all crisp whites and inky blacks, the words I hand-lettered for her, *The Love Dare*, are made of bold strokes and odd angles like graffiti. And, under the title, is a picture of Tony and Justin standing back to back, their arms crossed defiantly across their chests.

Dare us, their faces say, as if the world just told them that they could never fall in love.

I leave the boxes and take the package of samples back to government.

"You're late," Mr. Purdy informs me. "Got a pass?"

"No. I was doing *Gumshoe* stuff."

"That is an extracurricular activity, Mr. Peterson."

Mason catches my eye and smirks.

I don't wait for Mr. Purdy to send me to the principal. I've already signed myself up for a very long appointment. I just walk to my desk and hide the package of samples in my binder.

Mr. Purdy huffs and goes back to due process.

I pay attention. For once. Because, as a common criminal, I'm thinking due process is suddenly very important.

Walking into Dr. Taylor's room, I don't feel so awesome. Not when I see twenty boxes of *Gumshoe* magazines and Michael sitting on a desk next to them. Holland, Lia, DeMarco, and Dr. Taylor are standing around talking.

"You're here!" Lia says. "We were waiting to do the big reveal all together!"

"Yeah," Holland adds. "We've got sparkling cider to celebrate!"

"Oh," I say. *We are so not going to be celebrating.*

"You do the honors, Michael. You're the editor!" Lia says.

So Michael lifts a box onto the desk, and, with his car key, slices through the packing tape. He folds back the flaps and I get the feeling that I am watching this all unfold from a distance, like a fly on the ceiling.

Dr. Taylor stands back, his hands in his pockets with an air of confidence that there isn't a misspelled word or misplaced comma in the whole damn thing.

Michael also takes out a copy. Then Holland, then Lia, DeMarco, and me.

I watch Michael as he turns the pages, only to be distracted by a gasp from Holland. She must have been turning pages faster than Michael. I watch her eyes grow wide.

"What?" Lia asks. And soon she is leaning over Holland's issue, staring at the centerfold.

"What the hell?" Michael asks, spraying spittle and catching on.

Michael's question wipes the confidence from Dr. Taylor's face. He reaches for a copy too.

"I know you disagreed with us, Jamie," Michael says to me, his voice low but growing louder. "But that's no reason to ruin *our* magazine. Our hard work!"

"We didn't want gay smut in it!" Lia says. "We voted!"

"It's not smut!" Holland snaps.

"Whoa," DeMarco says real low.

Michael picks up another copy, flips to the middle,

and sees the comic again. "They're all like this?" he asks, his voice booming around the room.

"No," I say, and take the one from his hands. "We have a homophobic version too." I pinch the middle eight pages and give them a tug. The paper tears at the staples. The pages come free. I crumple the comic with one hand and give the magazine back to Michael with the other.

He's sputtering and wheezing, hatred for me boiling in the red-hot blood flooding his face. "You're a piece of work, Peterson!"

"So are you, Schnozbooger."

Michael lunges at me, his hands gripping my shirt as he gives me a shake.

"Go to hell." I shove him back, breaking his grip.

One of the girls yelps as he bumps into her.

DeMarco jumps out of the way as Michael lunges at me.

"Boys!" Dr. Taylor says, stepping between us.

I force my feet to stop and wrangle my clenched fist into my side. My chest heaves with the effort and my teeth grind together. I can hear my heart thudding in my ears, almost drowning out my thoughts. I'd been ready to punch Michael in his famous schnoz. But hitting a teacher? *No way.*

Michael, though, barrels into Dr. Taylor's outstretched hand.

"Enough!" Dr. Taylor shouts. "I will not tolerate this in my classroom."

Michael huffs and exhales a wet breath.

"Sit." Dr. Taylor points to two chairs on opposite sides of the room.

I sit in mine.

"Jamie," Dr. Taylor starts in on what I know will be a very long lecture. "You seem to have a problem respecting the decisions of your peers."

"They make bad deci—" I start, but he cuts me off.

"It isn't your place to judge others, you were sup—"

I jump in. "They're the ones being judge and jury." I point at Michael first, then include the others with a sweep of my arm.

"Jamie," Dr. Taylor warns.

But I continue, "They were the ones censoring *Gumshoe*, cutting stuff they didn't agree with."

"Only because we won't get funding next year because of his stupid-ass move!" Michael shouts.

"Language, Michael," Dr. Taylor says, his attention off me.

"Who cares about next year if *Gumshoe* doesn't reflect the diversity in our school?" I ask. "Doesn't tell our story, doesn't represent us? It's *Lincoln High's* literary magazine, not yours."

Dr. Taylor looks at me, listens.

"What about the awards?" Lia asks.

"I think Challis's story will help us win awards," I say, hoping it's true.

"Yeah," Holland says. "A gay graphic short? We will so stand out in the crowd!"

"You want to keep it in?" Lia asks as if the words taste rancid.

"Yes," Holland says.

DeMarco nods before saying, "Me too."

"What?" Michael asks.

"I vote we keep it," DeMarco says.

"But it's not up for a vote!" Michael says. "We *already* voted on it. And it lost!"

All heads turn to Dr. Taylor, as if he'll cast the final decision.

"The comic is in the magazines. We could take them all out, as Jamie demonstrated. Or we could sell them as is," Dr. Taylor reasons.

"But—" Michael and Lia protest in unison.

"Should we take another vote?" Dr. Taylor asks us.

"But, Dr. Taylor," Michael says, much calmer now. "We shouldn't change our minds because one person can't respect his peers or follow simple instructions. That's not fair."

"Okay, Michael. I understand that we should be fair," Dr. Taylor says. "So let me talk to Principal Chambers before we proceed. I don't want to step on anyone's toes by acting too quickly. Okay?"

Michael nods, satisfied. And as if the principal will, obviously, be on his side.

The classroom falls silent, as we each stew in our own juices. Michael and Lia look at me as if I am the devil incarnate.

I can't sit any longer. Not with them looking at me like that—like I'm a sinner of the worst kind and so beyond stupid that I can't follow simple instructions. I grab a stack of magazines from the box and stomp out of the room.

I am so steamed, I can't even think straight. With an armload of *Gumshoe*s and a burning desire to be right, I march out of Dr. Taylor's room and up one flight of stairs. I hear a chorus of laughter coming from room 302. I take one last look at the pink poster—the one that welcomes everyone. I inhale a deep breath and exhale slowly.

Then I step inside.

A cluster of students, mostly girls, and a few sophomore guys are sitting on desks and eating potato chips. The sophomore in a tie-dye tee sees me first.

Then they all stop laughing and look at me.

I hear my own heartbeat, feel a flutter of panic.

Surprise registers on Challis's face for a second before she smiles.

It's Eden who breaks the silence with an Ann Marie–style squeal. She jumps up and runs over—her arms out. Then she's hugging me, stack of *Gumshoe*s and all.

And I know what she's thinking. She's thinking I'm coming out. Okay, so I didn't exactly plan it that way, but, well. Heck. It's not like they care.

"You're squishing me," I say.

Eden lets go, looks up at me, and then says, "Hey, everyone, this is Jamie Peterson!" She drags me over to where the food is spread out on a desk, then starts in on introductions: "Juliet, Wesley, Alex, Madison, Stephanie, Hunter, Sam, and you know us." She points to herself and Challis.

"Welcome," Challis says. "You picked a great day to show up. We've got food."

I hear a little sarcasm in her voice, get that this is the last possible GSA meeting of the year, as well as the last possible one of my high school career. It's as if I'm three years late for the party.

The sophomore in tie-dye reaches over and offers his hand. "I'm Wesley."

I shake it. He's got a nice grip. *And dimples. I could get used to dimples.*

"We pride ourselves in being the most welcoming club on campus," Challis says. "Can I pour you a soda?"

"Um," I say, feeling a little dazed by all the attention. Then I remember why I am here. It's not to flirt with sophomores. It's to make an announcement. "No, thanks."

Challis looks hurt.

Eden looks confused.

"I can't stay," I blurt. "I just wanted to ask you guys for some support." I pass out copies of *Gumshoe*.

Challis flips to the middle. "You did it!" she shouts as she leaps off the desk where she was sitting. "You actually put my story in!"

Then she's hugging me, and we're bouncing up and down.

Soon everyone is thumbing through a copy, looking for Challis's graphic short. They fall quiet as they start to read.

"It's über-maginificent-amazing," Eden tells everyone.

When he's done reading, Wesley looks up at me. "What can we do?"

"Buy a copy," I answer. "Or five. Let the administration know that you appreciate diversity in our school's literary magazine."

"Yeah," Challis chimes in. "My story was rejected because it had gay characters, but Jamie here snuck it in under the radar—"

"They rejected this?" Wesley asks. "Why?"

"Some of the students didn't want to lose funding for next year."

"Give me four copies," he says, and pulls a twenty from his wallet.

THIRTY-FIVE

It doesn't take long for the art-geek girls to start talking about *Gumshoe*. The next morning magazines are being passed around art class. Ms. Maude even threatens to take Eden's away if she doesn't stop reading instead of working. Part of me hopes the gossip will build buzz and sell more magazines as soon as Dr. Taylor and Principal Chambers make a decision—because nothing would prove me right more than selling tons of copies. And part of me wishes the buzz would die down before Mason hears it.

In government, we're reviewing a chapter when Mr. Purdy gets a call. He listens, then announces, "James, your presence is requested in Principal Chambers's office."

I let my head fall into my hands. *This is it.* I'm in a shipload of trouble, because A) someone told the principal I knew who made Abe into a dick and I'll have to narc not only on the Redneck, but on all my friends, too; B) Dr. Taylor told the principal I hijacked *Gumshoe*, took it for a joyride, and sold it to my classmates like black-market contraband; or C) I published a gay comic, and in a matter of hours, my best friend will know I'm as queer as a three-dollar bill and forgot to mention it.

Chambers's chambers, here I come, guilty of D) all of the above.

"Mr. Peterson?" Purdy asks. "I said your pre—"

I jolt upright out of my thoughts. I put one hand on my diaphragm and try to stop it from jumping up and down. The fluttering is making me queasy. I grab my things with my other hand and stand, my chair screeching across the floor.

Mason turns around.

I find his gaze. Lock my eyes on his as I walk up the aisle, followed by a chorus of low "oohs" coming from the back of the room.

"You okay?" Mason whispers when I reach his desk.

I nod in an attempt to say that I am okay—even though I'm not—and the motion sends the room into orbit around me. I steady myself on the nearest stable object, Mason's desk.

His eyes fill up with concern, dark as molasses and as sweet as hot chocolate. I swallow, practically basking in his gaze as it warms my throat, my chest, my heart.

Then he smiles—not an all-out grin, but a genuine,

encouraging smile. One that says, *You can do this, Jamie. And I'll be here for you.*

My heart feels too big and my lungs too small, and I say, "I love you, man."

Only it didn't sound Brodie Hamilton cool. My voice comes out quiet, and not at all sarcastic—as if I mean it.

My face flames. And I leave the room before my clothes ignite and my ego spontaneously combusts.

I'm halfway down the hall before reality hits me. If I walk into the office with my heart racing, breathing fast, and turning green under a feverish blush, there's no way I'm going to pass a lie detector test. I stop in the restroom and splash my face with water. I dry it with the hem of my shirt while I hold my breath. When I'm done, I exhale slowly. I run my fingers through my hair so it looks just-right messy. Then I tuck in my shirt in an attempt to look respectable.

I walk into the office and tell the secretary my name.

"I believe Principal Chambers is expecting you. Third door on the left."

The dreaded Chambers's chambers.

I walk down the short, narrow hall, hoping I can catch a glimpse inside before I have to enter. The blinds on the glass part of the door are down, but the door is open a crack. I'm about to knock when I hear a familiar voice.

My mom's.

"Come in," Principal Chambers calls.

I push the door open and force myself to smile. It doesn't work.

"Hi, honey," Mom says.

"Jamie," Dr. Taylor says with a nod. He has several copies of *Gumshoe* on his lap.

"Hi," I squeak. There's one empty chair and I sit. I press my fingertips together as if in prayer, and then pinch them between my knees.

"We were just discussing your work with the school literary magazine," Principal Chambers informs me, as if I hadn't guessed. "It appears as if you published a submission without the other staff members' consent?"

I think this is a question, so I answer, "Yes. Challis Carmine is extremely talented, and I thought her graphic short was perfect for the magazine."

"But your peers didn't agree with you?"

"They voted to reject the piece." I refrain from adding "your honor" like people do in the movies.

"Please explain."

I look at Dr. Taylor. He was there. He could explain. But he just nods as if to say, *Go on.*

"Could you tell us why the other students rejected Challis's submission?" the principal repeats.

"At first they thought it was lacking in plot," I begin, knowing I have to bring up the other reason too. I close my eyes and try to form a sentence. "But it was also because of the—uh, the characters' orientations."

"So they didn't want an illustrated short story depicting homosexuals in the literary magazine?" she asks me.

I nod.

"But you put it in anyway?"

I nod again.

"Why?"

I pinch my fingers between my knees again and think back to how I told off Michael and Lia. I had been able to explain it then. But now, I don't know. I can't seem to get the words out. I shake my head.

"You pulled a stunt that could get you expelled before exams your senior year and you can't tell me why?"

"Expelled?" I croak.

My mother glances over at Principal Chambers and gives her head a minute shake. I've seen her do this with Frank when she wants to tell him to calm down, but I don't think Principal Chambers knows secret Mom code.

The words begin to tumble from my lips, tripping over themselves to get out, "*Gumshoe* is Lincoln High's magazine. It belongs to all of us, not just Michael and Lia, and I thought—I thought it should represent everyone, even the LGBT students. I couldn't let it be censored." I take a breath. "The *Gumshoe* staff . . . They were just worried about funding. You know, if the school board didn't like it, they might not fund the magazine next year. But I fixed that. I raised the pri—" I stop rambling when I realize that I didn't admit just to one crime but two. And a premeditated one at that. *Double crap.*

Pressing my lips together, I look around the room. Dr. Taylor is nodding, as if the pieces of my confession are falling into place on the timeline in his head.

"So while you were making changes to the magazine, you were also changing the price?" Principal Chambers asks.

"Uh, yeah."

"By how much?"

"A dollar. I sold some for five dollars instead of four."

"Wait, you're selling copies?" she asks.

"Yeah," I admit to yet another infraction.

"How did you get copies? Dr. Taylor and I have not made a decision yet."

"The printer gave me samples," I say. Then add to my rap sheet. "And I took a stack of them on Thursday."

Principal Chambers sighs as if she can't believe how stupid I am.

"I wanted to prove that students would buy them. And they did. Fifteen copies."

"And this money? Did it get turned in to Dr. Taylor?"

Oh my God. She just accused me of stealing! On top of everything else. No wonder I am in the principal's office with my mother and about to get expelled. "No. But I have it all here." I take an envelope from inside my binder and put it on her desk. "There's seventy-five dollars in there."

"So you didn't plan on profiting from the additional comic nor from the increased price?" Mrs. Chambers clarifies.

"No. That's the money. I was going to turn it in."

Dr. Taylor reaches for the envelope. He counts the money, down to the quarters that Challis paid for her copy with. "Seventy-five," he confirms.

At last Principal Chambers says, "Okay. Well, then I think that's all we need."

"Um?" I ask. "Am I . . . ?" I start. "Am I going to be expelled?"

"We don't make the decisions. The disciplinary committee does," Mrs. Chambers says to me. Then to the others she says, "Thank you for your time."

We all stand. My mom and Dr. Taylor file out the door first. Principal Chambers stays behind her desk.

"Jamie, should the disciplinary committee decide that this offense is punishable by expulsion, there's a chance you won't graduate," Chambers says, her voice like a warning. "So I'd recommend you keep your nose clean in the meantime."

"Yes, ma'am."

"The committee meets on Monday at noon." She taps a stack of folders on her desk as if to straighten them, but it sounds like a gavel. "And if you or your friends know anything about the Abraham Lincoln sculpture incident, I'll take that into consideration."

Blood drains from my extremities. *Does she know something?* I shake my head. *I can't turn myself in for that! I won't turn in my friends. And if you think I'd rat on Nick O'Shea? Think again.*

"Your diploma is on the line," she reminds me.

I walk out of the office, not sure what to do with the door. *Do I close it? Do I say good-bye?* I'm not up on principal-office etiquette. So I don't do either one.

My mom is in the lobby, being all polite and thanking Dr. Taylor for his time.

"Oh, Jamie," Mom says once Dr. Taylor has left. "I had no idea about this *Gumshoe* thing."

"It's stupid."

Mom tries to smile. She shakes her head. "It doesn't sound that way to me."

Her eyes grow glossy, and I'm torn between consoling her and wanting to crawl under the secretary's desk in utter embarrassment.

"I know I should be angry," she says. "But I'm so proud of you!" That does it. The tears wobble and then spill.

She's crying. In school. The secretary's desk is looking very appealing, but I don't crawl under it. Instead I man up and reach for her.

She hugs me, pressing her cheek to my shoulder. "You stood up for yourself—came out for what you believed in."

"Shh, Mom," I say, urging her to stop spilling my secrets. "It's fine. Everything's fine."

"You did the right thing," Mom tells my shirt. "Maybe not in the right way, but—"

I am holding my teary-eyed mother while she pours her heart out on the floor when a shadow fills the doorway and rumbles in like a storm cloud.

The Redneck.

I turn slightly, selfishly putting my mother between us.

His glare is as calm as the eye of a hurricane, as dark as a thunderstorm. My mother doesn't notice.

Over her shoulder, he mouths his favorite name for me, *Fagmag*, and I get the message. He's going to hurt whomever tattled on him for having his truck at the senior prank—and if that person was me—well, I better tell my mother I love her before it's too late.

THiRTY-SiX

I tiptoe into the house after school. I'd tried to not come home, but Eden had Bible study and I didn't need to practice for the concert. It wasn't like I could go over to the Viveroses' and try to mooch dinner because I can't possibly talk to Mason after what I said in government.

I know my mom is home and Frank is out of town—her SUV is in the driveway and his truck is nowhere to be seen. And I don't want to explain to her that my *Gumshoe* stunt wasn't really about coming out—at least not intentionally. She was so proud of me—like I did it to make a personal statement. How can I tell her that I am still not out? That I'm deathly afraid of telling Mason and how everything between us will change forever after I say it?

And I don't feel like talking about it.

I hear my mom in the kitchen, talking on the phone. She's here and so are the twins—their baby dolls and a grocery store's worth of plastic food are strewn across the living room carpet. One of them spies me as I toe off my sneakers and tiptoe toward the stairs, trying to avoid stepping on a plastic steak. It's a dog toy and it squeaks.

I put my finger to my lips, "Shh."

Surprisingly, she stays quiet.

"Good girl, Annie M," I whisper, figuring it must be her and not talks-up-a-storm Elisabeth. I'm stepping over the baby gate when I hear a little voice ask, "Amy?"

"What'd you say?" I ask.

"Amy," she says.

Weird. Elisabeth calls me Jamie. *Not Amy.* "Ann Marie?" I ask.

She nods.

Then I realize that my sister just said her first word. "Mom!"

Mom comes rushing in, clutching her phone to her chest. "What?"

"Ann Marie talked!" I say.

The panicked look on my mother's face falls away as she drops to her knees. "What'd you say, sweetie?"

"Amy," she announces, pointing at me with a chubby finger.

"Yeah," Mom says. "Jamie and I have some talking to do."

Damn it. I was hoping she might forget.

Then into the phone, she asks, "Did you hear that,

Frank? Your daughter spoke."

Frank's voice is muffled.

I wonder if he had hoped it'd be *Dada*. Elisabeth's was *Mama*.

"Say it again so Daddy can hear," Mom says, and holds out the phone.

"Amy," Anne Marie says.

This time I hear Frank laugh. And I think to myself, *Did she know I was trying to sneak to my room?*

"I'm so relieved," Mom says to Frank. "I know the pediatrician said not to worry, but she was so far behind Elisabeth. . . . Yes . . . Me too."

I escape while I can. I flop down on my bed and wish there was a restart button for the day because, God knows, I need to push it. *Why the hell did I have to say "I love you, man"?*

I hardly ever say "I love you, man" because I worry that people will think I mean it in the very real, very gay sense, and not as a joke. But I did. And I do. And I never should have said it. Not in the middle of government. Not to Mason.

Crap. All that stuff that happens to guys who are friends with gay kids? The jokes that they might be gay too? Those have probably already started circulating. Mason was counting on me—on our car—to get the hell out of Dodge. Forget the closet, all of Dodge was running out of ventilation right about now.

265

"Amy?" Mom asks, poking her head in around my bedroom door.

"Not funny," I say to the ceiling.

"She loves you," she says. "Her first word was your name."

I soften, look at her.

"Come downstairs?" she asks. "We need to talk."

I sigh and get up.

Mom and I sit on the couch where we can see the twins playing.

"There are better ways to do things, Jamie," she starts, patting my knee. "Don't get me wrong, I'm glad you stood up for what you thought was right, but you shouldn't have taken advantage of your position on the *Gumshoe* staff. The literary magazine was their baby too."

"Yeah."

"It wasn't yours to manipulate. It wasn't yours to use to make your own statement. You understand?"

I nod.

"You should have worked together with Michael and Lia and the others to come to a consensus."

"I know. But it wasn't going to happen. I felt like I had to—" I stop.

She waits for me, but when I don't continue, she touches my knee again. "It's a cute story. Flattering, huh?"

I don't understand.

"The boys in the story—they look like you and Mason."

My skin goes cold, like the air conditioning just kicked on. I lunge for my backpack, reach for a copy of *Gumshoe*. But I don't need to open the magazine. I know she's right—even without a pair of chunky black glasses and a mop of unruly hair, I can imagine Tony as Mason. *And Justin? She might as well have named him James.*

"You didn't notice?" she asks.

I shake my head. Once to the right and back to center.

"Oh, honey. It's probably nothing. Just me thinking of you two . . . ," she trails off.

"No," I say. "You're right."

"Mason's seen this, hasn't he?" Mom asks.

I shake my head. "Not that I know of."

"Well, you might want to warn him. He's going to see it eventually."

I don't tell her I can't possibly talk to him ever again.

"Jamie, you found time to come out to him, haven't you?"

I bite my lip. Feel the sting of tears prickling behind my eyes.

Mom reaches for me, pulls my head down to her shoulder.

I melt into her, cry as if the tears are the last of my ice-cube resolve. "I can't."

"Why not?" she whispers gently.

"I can't—I can't—" I sputter. "I won't be able to stand it if he—"

"He's your best friend, Jamie. I don't think he'll reject you."

"That and—" I think of how to explain it. Not the part about how he'll think that I am the world's worst best friend and that I don't trust him with a secret—my mom won't fall for that—but the *other* reason. My *other* fear. "But, like, what if he reaches over to, like, mess up my hair or something and stops. Thinks, *But Jamie's gay,* instead of what he usually thinks—just for a second. I don't think I could deal with that."

She squeezes my shoulders. "I see."

I swallow, slide out of her arms. The urge to cry is gone. Replaced with shame.

Because the pride is gone from my mother's face. *Why was she ever proud of me? Was she proud that I was gay? Happy that I finally came out?*

When I hadn't. Not even to my best friend.

THIRTY-SEVEN

The weekend between the first and second week of AP exams is a great time to disappear. If you don't call your friends, they don't notice. They're too busy studying. If you don't text your best friend, he'll think you've got your nose in a book. If you're ignoring your mother and hiding in your room contemplating becoming a hermit, she believes you're cramming for the calc exam on Monday. If you stumble down the stairs on Monday morning, looking pale everywhere except the black circles under your eyes, and your stepfather says, "What happened to you?" and you say, "Got my AP calc test today," he'll imagine you're a good student. But who in their right mind would study for forty-eight hours straight if they weren't going to graduate?

I just hope Principal Chambers will let me take the exam. It's in the afternoon timeslot. The disciplinary committee meets this morning, so I'll learn the status of my fate at lunch. Then, if I'm lucky, I'll be allowed to take the test. *Please, please, please,* I whisper to the clouds as I walk in from the student parking lot.

"Got your calculator?" Mason asks, landing a playful punch on my shoulder.

I nearly jump out of my skin. He doesn't know I'm avoiding him. "Yeah," I say. "You?"

"Got it." He pats his backpack. "You have a good weekend?"

"Studied a lot."

"So you weren't grounded-slash-babysitting?"

I frown, wonder what he heard.

"Principal's office? Friday?" he hints.

"Yeah," I admit. "For, um, well . . . ," I choke.

His eyebrows wrinkle with concern.

I stop walking and he does too. I just look at him. Look into his eyes and absorb every ounce of chocolate-cake softness before I say anything—because Mason is smarter than I am, and he'll be able to add things up. If I mention *Gumshoe* and how I put Challis's comic in without permission, he will add that to my announcement in government and calculate the truth. I. Am. Gay. And I've never told him. He'll deduce that I don't trust him. He'll have proof that I am the world's worst best friend. And that I'm in love with him.

I get the urge to wrap him in a bear hug and hold him. Hold on to him. So he can't leave me.

270

"Jamie?" he asks.

I shake my head. I can't say it.

"Dude," he says sympathetically.

And I think I might lose it. Right there in the quad in front of everyone.

I'm about to make a break for the privacy of the restroom when Wesley catches up to us in a blur of rainbow tie-dye. "Got any more magazines?" he asks, out of breath.

Wesley + Mason = Jamie is screwed.

I gulp back the lump in my throat, swear, then ask, "But you bought four *Gumshoe*s on Thursday?"

"Yeah. And they are the hottest thing since One Direction over at South," Wesley sort of explains.

Mason stifles a laugh as we walk inside.

"South Junior High?" I clarify. That was where Mason and I had gone.

"Yeah. Next year's sophomore class is so gay!" he says, following me down the hall.

And I think he means literally.

"So, well, I unloaded my copies and need more." He flashes me a dimpled smile complete with a skinny-shouldered shrug. It's adorable.

My face grows warm as the pit of my stomach drops a few degrees. *Is he flirting with me?* "Cool," I tell him, and busy myself with my locker combination before I think about it too much.

Mason leans against the locker next to mine. He's so close I smell Speed Stick and Scope. I glance over at him and get a dizzy feeling—hot and cold swirling together. I wonder what he thinks of obviously very gay Wesley. He presses his lips together between his teeth. *I know that look.* Mason's amused, like watching me with Wesley is an improv comedy act in progress.

I open my locker, and my hand brushes his arm. I jerk away as if my fingers got burned. He's so close, I can't think clearly. It takes me a second to remember what I was doing. "How many?" I ask Wesley, taking the last handful of magazines out of the shrink-wrapped package of samples.

"Four," Wesley says, and holds out his hand and a twenty.

I hand the magazines to him and put the rest back in my locker.

"Thanks, man."

"You're welcome."

"And nice to meet you," he adds, this time to Mason. Then he's off, bouncing down the hall like a six-year-old on espresso. Over his tie-dyed shoulder, he shouts, "Page twenty-seven!"

I grab a *Gumshoe*, flip it open, turn to page twenty-seven, and read a poem I had seen at least two dozen times before. I know what it says and snap the magazine closed.

"Do I get to buy one?" Mason asks in a whisper.

My whole body tingles as if he whispered it in my ear. "Uh, well, um . . . They aren't supposed to be on sale yet."

Mason's eyebrows go up as if to say, *Really? And how come I don't believe you?*

"But, yeah, you can buy one."

"Good," he says. "I want to see my poetry in print."

I know his name isn't in there anywhere. I would have memorized that poem.

"I can't tell you the page number," he says, "because you haven't sold me a copy yet."

Reluctantly, I give him a copy of *Gumshoe*.

He tucks a five-dollar bill into the pocket of my shirt and pats me on the chest.

The motion is like the opposite of CPR. It stops my heart.

"Hey," I say, noticing the time on a clock down the hall. "Good luck on your exam."

"You too," he says, and starts to walk away. He stops and comes back.

I wait.

"My poem," he whispers. "It's called 'At Night I Dream.'"

It's the title of a poem I remember—the one with the word *homophobia* in it—the one that made me decide to scan Challis's comic. "That was yours?"

He avoids my gaze and shrugs as if it's not important.

"You didn't sign it," I say.

"I know."

"But . . . ," I start, but I don't know what else to say. *But your poem started me on a path to Chamber's chambers? On the road to self-destruction?*

"I thought you might've guessed," he says to the floor tiles.

And with that, he leaves me standing there, remembering that I did think of him and his bilingual family when I read it. I turn to the page and reread, "a thousand words and ways to say it—simply, deeply, profoundly. *I love you.*"

He didn't mean me, obviously. The poem was about his family, not me.

I'm the one in love with him, not the other way around.

And if I'm not careful, we won't even be friends.

You and Me
by Wesley Osteryoung

You never see me,
even though every shirt I own
is brighter than a fire-season sunset,
more neon than Main Street at night.

I don't want you—
even though I think I might—
to think I'm too young, too awkward,
too out, to be considered your friend.

Maybe you just haven't noticed me yet,
even though I'm the only one
cheering for the marching band,
and waving a flag with a stripe of every color.

I don't blame you,
even though I wish I were
in your circle of I-love-you-man friends,
under your radar, on your mind.

THIRTY-EIGHT

The disciplinary committee reached a decision. My punishment? It's not so bad.

It's just the last thing I need right now: more school-work. I have to write a ten-page paper about censorship of books in schools and libraries—since I appeared so interested in the topic—while I am sitting in the library. With detention. And if my paper is satisfactory, I can walk at graduation and get my diploma.

After my calc exam and before detention, I swing by Dr. Taylor's classroom to turn in the twenty-five dollars from the rest of the *Gumshoe* magazines I sold—even though they were technically samples—because I don't want to get in any more trouble with Principal Chambers.

"Thank you, Jamie," he says about the money. "So, they're selling well?"

"Yeah," I say. "I think we have a hit."

"Good," he says. "I hope I wasn't too harsh with your punishment—I see where you were coming from regarding the comic and I don't disagree with you, just how you went about it."

Wow. Dr. Taylor agrees with me? "It's fine. And an interesting topic," I add, since the idea for me to write a paper on censorship obviously came from an English teacher.

"I've decided. I think we should sell the magazines as is," Dr. Taylor says.

Double wow.

"Which means we'll enter it for the awards that way too," he continues.

I resist the urge to do an end-zone dance. "Thank you. It means a lot—and not just to me."

"I know," Dr. Taylor says, returning to the papers on his desk. "I look forward to reading your paper."

"Yes, sir," I promise, and head out.

"Jamie," he says, calling me back. "I want to start selling them tomorrow, so can you man the table during your lunch hour? DeMarco has the lunch hour before you. Holland has zero-hour covered, and Michael volunteered for after school."

His words sound like music, sweet and satisfying. "Yeah, of course!"

"Lia's still upset," Dr. Taylor continues. "So I didn't ask her to participate. But she's welcome to."

I nod. I'd sit next to Lia every lunch for the rest of the year if I had to—as long as we were selling uncensored *Gumshoe*s.

I'm on my way to the library when I hear familiar shrieks—and from the location and from purple posters on the walls, I know it is the Japanese club party. And Eden. So I poke my head in the door.

Challis is writing something on the whiteboard, and Eden is trying to jump up and grab the marker, but Challis is writing high on the board.

"She's making my drawing pornographic," Eden complains to the group.

Several look up from reading manga and sketching on notebook paper. A girl dressed like a Pokémon giggles. She is drawing on the other whiteboard—and her artwork is pornographic. A spiky-haired redheaded boy is nestled between the legs of a blond, androgynous-looking character—their big eyes at half-mast.

It's enough to make me blush.

"Jamie," Eden pleads.

And I turn to inspect her drawing. Two boys caught in a hug but with thought bubbles. It isn't nearly as dirty as Pokémon's.

Challis adds to the second thought bubble, writing in what must be Japanese because I can't decipher the dashes and curves.

"Tell her to stop," Eden says.

"Challis?" I ask, sitting on a desk. "You owe me a favor."

Challis stops writing to look at me, her eyebrows straight lines. "A favor?"

"A week-of-detention, ten-page-paper favor. And if I don't get to walk, you're gonna owe me a whole lot more."

She pouts. "I do, don't I?"

I smile.

And she relinquishes the marker to Eden.

Eden pulls a chair over to the whiteboard, stands on it, and starts erasing.

Challis comes over and sits on the desk next to mine. "But you're the only one selling *Gumshoe*s. It's like the rest have been sent through the shredder."

"Nope," I say. "Taylor just told me we're going to sell them as is—with your graphic short!"

"Woo-hoo!" Challis leaps off her desk and opens her arms as if she's going to hug me. But then she stops, as if she thinks twice.

I wipe the unintentional girls-are-icky look from my face and open my arms.

"Thank you," Challis says in my ear as we hug. "Lincoln needed a little shaking up."

"Especially for our incoming sophomores—they're your biggest fans."

"Yeah," Challis says. "Next year the GSA is gonna kick butt."

"Wish I was going to be here to see it," I say, wondering if I would've come out if I had been among a supportive group of friends like them.

"Careful," Challis says, her blue eyes twinkling. "You might be."

"Hey," I say.

"Principal Chambers loves to hold the you-might-not-graduate thing over everyone's heads."

"I'll ace the paper," I say.

"Let me know if you need help," Challis says. "I've got tons of LGBT sites bookmarked on my computer— some about straight-washing YA lit."

I'm not sure what she means and what it has to do with my paper, so I say, "Yeah. Can you send them to me?"

Then, like a toddler wanting her parents' attention, Eden jogs over and points to her whiteboard.

"Aw," Challis coos.

I can't read the kanji. "Nice."

"It says, 'I've been looking for you all my life,'" Eden translates. "'Where have you been?'"

"And Raffi says"—Challis points to the other character and his thought bubble—"'Right here.'"

"Cute," I tell them, and motion that I want to speak to Challis alone. We step into the hallway.

"My mom said something when she saw *The Love*

Dare," I begin, because I need to know if she was right. "She said she thought the characters looked like me and Mason. Was that on purpose?"

Challis looks down at her shoes. They're the ones she wore to prom.

I tilt my head and try to catch her eye, but she doesn't look up.

Instead she nudges my sneaker with her toe and, barely above a whisper, says, "You were my inspiration."

"Inspiration?"

Challis's blue eyes meet my own. "You're a good person, Jamie. You don't care if someone's hot and popular or doesn't even have a best friend; you see them for who they are." Her fingers find my hand and squeeze it. "That's something. Inspiring."

"I don't feel it's my place to judge." I shrug. "Since I'm, well . . ."

She nods as if she understands the rest of my sentence. "I hope Justin and Tony didn't look *too* much like you—I left off Mason's Clark Kents and your freckles on purpose."

"Uh, thanks," I say, knowing those details won't change how people choose to see it.

Challis squeezes my fingers one last time and walks back in the classroom.

I walk to the library and find a table, my mind still on our exchange. I guess I asked for it, literally. I'd asked

Challis for a graphic short story and she drew me one, using my best friend and me for inspiration. I had promised her I'd get it in, but that was before I knew what it was about. Only after Michael and Lia read it, they rejected it. The rest of it was all me. Her story inspired me. It was like I was the one taking the dare, not my likeness in a comic book frame—I took the pen from her hand and wrote my own fate.

Now it comes down to Mason. He's got a copy of *Gumshoe* to decipher and decode. Add in a few clues from the art-geek girls, and well, he'll figure me out. The ball will be in his court. He'll choose to be my friend, or not.

THiRTY-NINE

Each morning that week, the Redneck calls me *Fagmag* in the locker room. Eden's friends gossip in art class. I sell dozens of *Gumshoe*s at the door of the cafeteria while Mason studies for more APs in the library. My exams are the regular ones, so I'll take them next week. After school, I report to the library to work on my paper and study for exams. The Redneck does the same. When I get home, my mom doesn't feel guilty asking me to mow the lawn or to run to the store or to watch my sisters—because it's McCall payback time. Eden calls and we talk on the phone. And Mason and I don't talk about my declaration in government or the comic in *Gumshoe*. In fact, we don't talk all that much, as if our last conversation—after Wesley and over *Gumshoe*— was our last. So even though I try to fool myself with the idea that I'm avoiding *him*, it could be that he's avoiding *me*. Or maybe he's just had enough of my crap.

Thursday afternoon, I'm shoving my computer into my backpack in preparation for my mad dash out of detention when the Redneck blocks my path. I dodge right and reach for the door handle in vain.

"Fagmag," he growls.

I freeze like a deer in the road.

"I thought we had an agreement." He points a sausage-like finger at my solar plexus.

"Yeah, Nick, we did," I say with all the false confidence I can muster. "I didn't narc on you and you didn't narc on me."

He thinks for a long minute.

I think I can see gears turning behind his big freckled forehead.

"Uh-uh," he decides. "I still got effin' detention."

"Me too."

"So you ratted on me." He pokes at my chest again.

I shake my head, play it cool. "Nope. Sorry."

This clouds his sky-blue eyes. "Yeah, you did."

"Nick," I say. "I didn't tell on you. Your truck was at the school that night. Someone saw it."

"Well, I'm gonna tell my parents you're not Eden's boyfriend."

"Go ahead," I say because it's true. "But that'll piss her off. Big time. And, well, I'm not gonna stick around to see that go down."

He's still thinking, so I edge around him and out the door.

I hear a guttural sound behind me and imagine the Redneck, changing colors like a stoplight—from red to yellow to green, swelling to the size of a silo and roaring like the Incredible Hulk with a Hummer crushed in each fist. I imagine what he'll do to me and break into a run.

In art on the last day of classes, the room looks bare. Drawings and paintings have been taken down from the walls. The still life has been disassembled, the wax apple and peacock feathers returned to the back corner. I feel a little pang of this-is-really-it for my last day of high school.

Our self-portraits and accompanying artists' statements are due. We also have to clean off our shelf and return the supplies we borrowed. I turned in my self-portrait with my artist statement about what it all meant taped to the back. It's all psychotherapist mumbo jumbo that I'm sure Ms. Maude will think is deep. Even though, in reality, it's just the thesaurus in Microsoft Word, because the truth isn't something you type up and turn in.

My shelf is a mess of sketches, so I'm sorting keepers from trash, sliding the latter into the blue recycling bin, when the room falls silent.

DeMarco looks over at me as if to ask, *What's going on?*

We turn around to see that the art-geek girls have gone mute.

"Finally," DeMarco mutters, and goes back to recycling old assignments.

The girls are in a tight huddle, all of them looking down at something.

"Oh my God!" Sharpie girl whisper-shouts. "They are so adorable!"

"It looks just like them!" another adds.

"I don't know, Eden," Challis says. I see her blond head shaking in slow-motion.

"You don't like it?" Eden asks.

Challis's head revs like a lawn mower, shaking faster.

Then there's a ripping sound. A crunching, crumpling sound. And a collective gasp.

Challis's long arm emerges from above the circle of girls, a piece of paper in her fist. Eden lunges for it as Challis steps out of the huddle. "Challis!" she shouts. "That's mine!"

"Girls?" Ms. Maude asks.

But neither of them pay any attention to her. Challis marches toward me like an advancing army of one. Eden jogs beside her and jumps to try and reach the paper. When this doesn't work, Eden grabs Challis by the waist and digs in her heels.

Stopped in her tracks, Challis tosses me the ball of drawing paper. As it spins through the air, colors flash from within the folds.

I catch it.

Eden's green eyes go wide behind her glasses. She lets go of Challis and bounds over to me. "I don't think you want to see that, Jamie."

I palm the balled-up paper and hold it behind my back so she won't grab it. "Why?"

"I just drew it, like, without thinking."

I can tell a lie when I see one. "That so?" I ask. "Then why the geek-girl convention?"

"Please, Jamie," Eden whines. "Please don't look at it."

Slowly, I unfurl the mashed corners, and reveal the offending image. It's damn near perfect. The lines and the colors. The post-prom hotel room. The hazy, romantic atmosphere. The disheveled bed. The trail of bow ties and boutonnieres that litter the floor. The kiss—steamy yet sweet. The hands drawn in exact detail, tanned and strong and caressing my freckled cheek.

It looks exactly like me.

And Mason.

FORTY

Instead of hanging out with my friends and joining in on the last-day-of-senior-year craziness, I'm alone in my room after school. I pull the crumpled ball of drawing paper from the bottom of my backpack. I gently pull on the edges as if I'm unwrapping a gift the size and shape of a heart. I smooth the wrinkles against my knees and see the drawing by the light of my bedside lamp—this time without an audience. Without Challis's scorn and Eden's horror, I don't feel the need to be shocked by the picture. Instead I let myself slide into it. I inhale, imagine I smell Mason's Speed Stick and the starch on his shirt collar. I close my eyes and my room morphs into a dimly lit hotel room. I press my face into his hand, lean into the kiss just as Eden drew it—fan art, fairy tale, and daydream merged into one.

This. This is what I want, who I want to be. I want Mason to be my more-than-friend. I want to kiss him, hold him, protect him from the storm of words his father unleashes on him. I want to be his everything. But I can't, so I fold the picture in half and put it in my nightstand drawer, where it will be safe from the prying eyes of the art-geek girls. And I wonder, *How can the art-geek girls and I want the very same thing? And why do we want it so badly?*

I don't have answers. I just know that Eden's drawing isn't supposed to exist—wanting something in the privacy of your own heart is different from advertising it with art. The art has the power to be public, to be out in the world, where it can hurt someone. And that someone is Mason. If he's straight, it'll sting. If he happens to be bi or gay, it will out him against his will. And no matter what he is, the drawing has to stay hidden for the sake of our friendship.

I know I need to say something to Eden—and it won't be that I like her drawing. I've been around my mother long enough to know that this is one of those situations that requires a conversation, but I don't know what to say. Not yet.

Inevitably my phone buzzes in my pocket as I push tater tots around a lake of ketchup on my plate. Ann Marie is screaming, and Elisabeth has made mashed potatoes out of her tots, only they are a disgusting shade of pink due to the ketchup. My mom is in the other room on the phone with Frank. I lift Ann Marie from her booster seat with one arm and fish my phone out with my free hand. "Yeah?"

"Hi, Jamie. It's Eden."

"Hey," I say, and bounce my sister on my hip.

"Is this a good time?"

Elisabeth takes a handful of mashed tots and puts them in her mouth. My stomach goes queasy, but I don't stop her. "We're eating dinner. Or we were eating dinner."

"Oh," she says. "I can call back later."

I think about the drawing. And, knowing I need to talk to her about it, my stomach feels worse. I'm clearly not ready to talk. "Maybe it'd be better if you didn't."

"But, Jamie, I—I'm sorry!"

Ann Marie wails in my other ear.

"Please let me make it up to you. I didn't draw it to hurt you."

"Look, Eden. I don't know how I feel about it."

"Um, you're pissed. Angry. You think I'm stupid. And insensitive."

"What?" I ask her. *I was supposed to say those things.*

"I have an older brother," she reminds me over Ann Marie's whimpering and Elisabeth's banging on her tray for more food. "He doesn't communicate so well either."

"Okay. Yeah. That's how I feel." I pick up my plate and slide my uneaten tater tots onto Elisabeth's.

Eden's quiet for a minute, then asks, "You want to

go to the senior bash?" meaning the alcohol-free, school-sponsored party with the pool and the rock wall.

"I'm not in the mood," I say, because I *am* angry and I *do* think she's insensitive.

"I'll be your date," she offers.

"Not helpful," I say, even though I know this is probably the only senior party her parents will consider letting her attend. And if I were being a good friend, I'd take her. But she hasn't exactly been a good friend either. So it's not like I owe her anything.

"Why not?" she asks.

"Eden." I sigh. "I don't want to see you right now."

"Jamie," she says. "I said I was sorry."

I sigh, knowing I should accept her apology and have that talk. But I don't feel like it.

Silence.

I try a different tactic. "I really don't want to see Mason. Bahti said they were going together." Bahti invited me to be the third wheel.

"So you don't want to hang out with me and you're avoiding Mason. What *are* you doing?"

I look at Ann Marie's tear-streaked face, considering a total meltdown. "Nothing."

"That's pretty pathetic, Jamie. It's the last day of school, senior year. You shouldn't be alone doing nothing. Let me be your friend. We'll have fun."

She sounds desperate.

And I do sound pathetic. I start to cave. "I *could* use a distraction."

"So how about a movie? Nice and quiet. My place."

"Yeah," I say. "I guess."

Watching movies makes me think of Mason. And the popcorn makes me think of Mason. Okay, everything makes me think of Mason—or maybe I'm thinking of Mason 24/7 and the other things are just getting in the way.

So avoiding him is a good policy. It's better than having a friend crush on him, telling him *I love you, man* in government, and handing him a copy of *Gumshoe* with *I'm gay* practically printed in the centerfold. If I don't see him, I'll have to stop thinking about him and I won't have to talk to him. So then he'll never ask about what I said in government or why the hell didn't I come out to him like a normal person instead of publishing it in *Gumshoe* like a freaking idiot? And I won't have to hear him tell me, *Jamie, you're the world's worst best friend.* Or, *It's cool you're gay and all, but I don't think we should be best friends anymore.*

Eden and I make plans to spend the weekend together so I can pretend everything is okay between me and Mason—even though it clearly isn't—and give us a chance to talk about her drawing.

On Saturday morning, we decide to study for exams, and I know the perfect coffee shop where we can get away from big brothers and little sisters. So I drive downtown.

When we're stopped at a red light, I ask, "Why'd you draw it, Eden?" She doesn't answer, so I look over at her. "The picture?"

"I know now that I shouldn't have done it—drawn it," she says to the passenger-side window. "But I just had this picture in my head—a picture of what *should* have happened—what didn't happen because I let you take me to prom when you should have asked him."

"I asked you to prom," I say. "On purpose."

"I know you did. And I had a great time." She turns my way and touches my arm. "But, well, I had this fairy tale in my head. So I drew it—it was in my sketchbook. My private sketchbook."

"But you showed it to Challis and the art geeks," I remind her.

"Yeah," she admits. "But only because it turned out so good."

It was good. It looked exactly like us—well, us if we were in a comic book.

"You know what it's like to like someone who doesn't notice you?" she asks shyly.

Actually, I've been having the opposite problem. Mason noticed me all right, because I, well, opened my big mouth in the middle of government. But I nod anyway.

"I wanted her to notice me." She almost chokes on her confession.

"You wanted Challis to notice you?" I whisper.

She nods. Hiccups. "She's such a good artist. I—I wanted to impress her."

"And it all backfired?" I ask.

"She ripped it out. Crumpled it up." Eden swipes at a tear.

"Um, yeah," I say, because I'm kind of with Challis on this one. "Because your drawing was of me! Kissing Mason."

"I know."

"So it wasn't about you and Challis. It was about me. Did you think about that? How I might feel?"

"Yeah," she says. "I was thinking of you. And how you should get your fairy tale. How you deserve to be happy."

"No. If you were thinking of me—the real me—if you were, you would have known it was wrong to draw us like that. We aren't some fictional couple you can slash together. We're people. Real people!"

"I know," she says, wiping another tear from under her glasses. "It was stupid for me to want you to have a happily ever after, even if it was just on paper."

"Happily ever after?" My voice jumps up an octave. "That's jumping the gun. I'm not even *out* to Mason."

"I know you like him. And face it, you need to do something about it."

"No. I. Don't!" The light changes, and I press the gas.

Hard. Slam it into second.

Eden grabs the door handle. "What?" she shouts over the engine as I jam it into third. "You don't think he knows you're gay?"

The speedometer inches up over the speed limit as I shift into fourth gear. "No," I repeat. "No. No. No."

But she has a point. Of course he knows. Everyone knows. Michael, Lia, Holland, DeMarco, Dr. Taylor, Principal Chambers, Eden, Challis, Wesley. And the Redneck.

"You said you were going to tell him," she says. "And slow down!"

"I tried," I admit, and get the feeling that I'm losing this argument. I let up on the gas. "But I couldn't do it."

"But you have to."

"I know. But what if he doesn't want to be friends after?"

"What?" Eden asks, then jumps to conclusions. "You think he's homophobic?"

"I don't know."

"Mason is not homophobic. Give him more credit."

"But Lia?" I ask about her former best friend who went AWOL when Eden came out, hoping to make my point.

"No, Jamie," Eden says. "Mason is not like Lia. He, like, touches you all the time."

"Does not," I protest, but memories flood my mind:

Mason messing up my hair, Mason caressing my neck, Mason resting his forehead on my shoulder. I'm lying.

"Okay, he doesn't," she concedes.

"Not like you're thinking," I clarify.

"Okay, okay. Mason isn't gay and he doesn't like you."

"Thank you," I say.

"It was all a fan-girl daydream, okay?"

I don't acknowledge this.

She tries again. "Just a little fan-art fairy tale."

"Okay," I say. "Now can we forget it ever happened?"

"Yeah," she says.

"Because I'm not giving it back. No one will see that damn drawing again."

"Got it," Eden agrees. Then she asks, "Friends?"

"Friends," I say, and nudge her with my elbow.

The pedestrian traffic and the lack of parking near our destination indicate that the Saturday market is in full swing. Eden decides to bail on our plans to study in favor of shopping, so I park behind my mom's office and we walk over to Eighth Street. Twenty minutes later Eden tugs on my hand and pulls me into a booth selling pastries. "What do you want?" she asks.

"Blueberry muffin," I say.

She pushes a loaf of bread, a paper bag containing a

jar of local honey, and a bouquet of flowers into my arms. "A chocolate croissant and a blueberry muffin, please," she tells the baker, and soon we are looking for a bench to sit and eat.

"Bookstore!" Eden says with her mouth full, pointing excitedly down the street.

"Next stop?" I ask, peeling back the paper from the bottom of my muffin.

"Definitely," she agrees.

I feel a little lost in the bookstore—not sure where to start and not wanting to explain to anyone my utter lack of reading anything that wasn't assigned since junior high (when I finished the Harry Potter series). But Eden appears to feel right at home. She zooms over to the young adult section and plops down on the floor, her bread, honey, and flowers piled around her as if she's moving in. She pulls out a handful of graphic novels and starts reading. And I get the feeling we're going to be here awhile.

I skip the girls-in-flowing-dresses section, the display of girls-with-swords books, and another of girls with mermaid tails. I find myself in the children's section and half look for a bedtime story for my sisters—preferably one without Disney princesses and that I haven't read a million and two times, but I know I won't be buying a book. Not with the five dollars I have left in my pocket.

Near the register is a collection on nonbook items. I try on a finger puppet, spin a display of magnets, and run my fingers through a basket of buttons. Most have silly quotes on them, others silhouettes of Sherlock Holmes, and a few the rainbow flag. I pick up one of the rainbows and run my thumb over the smooth surface.

My stomach feels queasy, but not in a bad way, as I imagine myself at college. Where I'd pin this to my backpack. And never have to say a word.

I'd be that guy in my self-portrait—the confident, who-I-want-to-be one with the squarish Adam's apple and his eyes on the future—asking guys if they want to study or grab a cup of coffee. I'd meet people. Maybe find someone special and fall hopelessly in love with him. Not Mason, obviously. I picture the four of us hanging out: me and a boyfriend, Mason and a pretty, dark-haired girl who adores his every move. I'd be happy for him. Happy he found someone.

The bookstore employee looks up from shelving books and asks me, "Can I help you?"

I look down at the circle of stripes in my palm and take a deep breath. "Just this," I tell her, and hold up the pin.

"Sure," she says, and walks to the cash register. She punches a few keys and says, "A dollar six."

I hand her the five and she counts out my change.

"You need a bag?"

I shake my head and take the change and my receipt.

"What'd you get?" Eden asks from her seat on the floor.

"Nothing," I say, but show her the small button.

"Pretty," she says with a smile. "And so not nothing."

FORTY-ONE

"You can answer that," Eden tells me when my phone rings.

"But—"

"Here." Eden grabs my phone.

"Good afternoon," she answers like a secretary. "Jamie Peterson's phone."

She listens for a moment, then asks me, "Where the hell are you?"

"Downtown, with you," I say.

"Oh," she says. "I thought you wanted me to lie."

I take the phone back.

"You're with Eden?" Mason asks, sounding a little wounded.

"We were going to study at Flying M, but the market's going on," I explain.

"So we're shopping," Eden says.

"Yeah, um," Mason says. "I was wondering if you

wanted to catch a movie."

Eden wiggles like a happy puppy. *Yes,* she mouths through a big grin.

But I feel kind of bad, dumping her for him. And I'm not sure I want to be alone with him. "Can Eden come?" I ask.

Eden's face switches channels. She shakes her head.

I shoot her a give-me-a-break look as Mason says, "Yeah, that'd be great. Meet you there? I've got my mom's car."

Back in my car, Eden says she shouldn't be chaperoning our date.

"It isn't a date. Besides, I was avoiding him," I tell her. "Until you answered my phone."

"You aren't good at avoiding people," she says. "Especially Mason."

I sigh. She's right. Part of me can't wait to see him, can't wait to feel his fingers rub my head as he messes up my hair.

"So you gonna talk to him? About what you said in government?"

I wonder, briefly, how she knows. But remember everyone knows. "Um, no."

"But what if this is *the date?* What if he does one of these?" She yawns and stretches, letting her fingers fall on the back of my neck.

"Why would he do that?" I ask.

"Um, because he likes you?"

We just went over this. We agreed to drop it. I sigh and decide to put an end to this conversation. "I saw him kiss a girl. On the mouth. With—never mind."

I don't need to look at Eden to know she's shocked. "He was sitting in a tree? With who?"

"Bahti."

"No way!"

"Yes way."

"Not important." Eden dismisses my reasoning. "Lots of gay boys kiss girls. It's lips-are-lips logic."

I've never heard of that. "I don't kiss girls," I tell her.

"That's because you're saving yourself."

"No," I say, and almost say exactly why I don't kiss girls—it's gross—but stop before I hurt her feelings. "I don't like lip gloss."

"Maybe Bahti wasn't wearing lip-gloss. . . ." Eden trails off.

Mason meets us with an ear-to-ear grin. He's wearing a cowboy-inspired plaid shirt that's a little tight across his shoulders—something that didn't migrate from Gabe's side of the closet in time—and cargo shorts.

My stomach does a little dance—happy and sickening—and I smile back.

"Jamie!" he says, giving me a hug-slash-thump on the back that has Eden shooting me I-told-you-so glances over her shoulder as we walk toward the theater.

"Alien invasion?" Mason asks, stopping to read the movie titles on the marquis. "Or rom-com?"

"Aliens," I answer before Eden has a chance to. She'd probably choose the romantic comedy and try to make this into that date that's never going to happen.

Although, contrary to my not-a-date plan, I do bum some money for a ticket and a soda off Mason, but I'll pay him back.

Mason is in his movie zone and I am in mine. He's got his large bucket of popcorn, extra butter, on his lap and an orange soda in a cup holder on the far side. I'm slouched low with my sneakers wedged between the seats in front of us, sipping on my soda while the aliens plot to take over the planet. Eden is sitting on my other side, snuggled deep in her seat and leaning close to me. Her eyes are wide behind her glasses—probably because she doesn't see too many rated R-movies and these aliens are creep-tastic.

I steal a handful of popcorn from Mason without asking and eat it all at once. Then I focus on the movie, secretly wishing that the cute guy won't bite the dust or make out with the hot chick.

Cute guy is frying aliens with his laser gun when Mason's bare arm brushes mine. It zaps me out of the moment and into the next galaxy.

My heartbeat quickens. I jerk away.

"Dude," Mason says. "That scared you?" He means the slimy alien that just jumped up behind the cute guy in the movie, not the touch of his arm.

But I just nod.

FORTY-TWO

Our government exam is on Tuesday afternoon, so I know I'll see Mason at school. Basically, we haven't been alone together, so my plan is working. We haven't talked about my declaration or about *Gumshoe*. And that's okay with me.

I'm putting my notebook and my phone in my locker—we can't have anything in the exam room but pencils and a water bottle—when Mason plops down on the floor at my feet.

He leans back against the lockers and says, "I'm starving."

"Hey."

"You hungry?" he asks, and opens a plastic bag from the grocery store where his mother works.

"Yeah," I say. Stupidly, the cafeteria is closed during exam week, and I forgot about it. So I didn't have lunch.

Mason pulls out package of tortilla shells and another

of sliced cheese. He's beginning to look like a godsend in a gray mechanic's shirt. He spreads the plastic bag on the floor and puts his loot on top of it. He adds a bottle of orange soda, an apple, and a can of chiles.

I sit cross-legged on the floor, facing him.

He folds a piece of cheese into a tortilla and takes a bite.

I help myself to one, then ask about the can of chiles. "How are you gonna get that open?"

"Pocket knife," he mumbles through the food in his mouth.

"A knife? In school? Are you crazy?"

He is. He shifts and pulls a Swiss Army knife from his pocket.

I look up and down the partially empty hall.

"They aren't gonna do anything," he tells me. "It's the last exam."

I give him a look. He might not have been in Principal Chambers's office five times in the last two weeks, but I have.

"And, if they do, they'll have to find someone else to speak at graduation." He opens a little hook-shaped device from the knife and begins wiggling it around the rim of the can.

I watch in wonder. I'd never seen a can opened without a can opener. "I didn't know you were a Boy Scout."

He peels the lid back and fishes a pepper out with his fingers. He makes another taco.

Then something he said sinks in. "Wait, you're really speaking at graduation?" I ask.

"Salutatorian."

"What are you gonna say?"

"Thanks, everyone, for slacking off this year and making me do this crappy job."

"Huh?"

"I have no idea how I ended up second in the class," he says. "Last semester I wasn't even in the running. I mean, I'm in Mr. Purdy's government class with you."

"Um, thanks?"

"It's not AP," he explains. "You have to take all AP classes to get a perfect GPA."

I nod. I had only AP calc, and it threatened to bring my grades down, not up.

"So a bunch of people must have screwed up last semester, or I'd never be where I am—not with a regular class." He takes a swig of soda and hands me the bottle.

"Last semester?" I take a drink. "That was when the flu hit during exam week."

Mason slaps his knee. "You're right! Everyone was sick."

"I was."

"So I owe my class rank to the the flu?" Mason says. "Nice."

"Does Bahti know?" I ask. Because she's gonna know. At graduation.

"I sure as hell didn't tell her. It's not like I'm going to Berkeley," he says.

There's a sarcastic tone in his voice, and I know he's kidding. But I can't help thinking, *Why not? If you're so smart, why not?*

"I know what you're thinking," Mason says, pulling another dripping chile from the can and adding it to his third taco.

I play dumb.

"I *want* to go to WSU, not some hoity-toity Ivy League school. Not for undergrad."

That's right. He's going to grad school.

"Besides," he says with a gooey, cheesy grin. "This way we get to go to college together."

I smile back, my chest as light as a helium balloon.

Then, like a pin to my solar plexus, Mason asks, "You sell a lot of *Gumshoes*?"

I deflate, then mumble, "More than last year."

"It was the graphic short, wasn't it?"

I shrug and take a bite of taco shell and cheese.

"Jamie?"

My teeth clamp down on the inside of my cheek. I yelp in surprise.

"You okay?" he asks.

I nod and cradle my face.

"It was good," Mason says.

My mind whirs, trying to catch his meaning.

"Challis's story?" he prompts.

"Not stellar," I say, trying to throw him off my tracks. "Maybe a little lacking, plot wise."

He looks confused. "You got a week of detention for something you didn't even like?"

Damn it, he's persistent. I try another tactic. "Challis worked really hard on it, and I didn't want to let her down."

His eyes catch mine, hot-fudge pools that seem to say, *Talk to me.*

"She's a little weird," I say about Challis because I can't talk about myself. "But we're sort-of friends—she's in my art class—and I sort of asked her to draw me a story—told her I'd get it—"

"Jamie," Mason gently interrupts my babbling. "You're sort-of friends with everyone."

"But I didn't know what the comic was about until after I promised," I say.

"Yeah?" It sounds like a question.

"Yeah," I scoff, because that is the truth, the very last shred of it, but the truth nonetheless.

He smiles sadly and shakes his head.

He knows I'm lying about not liking it.

Mason stops pushing. "I wouldn't want Challis to have it out for me, either."

An Elegy to Lincoln High
by Brodie Hamilton

The stadium lights fade to blue
as night reclaims its rightful place—
the game played, the season over.
Six wins. Three losses.

My jersey no longer mine,
passed on to the next guy,
my seat in the cafeteria,
my locker and textbooks too.

Old people say these are
the best days of our lives,
the times we'll always remember—
as if the rest of life sucks.

Jealous people say
jocks like me peak in high school—
and end up selling mattresses,
cell phone plans, or used cars.

But I say farewell, Lincoln High.

Thanks for the football,
the rockin' group of friends,

and the beautiful girls—
you know who you are.

Thanks for the starting gate,
the push out the door,
the drive to do something better,
bigger, and to leave you in the dust.

FORTY-THREE

Graduation is on Wednesday afternoon at the big basketball stadium at Boise State.

I'm all decked out in a shirt and tie, the dress shoes my mom bought me when I told her I was wearing my Converse, and a black graduation gown that reminds me of a Hogwarts robe. I have my trumpet. (The band is playing the national anthem.) And my parents have successfully herded the twins into both their dresses and their car seats.

They drop me off near the stadium and then go to find a parking spot.

I join the crowd of seniors, some of whom—Brodie and Kellen—are totally pumped and bouncing around greeting people with fist bumps and high fives. Others seem bored, as if they're thinking, *One walk across the stage and I'm gone.*

"Peterson!" Brodie says.

"Hey, man."

"Where's Viveros?" he asks, holding out his fist.

I shrug. I don't see Mason. "Maybe he had to go do salutatorian stuff?"

"Nah," Brodie tells me. "We did that this morning."

"You're giving a speech?"

"Class president official business," he says, pinching the lapels of his suit.

"Sounds good," I say with an *oof* as Kellen drapes a meaty arm over my shoulders.

"Dude," Kellen says. "So glad I don't have to speak— that stadium's effin' huge."

"Me too," I agree, lifting my trumpet case. "I'm just playing in the band."

"Cool," he says, then releases me. "Brodie here's gonna read his 'Elegy to Lincoln High.'"

"Nah, man," Brodie says. "Chambers says I couldn't read it."

"But it's, like, a published work of art," Kellen says.

"It doesn't have quite the right tone for a graduation ceremony," Brodie says in his snooty principal voice.

Kellen and I laugh.

I spy Eden and wave two fingers her direction.

Kellen follows my gaze. Then he thumps my back. "I love you, man," he says instead of good-bye. It doesn't mean anything—not like when I said it to Mason in government. That's the thing. There are three ways to say *I love you, man*.

The first one is an announcement, said at full volume and often accompanied by a swear word. It's sort of *Thank you,* sort of *You're cool,* with a little *And damn, you make me look good* thrown in. This is how Kellen said it.

The second one is a diss, said with four and a half tons of sarcasm and most likely a reference to the father, son, or Holy Ghost. There's no sort of about it. It means *I hate you right now.*

The third one comes wrapped in caution tape. It is said quietly and on its own, without any adjectives. There's no "sort of" to this one, either, because you mean it.

Like, well, I did.

Mrs. Templeton waves down those of us in band. She ushers us inside. We unpack our instruments and assemble them, playing random notes and getting nervous.

"Ladies and gentlemen," Mrs. Templeton shouts over the noise. "Your music is all on your stands—and, seniors, please leave it there when you join the rest of your class. You will also leave your instrument with your stand partner. Understand?"

I nod. It's not like I want to be carrying my trumpet when I walk across the stage.

"I'll be at school all next week so you can pick them up."

More nodding.

"Ready?" she asks.

"Ready!" we shout.

And Ms. Templeton shows us out to the auditorium floor.

I look up at the seemingly endless rows of seats—almost all of them filled with bodies. I look around for my mom and Frank and the girls, but don't see them.

After we play the national anthem, I join the seniors in the bank of chairs in the middle of the floor. The seats are alphabetical and a few empty ones are scattered here and there. I watch Bahti find her seat among the *R*s and calculate where mine might be.

Then I see it. *L, M, N, O*—Eden O'Shea. Nick O'Shea. *P.* Jamie Peterson.

I'm next to Redneck.

Too bad I'm not next to Eden. She's on Nick's other side, her head bent down.

I pull my Hogwarts robe close around my legs and sidestep down the row past Eden. I try to catch her eye, but she doesn't look up. I touch her shoulder and wait for a response.

"Move it, Fagmag," Nick mumbles.

Eden elbows him, then glances up at me. There are tears in her eyes, streaks on her face.

I want to ask what's wrong, but Nick glares at me. I'm the only band member still not seated, so I pick up my program from my chair and sit as quickly as possible, not looking at the Redneck. As soon as I sit, I discover that I have a problem. Nick takes up a lot of space. I squeeze my arms to my sides, afraid of touching him, and press my legs together, as far away from him as I can get. I sit as still as possible and grip my rolled-up program so tight, it crushes in my hand.

The Redneck sees me do this and snorts. I hear him exhale, an insult on his breath. I scoot my chair closer to the girl on my other side and try to concentrate on Principal Chambers.

"It is my pleasure to be here this afternoon with all of you," she begins. "This is my favorite part of being an educator—seeing our seniors walk across this stage on their way to bigger and better things."

She babbles on sentimentally and, finally, introduces Brodie.

Which shoots the senior class to its feet. We whoop, clap, and whistle.

"Oh," Brodie says into the mic. "Wow."

Our cheers die down as he starts in on his speech about how wonderful we are and how the last three years have been a roller coaster of ratcheting expectations, amazing highs, thrilling rides, and heartbreaking lows. He mentions losing the homecoming game and being crowned prom king. And, when he's done, we cheer for him as if he's bursting through the paper banner and running onto the field. I wish I still had my trumpet, so I could make some major noise.

Especially when Mason steps up to the mic.

"Thank you, Brodie," he says. "Superintendent Owens, Principal Chambers, family, friends." Then in Spanish. "*Gracias . . . familia, amigos.*" Adding, "*Lo siento por mi acento. Lo sé, es horrible.*"

My mouth drops open. It's been years since I've heard him say more than a word or two in Spanish. And I wonder what it means. *That he forgives his father? That he's calling a truce? That he felt bad for the grandparents in the audience that don't speak English?*

I can't read his face. He has the same look that Brodie did, a pasted-on smile edged with nervousness. His black plastic glasses catch the stage lights. A crisp white collar of a dress shirt and the wedge of a red silk Windsor knot shows above his gown, and the springy ends of his curls are escaping from under his mortarboard.

"Out in the real world," Mason is saying, "we won't have Coach Callahan telling us to work out and eat healthy or Ms. Maude trying to cram a little art and culture into our diet. We won't have Principal Chambers telling us our T-shirts are offensive or Mr. Purdy telling us"—he pauses—"well, we won't have Mr. Purdy."

The stadium rolls with laughter.

"Aw," Mason says. "Mr. Purdy, I love you, man."

Beside me, the Redneck laughs, but not at Mason's speech. I get a bad feeling and inch so close to the girl on my left that I am practically sitting on her lap.

"Nick," Eden hisses.

Then the Redneck hands me his program. It's printed on letter-size paper folded in half, but it looks the size of a Post-it in his meaty, Idaho farm-boy hand.

Eden leans forward and shakes her head as if to warn me of something.

I take it anyway. And, not knowing what to do with it, I page through it. There's a list of our names, and, next to them, the colleges we're going to, or the divisions of the armed forces, and the scholarships we received.

Taking a wild guess at why he gave me the program, I look up his name. It's alone on the line after Eden's. She's going to NNU, but Nick's line is blank: no college, no service, no scholarship. That can't be why he gave this to me.

I know what's next to my name—my little marching band scholarship for when I play for the U of I Vandals. And see that Mason won several academic scholarships.

I turn the page, and the Redneck whispers in my ear, "I love you, man."

FORTY-FOUR

I feel cold all over. My teeth practically chatter. My hands shake and the program shivers. There, in the centerfold, is the drawing.

Eden's drawing.

It isn't wrinkled like the one I pried from Challis's fingers. It's color-copied or was printed using a laser printer. And stapled into the program.

It has a caption now. *I Love You, Man.*

And Mason's voice echoes it as he finishes the translated part of his speech. *"Te quiero, güey."*

Real funny, Redneck. *Way to scare the bejesus out of me. Put a copy of your sister's drawing in a program and then hand it to me.*

I look at him.

And when I do, he snorts half a laugh.

I look at Mason onstage. His plastic smile is firmly in place, lacking the zap that stops my heart.

But my very next thought does that trick. The temperature in the auditorium drops another ten degrees as I imagine a copy of the drawing in every program.

I lean forward, peer around my next-door neighbor, past Juliet Polmanski's empty seat next to her, and down the row of students. No one looks back at me. I look the other way, around the black mass of Nick's robe, but Eden doesn't look at me either. Her eyes are squeezed shut as if she's trying to turn off the flow of tears. I look over my shoulder and catch Bahti's eye. She makes a face that seems to say, *I'm sorry.*

So I look.

And sure enough, there's one stapled in my crunched-up program.

And one in my neighbor's.

Oh. God.

Oh. God. No.

I look up at the rows of people surrounding us and begin to feel like an exhibit at a zoo. I feel the sting of tears forming behind my eyes. I blink and find Mason's face behind the podium. His smile is more relaxed, more real. He obviously hasn't seen his program. Yet.

He's wrapping up, "Seniors!" he shouts. "We're outta here! ¡*Hasta luego,* Lincoln High!"

Kellen is the first to jump up, clapping. And then everyone around me joins in. While everyone is cheering, whistling, and whooping, I stay seated, my face buried in my hands. Silently, I chant my new mantra to their impromptu rhythm. *Oh. God. No. Oh. God. No.*

The stadium goes quiet, and an unfamiliar voice is amplified over us.

"Good afternoon, everyone!" it says. "I'm Juliet Polmanski."

Part of me wants to look up, verify that it is her—since I've never heard her say more than "I'm sorry" and "Excuse me." But my own personal hell seems better suited to the dark, even if it's just the palms of my hands. *Oh. God. No. Oh. God. No.* Because there's no place to hide. No desk or table to crawl under. No stuffy closet. No tomorrow.

"As you can imagine," Juliet says, "I've spent the last who-knows-how-many nights reading commencement speeches and trying to figure out what to say. This speech is supposed to be about looking forward to our future, but all I've been thinking about for the last three years is our past. It's been a long road for me, for all of us who knew my brother."

Silence falls over the crowd, no doubt because everyone is thinking of Jordan.

The mood turns somber, and I wonder if it was better when all she had to say was "I'm sorry" and "Excuse me." Because right now they seem like the only words to say to Mason. *I'm sorry I screwed up your life. Excuse me, I didn't mean to make you the focus of the worst prank in the history of Lincoln High. I know this wouldn't have happened to you if it weren't for me. I'm sorry. Excuse me, I'll be leaving now. I'll get out of your life. So I won't ruin it further. Not with my stupid, babbling mouth. Not with the way I look at you. Not with my totally-out-of-bounds friend crush on you. Not with our portrait in your graduation program. I'm sorry.*

I'm sorry. I'm sorry. I'm sorry.

"Our Lincoln High experiences were all different. Some of us saw our high school years from the stage, others from the orchestra pit, the basketball court, the field, the stands. Some of us watched it from the back of the classroom or from behind a book. . . ."

From the closet? I wonder, my face still in my hands. But she doesn't mention it. Probably because closets are not safe. If you don't come out yourself, you're dragged out, kicking and screaming.

"No matter your vantage point," Juliet continues, "you'll walk out of this stadium this afternoon with more than an empty leatherette folder—don't worry, you'll get your diploma in the mail. . . ." She pauses for the obligatory laughter. "You'll leave with a heart full of memories. Like the evening of the snowball dance when the . . ."

Even with the microphone, Juliet's voice fades to oblivion, getting lost in the stars that cloud my eyelids. I don't want to think about memories. Because Mason is in every one of them, from the first day of sophomore year (the first time he had to wear glasses to school) to senior prom (the first time he kissed a girl) to today (the last time he'll ever talk to me). I feel the sting that comes before tears. *Oh. God. No.* I inhale a ragged breath. I will away the urge to cry. When it's safe, I look up from my hands.

"I think we've all learned that life is short," Juliet says.

Not short enough.

"So we shouldn't waste it, but instead we should embrace the amazing opportunities before us, like college, jobs, the Peace Corps, and serving our country. We should hold on to the good things—like our friendships— and tell our friends, 'I love you, man.'"

My lower lip wobbles traitorously, and I bite it in order to keep it still.

I hear Eden sniffle from Nick's far side, and my neighbor swipes at a tear, smearing mascara across her cheek. *The three of us are going to be a blubbering mess in a matter of minutes.*

"We should keep moving ahead," Juliet says, "no matter how impossible it seems, no matter what you've lost."

Really? I ask her silently, because I'm not so sure. I feel like in losing Mason, I've lost everything.

And then she wraps up her speech with, "And even after all this time, filling our brains with formulas, history, and theories, I hope that each and every one of you will follow your heart, for it is bound to lead you on an incredible, breathtaking journey."

I watch Juliet's face break into a beautiful smile and feel for a moment that she is looking at me. Until the people in front of me rise, clapping and shouting. Their gowns form a curtain of privacy around me, as if to shelter me and the fragile smile she imparted on my own lips.

Juliet lost everything. I think back to her poem in *Gumshoe*, about Jordan's cross on Highway 16, and wonder how she ever managed to smile like that—not nervous, not pasted on, but a real smile. Maybe losing someone close to you isn't the end of everything. Maybe it makes you stronger.

When they sit down again, Juliet, Brodie, and Mason are no longer onstage. Juliet slides into the empty chair on the opposite side of the girl next to me.

"Good job," my neighbor whispers.

I whip my head around to Bahti's row, where I know Mason will also be seated.

His back is toward me as he picks his way between the seats. He pauses by Bahti, and I watch as she takes his hand, holding it for a minute until he scoots down two seats and their arms don't reach. He bends to pick up the program on his seat and then sits down.

The girl next to him whispers something.

And he opens the program.

His tassel slides down, swings in front of his face, but I can see his lips suck in air between his teeth, almost as if he finds the picture funny. But the next second his expression changes as he clenches his jaw.

Slowly, he closes the program and looks up.

It takes every ounce of strength in me to fight the urge to jerk around in my seat. I hold his gaze.

He mouths a question that ends in a swear word.

My face crumples and my shoulders hunch. I mouth back, *Sorry.*

FORTY-FIVE

My robe is as hot as the massive lights burning down on the stage. My shirt and tie choke me. My stomach buzzes. My new shoes pinch. The backs of my knees itch. And I will have to get my picture taken. Then I'll have to stand up in front of every single person I know and walk across the stage. I rub my face with my hands, wish I could splash it with cold water. Closing my eyes, I try to summon my courage.

My neighbor nudges me.

I blink.

"Jamie," Juliet pleads. "Go!"

"Huh?"

"Go!" she says, and points to a few students lined up by the photographer's backdrop.

I recognize the Redneck, his robe barely brushing his knees.

"Sorry," I say, rushing over to join the line, but only because she wanted me to.

From my new vantage point, I can see Mason. His row is still seated and he's looking down, as if he reading his program. Or maybe he's praying for this whole thing to be over.

"Smile," the photographer says.

I try, and grip the roll of fake diploma too hard. It crumples in my hand.

The flash fires and I'm momentarily blind. Then I'm in line again, shuffling toward the stage as names are being called. *Iliana Maria Muñoz. Cameron Gabriel Nash. Joshua Bradley Newton.*

I give the Redneck plenty of space as we near the stairs. I look over my shoulder. Mason is standing in front of the photographer, the now-crunched fake diploma in his hand. He doesn't smile. The camera flashes anyway.

Ms. Maude signals it's time for me to go, and I stumble up the stairs.

I blink back the glare from the stage lights as Principal Chambers holds out her hand for me to shake. I take it, a handful of icicles compared to my own sweaty palm.

A man says my name into the microphone, "James Laurence Peterson."

I blush even hotter, walk a little faster. Wanting nothing more than to get this over with.

Then I hear it.

My classmates erupting in a storm of applause, shouting my name as if I were some sort of Lincoln High superhero, instead of the kid who just ruined his best friend's life.

FORTY-SIX

We toss our caps into the air, scramble to pick them up. Then it's over.

Thank God.

We file out into a courtyard, away from the blinding lights and stifling heat. I unzip my robe and loosen my tie. I'm unbuttoning the top button of my shirt when Eden rushes over.

"I can't believe Nick did this!" She shakes a torn program at me. "I'm so gonna kill him!"

I nod absently and look for Mason in the crowd. I don't know if I want to talk to him or not, but I have to know if he's okay.

Eden calms down a notch, seeming to understand. "Over there," she says, and points.

Then I see him, talking to Brodie and Kellen. He's still standing and seems all right.

He turns and looks right at me.

A swarm of honeybees buzz in my stomach, and I fight the urge to turn and run.

In slow motion Mason claps Kellen's shoulder. Then he drifts toward Eden and me.

The bees buzz and sting. My throat swells up. I can't breathe.

"Jamie!" he calls.

With this, our classmates stop talking—the only sound is the buzzing in my ears.

I feel Eden's hand on my back, pushing me toward Mason.

He hugs me and thumps my back, and I return the gesture robotically, not knowing what else to do.

"Jamie," Mason says again.

I look past the glare of sun on his glasses. His eyes are bright, sparkling with energy. And he's close. So close to me.

"Jamie." This time he says it at a whisper. "I'm ready. Are you?"

I search his face for an idea of what he's talking about. It's inches from mine and on the verge of a smile. *A smile?*

"You want to do this?"

I don't know what he's talking about until his hands close around my ears, his thumbs pressed to my cheekbones, and the tips of his fingers wrap around the hot back of my neck. Then I get it. *Oh my God,* my scrambled brain thinks, *he wants to kiss me!*

And suddenly I can't wait any longer.

"Hell, yeah," I reply, and reach for him. I close the gap in an instant and press my lips into his. Too hard at first, but I figure it out. I kiss him. His lips are soft and warm and vaguely sweet.

At first the crowd is pin-drop silent.

He kisses me back.

My mortarboard tumbles to the pavement.

Our lips part.

A chorus of low oohs begins. Then a series high-pitched whistles, with one "woo-woo-woo" that sounds like Brodie.

So we don't stop kissing.

FORTY-SEVEN

But we do stop kissing. Because a girl's voice rings out, bouncing off the hard cement walls. "You had no right!"

Mason and I turn to see Eden and the Redneck squaring off a few yards from us. We stand there, our arms still around each other as if we are holding the other one up.

"Why'd you draw it," the Redneck asks, "if you didn't want people to see it?"

"It was personal!" she shouts.

"Yeah." He laughs. "A personal moment between two fag—"

She slaps him.

His head jerks right, her handprint on his cheek burning as bright as a red neon sign until the rest of his face catches up.

His hands ball into fists as big as sugar beets, and Eden's eyes grow wide.

Oh my God, I think, my fingers gripping Mason's robe. *He's going to hit her.*

The Redneck's forearm muscles tense, release, and tense again, his face glowing redder with each squeeze.

Eden seems frozen between anger and fear.

Mason's muscles go rigid, as if he's ready to pounce.

"You worthless piece of homophobic crap!" Challis's voice cuts through the crowd. "Back the hell off!" Then Challis is all up in the Redneck's face, slamming her palms into his gorilla-wide chest.

The Redneck growls like a pit bull, drowning out her insults.

She shoves him hard.

He doesn't budge. Then, after a beat, he turns and stomps away.

Challis gives his retreating back a single-finger salute and puts an arm around Eden.

"I can't believe he did that," Eden mumbles. "He doesn't even write his own English papers."

As if drawn by the shouting, families start to trickle in around the corners of the stadium, infiltrating our sea of black hats and gowns with bits of colors—dads in red power ties, sisters in pink party dresses, brothers in orange-and-blue BSU jerseys, and moms in printed blouses.

I let my arms fall to my sides and Mason does the same. We stand there, taking in the wave of people.

My mind plays a game of mix-and-match, matching parents with my classmates: Holland's mom is a tank-top type, her father a burly blond with more tattoos than shirtsleeves.

The Schoenbergers are dressed in black, Michael's dad in a suit and his mom and sister in dresses.

Challis looks around hopefully, as if she is trying to spot someone, anyone with a blood relation. She bites her lip as her eyes grow glossy with realization that they hadn't come at all.

"You see your folks?" Mason asks me.

"No, you?" I reply as my eyes snap back to Challis.

She's wrestling out of her gown. The zipper is stuck and she yanks the gown off over her head. Her hat falls to the asphalt. She balls up the flimsy nylon robe and shoves it into a trashcan. Then she scoops up the mortarboard and tosses that too. Only the square hat doesn't fit in the round hole. So she leaves it there, the gold tassel fluttering in the breeze, and walks away.

Mason points to where the crowd has shifted to reveal our parents—both pairs plus four siblings and my grandma and Stan—all together. My biological dad couldn't make it. And this makes me think of Challis.

"I'm not ready for this," Mason whispers.

I know I should be thinking about him. About us. About what this all means, but I can't concentrate. "One minute," I tell him, and squeeze his hand. Then I jog to the trash can, pick up Challis's mortarboard, and pull the tassel free. I put it in my pocket, thinking that maybe, someday, she'll want it back.

In a flash I'm back at Mason's side. "Sorry."

"You think they saw?" He juts his chin at our families.

"The picture? Or us . . . ?"

"Both?"

"Probably," I say. My mom is sagging under the weight of one of the twins in her arms, so she's probably been standing there for a few.

Mason swears in Spanish.

"It'll be okay," I tell him, and hold out my hand, palm up and open—there if he needs it.

Mason takes it. His grip so tight, my knuckles abrade one another.

We dodge a hugging knot of Polmanskis and another of Quincys. Our hands cementing themselves together with heat, sweat, and fear—bonded as we approach our own knots of family.

My mother is beaming, Frank is smiling. Grandma and Stan look out of place.

Mason's father is scowling.

One of the twins spots us and wiggles free from my stepdad's arms. She trips toward us and the other follows. Mason and I catch one twin's little hand with each of our free hands. They tug us back toward our families.

That's when I see Mrs. V brushing tears from her eyelashes and Mr. V's grip on her shoulder.

"Congratulations, sweetie," my mom says, hugging me long and tight. "You did it!" I don't know if she means graduating or coming out. I've let go of my sister and Mason, but I don't remember when I did.

"Congrats, Jamie," Frank says, giving me a *thunk* between the shoulder blades. He picks up one twin and at the same time, reaches for the other's hand.

I offer to shake hands with Gabe, but he pulls me into a hug. He passes me to Londa and goes back to teasing Mason in Spanish.

Over the top of Londa's head, I watch my mom watch Mr. Viveros.

"Congratulations, Jamie," Londa says. "I'm gonna miss having two little brothers—you'll visit me in my new apartment?"

"Of course," I say to her, but my eyes flick to my mom.

She gives Mason a motherly hug, whispers something in his ear. He nods. She pulls him close again, holds him for a long time. Then she says to his parents, "You should be proud, a college-bound high school graduate!"

They nod and mascara-tinted tears dislodge themselves and roll down Mrs. V's cheeks. Mr. V's face is stony, not a flicker of emotion crosses it, and I get the feeling he's thinking about the one thing no one is saying out loud: his son is gay.

"We've gotta go," Mason says quickly. "See you at the party, okay, Jamie?"

"Yeah," I say, my heart heavy with what I imagine will happen when he and his father are no longer in a public place.

FORTY-EICHT

My mom puts an arm around my waist and rests her head on my shoulder as we walk to our own vehicle. My grandmother and Frank are walking in front of us, each carting one of the twins on a hip. Stan trails behind.

"That was one helluva way to come out," Mom says, and I know she saw us.

"Mom!" I scold.

"*Gumshoe* was pretty good, but phew, that kiss was better."

"Mom!" My face warms with embarrassment.

She gives me a squeeze. "I'm so proud of you."

We're quiet for a moment as we wait for Frank to get Ann Marie settled in her car seat, and it occurs to me that maybe Mom hasn't seen Eden's drawing—maybe the picture was only in some of the programs—maybe she doesn't know that our coming out wasn't exactly our idea.

"Mason, though . . . ," Mom says. "That surprised me."

"Me too," I agree. "But these girls in our class, they seemed to know."

"Really?" she asks.

I pull my program from my shirt pocket, unfold it, and hand it to my mother.

She's confused.

"In the middle," I say.

She pulls the wrinkled pages open, squints in concentration at the drawing. Then she covers her mouth with one hand, but I can tell her lips are an O of surprise. "These girls, they did this?" she asks. But she doesn't wait for me to answer. "Oh, Jamie! Honey."

I practically catch her as she falls onto me—her arms open and eyes welling with tears. "Baby," she says, the word—fortunately—muffled by my shoulder.

"Carrie?" Frank says her name, ducking back out of the SUV.

"I should've had you transferred," Mom mumbles through tears. "I knew that school was trouble. Knew it all along."

Frank gives me a what's-she-talking-about? look.

"It's okay, Mom," I say. "We're okay."

She pulls away and looks up at me. "But the school, they should— They should—"

I shake my head. "School's over. It doesn't matter."

"But—"

"Mason and I are fine," I repeat for her sake, but deep down I get the feeling that I'm lying. "We're fine."

And all through dinner—my grandmother has made real food—I keep thinking about the stone-cold look on Mr. Viveros's face.

After dinner my phone buzzes in my pocket. It's Eden. I don't answer.

A text comes in:

Please pick me up. I need to talk to you.

I know I need to talk to her too. But I don't feel like it. Not now. Not in the mess I'm in. Not while I'm worried about Mason. I don't reply. I just scrape my untouched plate into the kitchen trashcan. I put it in the dishwasher, a swirl of mashed potatoes and a matching one of gravy still clinging to it.

I glance up to find my mom looking at me, a worried smile on her face. "Mason?" she asks.

I shake my head. "Eden."

"What did she want?"

"To talk." I sigh.

"That's girls for you," Mom says. "It's what we do best."

I know what she's saying, that she's here if I want to

talk about it. "Thanks, but—" My phone buzzes again. I look at the screen and wish this message would be from Mason and not Eden.

Can I come over?

Mom looks at me as if she wants it to be Mason as much as I do. I shake my head, and her face falls to what I imagine is a mirror of my own expression. I feel her pity and want to shake it off. So I text Eden back.

No. I'll pick u up. For Brodie's party.

Eden bawled like a baby all the way here, saying over and over how sorry she is about the drawing. I let her, because I needed to hear it. Not the crying, just the apology. Then, when we got to the party, she disappeared into Brodie's bathroom and has been there for the last twenty minutes. I guess I got what I wanted: to be alone. But I can't stand it. My stomach is a mass of writhing worry. And even though the party has barely begun and I know that Mason's probably still eating dinner at the Viveros-no-phone-zone dining-room table, I text him.

Hey, can't wait to see you.

Too tacky. I hold down the delete button.

Thinking of you.

Even worse. Delete.

Hope you're hanging in there.

Is that a sexual reference? Or a kitten poster? No. Delete, delete, delete.

Finally, it's Eden who saves me when she emerges from the bathroom, her eyes still ringed with red.

"How do you send a text to someone you kissed and really want to be your boyfriend but you aren't sure he feels the same way?" The words bypass my brain and tumble out of my mouth.

She takes my phone from my hand. "You don't."

"But—" I reach for it before her words sink in.

"Some things are better explained in person." She closes my phone and hands it back.

"You don't have to disappear," I tell her while we wait for Mason. "I'll explain about the drawing. You won't have to." We have a clear view of both the gate and the French doors, but we're standing away from the noise of the fire pit and barbecue.

"Thanks, Jamie," she says. "But I'm gonna pass. I think you two need time alone."

I know. But I'm not sure I'm ready.

Forget butterflies. I've got a nest of yellow jackets

down there. I don't know what to do. What to say. Or how to act. *What do you say after you kiss someone? What did that kiss mean?*

"Stay?" I ask. "Please."

"Okay."

I spy him. He's wearing a white button-down shirt—probably from Gabe's side of the closet—as if he hasn't changed his clothes, just taken off his tie. The sleeves are rolled up, and his tan forearms are bare. He looks okay. Actually, way better than okay.

My heart melts and my palms get sweaty. I wipe them on my shorts and check my antiperspirant.

"You're fine," Eden assures me. "And you smell good."

She starts edging away, as if to start her disappearing act.

I grab her hand. Make her stay.

Mason sees me and smiles as bright as the first star on the horizon.

I hang on to Eden for balance, weaving my fingers into hers.

She tugs me toward him. "Hey, Mason," she says cheerily.

"Hey," he says. Then he sees our hands. And his eyebrows wrinkle with a question.

I untangle my fingers from Eden's.

"I was just leaving," she says.

"See you," Mason says to her. But the eyebrow question marks remain.

"I—I, uh," I stammer, trying to explain. "Um, I mean, earlier—that was, yeah. But I guess, I'm worried—I don't know, I want to, you know, but—"

"Jamie," Mason says. "You're babbling."

"I know, it's just—" I inhale. Try to make the words make sense. "Are we—are we more than friends?"

He steps closer, his brown eyes locked on mine. "That depends . . ."

I hiccup more air into my lungs, stammer more nonsense.

His voice is steady when he finishes his sentence. "If I'm still your best friend or if Eden is."

"You are," I say.

"Good." He nudges the grass with the toe of his dress shoes. "You know, because I was sorta feeling replaced."

Oh. Yeah. I reach for him and touch his arm.

He steps closer, not hugging me but resting his forehead on my shoulder, like he did that night it rained. I wrap my arms around him.

"Sorry," I say. "It's just—it was hard to be around you *and* in the closet. And Eden . . . Well, Eden knows everything. I could talk to her."

"I know," Mason mumbles into my collar. "I wanted to come out to you, tell you the real reason I didn't want

344

to date in high school." He chokes on the words. "But it just got too damn complicated."

"You're right," I say. "Way too much drama."

Mason chuckles, and I feel his shoulders shake. I join in. Soon we're laughing so hard, we edge right back around to crying. My stomach muscles spasm, and I clutch my gut as another peal of laughter rocks through me. Mason claps a hand on my shoulder and I tumble into him. We totter for a moment, then fall onto the grass—Mason on his back and me on my side and pressed into him. We duck our heads, embarrassed and laughing.

I peek out from under my fingers to see Kellen raising a can of beer as if he's giving us a toast. Brodie does the same, followed by an "I love you, man!"

I smile back and raise my empty hand as if I have a can in it. "Love you—"

But Mason pulls my hand down. He's still laughing when he says, "You're such a flirt."

"Sorry."

"Don't be," Mason says. "Just flirt with me next time."

"I promise."

He edges up on his elbows, his face dangerously close to mine.

My stomach is knotted up from laughing, and my lungs are working overtime to catch my breath. So when he rolls toward me and kisses my lips, a million mixed-up signals course through my neurons. I'm dizzy. Breathless. Speechless. Ice-cold. On fire.

I don't let him stop. I reach for his face, pull him over onto me.

Someone yells, "Get a room," but we ignore them and keep kissing.

Until we both start giggling. My face is burning.

"How many creepy stalker girls are staring at us right now?" Mason whispers.

"Um. All of them."

He takes a deep breath, as if to prepare himself for something. Then he stands and offers me a hand.

I take it and he pulls me upright. I don't let go.

Mason motions to the cluster of people around the fire pit. "Do they look a little cozy?"

I follow his gaze and find Eden and Challis, their heads bent together as if they were whispering. *Oh my God*. They have their arms around each other. *That's new.*

"I don't trust them. They're up to something," Mason says.

"They're fine," I say as they pivot and then walk toward us.

"Hey," Challis says.

Mason doesn't respond but looks away instead.

I don't know if I've ever seen him go shy before. "Hey, you're here," I say to cover for him. I had hoped she'd be here but wasn't sure she would be.

She shrugs. "Nice party."

"I have something for you," I tell her. I pull her tassel from my pocket and hold it out.

She stares at it, then looks at me.

"I thought you might want it, you know, someday."

"You saved my tassel from the trash can?" She takes it from my hand and looks at it.

"Yeah."

"In the middle of the crappiest day of your god-damned life you pulled my graduation tassel out of a trash can?" she repeats her question.

"It wasn't *in* the trash can," I say, avoiding her question because the jury's still out on if this is the worst—or best—day of my goddamned life.

"Can you be any more perfect?" she asks.

Eden shakes her head. "He's adorable. I told you."

"Thank you," Challis says to me. "But this isn't why we're here. We came to apologize—to both of you."

Mason's eyes flicker up from the grass.

"Mason," Eden says. "I'm so sorry about the picture. I drew it because I wanted you two to get together—wanted everything to be a fairy tale—but I didn't mean for everyone to see it. I just wanted to show Challis and a few friends. That's all."

I look over at Mason.

"Yeah," he says. "Fine."

"It's not your fault Nick made copies and stapled

them into the students' programs," I tell Eden for Mason's sake. "Heck, I can't even believe he thought of that."

"He got the idea from *Gumshoe*," Eden says.

I cringe.

"Brilliant," Mason says.

"Apology accepted," I say to Eden. Then I say to Mason, "We talked about this—how it wasn't Eden's brightest move."

"I won't do it again," Eden adds, then smiles a little. "No more fan art for real people."

But Mason doesn't respond.

And Eden's smile fades.

I know Mason won't accept her apology, and I also know not to push him. Not today. I shake my head and Eden seems to understand.

"See you," she says. "And Challis is giving me a ride home, so you don't have to."

"Okay," I say.

Then Challis slips a supporting arm around Eden and they walk away.

Mason watches them go, then wanders a few yards to a cooler. He rummages through the ice and chooses a can of beer for himself, then asks me, "What do you want?"

"Soda," I say.

We find a pair of patio chairs away from the crowd and sit. Our knees touch and a million questions bubble up in my brain. *When did you know? Why didn't you tell me? Did you know I had a crush on you? Is your dad gonna kick you out? You want to get naked?* I press my lips together. I don't ask any of them yet, but instead I say, "So, McCall?"

"*So* didn't turn out like I planned," he says. "I wanted to see what it'd be like to be a couple. Where no one knew us. Where no one assumed we were straight."

I nod.

"I thought it'd be amazing." His voice is a whisper. "I thought I'd have the *cojones* to come out."

"But I was a complete and utter asshole?" I ask.

"Something like that," Mason agrees.

"Sorry," I say. "It would've been epic—if I hadn't screwed it up."

"I think we both did a little screwing up," he says, and treats me to a smile.

"Maybe," I agree. "I was going to come out to you, too—but I thought it might make the ride home a little uncomfortable."

"Or the night a little more interesting?"

My face flushes warm at the thought. "You're the one who climbed into bed with me!"

"Earth to Jamie," he says, teasing me.

"I didn't know. I mean, you were kissing Bahti at prom."

"Just for practice, so I wouldn't screw up my first *real* kiss," he says, fueling my blush. "So how was it?"

"Flippin' awesome," I say. "Except maybe for the audience."

Mason chuckles and shakes his head. "Kinda like your favorite comic."

"Kinda," I agree, thinking back to our look-alikes, Tony and Justin.

Mason leans forward and, with his lips brushing mine, he whispers, "I thought it had plenty of plot."

I don't so much hear him as feel his lips move, sending a current of desire down my spine. "Me too," I mumble as I kiss him. Someone turns up the stereo and Maroon 5 blasts from the speakers. People start dancing on the deck. With the music making it impossible for someone to overhear our conversation, I ask. "When did you know you were gay?"

"Dunno." Mason takes a swig of beer. "At first I thought I was just late to the party. You know, like when Brodie was kissing girls in sixth grade, I wasn't interested. I thought I would be, eventually. Turns out I wanted to be invited to an entirely different party."

"So you said you didn't want to date in high school."

"I should have said I didn't want to *come out* in high school."

"I didn't either," I whisper.

"And you so blew it!"

"Seriously, did *everyone* know?"

"And then, when you said 'I love you, man' to me in

government, I wanted to climb over my desk. Kiss you right there. In front of Mr. Purdy and the whole effin' class!"

That grin tugs at my lips again.

"But you looked like you were about to die." His eyes melt into molasses, his lips slack with empathy.

My smile fades. "I was."

He reaches for me, wraps his fingers of his left hand across the back of my neck, and tilts my forehead down to meet his. We stay like that. Hunched over with our foreheads touching.

I try to say something. Anything. But my head is swimming with the memory, and the back of my neck is hotter than day-old sunburn.

Mason shushes me, his eyes all dark and deep behind his glasses. "I love you, man," he whispers.

I stare at him, at his face an inch from mine.

He missed a hair when he shaved, half an inch from the corner of his mouth. One lens of his glasses is speckled with hard water spots, and he smells like beer tastes. But somehow, he's perfect. My every daydream come true.

"I love you, too," I tell him, and let the music surround us as we fall silent, as if to let the moment soak into our skin.

When the song changes, I ask, "So you knew about me?"

"Um, yeah," Mason says.

"When?"

"When did I figure out you were gay or when did I notice you had a crush on me?"

My face warms. "The first one," I say, still too embarrassed to admit to the second.

"I dunno, maybe sophomore year—you *so* didn't like girls. They made you squirm."

"And you didn't say anything?" I ask.

"God," he says. "I wanted to. But you never seemed ready."

"I tried to tell you, but I always chickened out. I didn't want anything to change between us—didn't want you to think of me differently after I came out."

"You meant different *bad*?" he asks. "Because, well, I think everything just changed."

"It did, didn't it?"

"In a good way. I hope."

"Different but good. Really good," I agree. "Except, um, your dad. He looked upset."

"He's a piece of work."

"What did he say?"

"More like what didn't he say? Mom had this nice dinner planned—and he just wouldn't shut up. Ruined Mom's dinner."

"Sucks," I say.

"He's why I didn't want to come out in high school. I was afraid he'd kick me out." Mason puts his beer down in the grass.

"Did he?" I ask.

"Pretty much," Mason says with a shrug.

"You don't care?" I ask, shocked. I'd be freaking out if I were about to be homeless.

"I care. But, at the same time, I've always thought it'd happen. I've got my scholarships, financial aid, that job with Sal." He ticks off the pieces of his plan on his fingers. "I was gonna leave in August anyway."

I see it now, all the calculations, the notes in French in his day planner, all the parts. But there's a missing piece. It's the end of May, not August. "But it's not August yet."

"Londa's moving in with some friends from school. Said I could crash on their couch—if I bought them a couch." He laughs.

I try to smile, but I must look worried, because Mason takes my hand. "And tonight?" I ask.

"Your mom said I could stay at your place. I mean, if it's okay with you."

I feel a smile spread across my face as if to reveal every crazy amazing thought that runs through my brain.

"That's exactly what I was thinking," Mason says with a grin of his own.

I want to laugh at this, but I need to know that even if he's kicked out of his house, he'll be all right, because I might not be able to stand it if he isn't. Especially if it's all my fault. "And after that? You'll stay with Londa? And in August you'll come to college with me?"

Mason looks me in the eye. "I'll be okay, Jamie, as long as I have you."

I hold his gaze until he's too close to focus. My nose brushes his and our lips meet in what feels like—not slow motion—but every moment in my life and the lack of time all together.